MY INVISIBLE
HUSBAND

MY INVISIBLE HUSBAND

SHEILA M. GOSS

URBAN BOOKS
www.urbanbooks.net

URBAN SOUL is published by

Urban Books
10 Brennan Pl.
Deer Park, NY 11729

ISBN 1-59983-007-8

First Printing: December 2006
10 9 8 7 6 5 4 3 2 1

Printed in the United States of America

I

CHARADES

Oh, what a tangled web we weave, when first we
practice to deceive.
—Sir Walter Scott (1771–1832)

1

"Congratulations on your wedding, Nikki."

"Thank you," Nikki Montana replied as she looked up into the eyes of her coworker Kenneth Capers.

"When will we get to meet the lucky groom?" Kenneth asked as he ate the last bite of cake on his plate.

Her eyes darted downward as she repeated to him the response she had rehearsed and given everyone all day. "As soon as his schedule allows, I'll bring him up to the office for everyone to meet."

Nikki thanked everyone for coming to the wedding shower her manager insisted the department throw for her. As an account executive at Midas Touch, Nikki was responsible for coming up with innovative advertising campaigns. Her accounts consisted of small to global companies in all types of industries. She had been receiving gifts from her clients all week. Deep down inside she felt guilty about accepting the gifts her coworkers and clients so thoughtfully picked out. She glanced at her watch. Her plane for Las Vegas would be leaving in less than twenty-four hours, so she knew she had to get home to do some last-minute packing. And when she returned to work a week later, she would be a married woman.

Some of her coworkers helped carry her gifts to her car, congratulating her once more along the way. For the rainy season of April, it was a beautiful sun-shining spring day, and under normal circumstances she would have driven with the top down on her convertible candy-apple-red BMW, but today she had to worry about the trail of gifts and cards that she could possibly leave down the highway. So the windows being partially rolled down would have to suffice.

As Nikki stopped at a red light, the passenger in a midnight-blue SUV that was stopped next to her attempted to flirt with her, but she ignored his advances. As she sped away, she heard him yell obscenities at her.

"That's why I didn't acknowledge your existence," she blurted out.

She drove the rest of the way home listening to one of her favorite Dallas radio stations. *The Drive at Five* radio mix always calmed her nerves during rush-hour traffic.

When she pulled into the driveway of her two-bedroom ranch-style home, she spotted a familiar car, belonging to none other than her best friend, Charlotte. Nikki had hoped to avoid Charlotte until after her return trip from Las Vegas, but luck wasn't on her side.

Nikki got out of the car, deciding to come back for the gifts and cards later. When Charlotte saw Nikki get out of her car, she got out of hers as well. The two greeted each other without speaking a word, but with a hug only. Nikki could sense that Charlotte wanted to explode with words, but as she followed her up the sidewalk and to the doorstep, she stood silently until Nikki unlocked the front door and the two entered.

"How could you plan on sneaking to Vegas without a word?" Charlotte said, closing the door behind her. "I had to find out from your sister that you were leaving in the morning."

Nikki knew that she wouldn't be able to keep her secret

for long and really needed someone to confide in. "If you give me a minute to get settled, I'll explain everything," she said, setting her keys and purse down on the living room end table.

Charlotte crossed her arms and responded with an attitude. "You'd better, because we've been friends far too long for me to hear about this from someone else. This really hurts. I thought we were close, but I guess I was wrong."

"Calm down. I'll explain it all in a minute," Nikki announced, trying to calm her friend.

Charlotte rolled her eyes. "Whatever. You definitely have some explaining to do, missy."

"Make yourself at home," Nikki said, as she headed toward her bedroom. "I'll be right back."

When Nikki returned to the living room she could hear some rustling around in the kitchen, where Charlotte was making herself a turkey and Swiss cheese sandwich. Nikki went into the kitchen and took a seat on one of the wooden bar stools at the island and sat silently until Charlotte finished making her sandwich and joined her on the bar stool.

She and Charlotte had been friends and inseparable since first grade. Although they each had siblings, they were more like sisters. They were both five feet eight inches tall and wore their hair in a short Halle Berry style that was made famous years ago. Although both were attractive, Nikki's breasts were larger and her sparkling hazel eyes usually captivated most men. Charlotte, on the other hand, was well proportioned and had legs to put Tina Turner to shame. When it came to dealing with issues, especially issues that involved men, they were complete opposites.

Nikki cleared her throat. "I know what I'm about to tell you might sound crazy, but please hear me out before you interrupt."

Charlotte took a bite of her sandwich and after swallowing said, "Sure." She continued to eat while listening to Nikki.

"I'm going to Las Vegas because everyone thinks the ring I'm wearing is an engagement ring."

"Okay, I know that much," Charlotte said in a nonchalant tone.

"And they think I'm going to Vegas to marry my fiancé."

Charlotte almost choked. "What in the world? What fiancé? How could you keep something like this from me? Who is he? Do I know him?"

Nikki waited for Charlotte to stop blurting out questions. "Are you through so I can finish?"

Charlotte took a sip of her drink. "Go ahead," she said as she looked at Nikki in amazement.

"The key word is everyone *thinks*. I'm tired of everyone asking me about my personal life . . . asking me when I'm going to settle down. The idea hit me after I saw this lady do it in a movie."

"Uh-huh," Charlotte said as she stared at her in disbelief. "The idea of what?"

"If everyone thinks I'm married, maybe they'll stop asking me about my love life. Then I can go on with my life worry-free. I won't have to worry about being thirty-four and unmarried. And I sure won't have to listen to the countless questions about why, when, et cetera."

Charlotte put her drink down and pushed her plate away. "So you're telling me you've planned a fake wedding and everyone, including your family, thinks you're going to Las Vegas to get married?"

"Yes," Nikki said, putting her head down in shame.

Charlotte looked at her with such pity before bursting out into laughter. "Girl, are you crazy? How in the world do you think you're going to pull it off? You do have to come back. And when you do come back, without a husband, I might add, what will you tell everyone?"

"Actually, I've told everyone he travels a lot and when he's in town, we only have time for each other."

"You've been setting this up for a while. I thought you bought the ring to ward off men you didn't want to talk to. I never thought you would do something this stupid."

Nikki defended herself. "I don't think it's stupid at all," she said, getting up from the bar stool and pacing. "Besides, I'm due for a vacation and this will keep people out of my business, especially the people at the office. Now maybe my director will stop flirting with me every chance he gets."

Charlotte shook her head and said, "I can see you telling those busybodies at work, but did you have to lie to your own family?"

"You know my family. They're as bad as my coworkers," Nikki said, throwing her hands up. "You know for yourself that they're always asking me when I'm going to settle down. I'm sick and tired of being made to feel like something is wrong with me because I'm not married."

"I hear you, but still this is going to backfire and then what?"

"This will bide me some time. I can always tell them it didn't work out and I got a quick divorce."

"Sounds like you've thought of everything."

Nikki walked toward the side door of her house, which was off the kitchen. "I sure did. Now help me get my wedding presents out of the car."

Charlotte shook her head and began to chuckle. "Girl, all I can say is you're something else and watching you work your way through this one is going to be good!"

Nikki's trip to Las Vegas was filled with gambling and shows. In addition to enjoying Las Vegas, she rented a car and drove to Los Angeles to do more sightseeing. On the plane ride back home to Dallas she closed her eyes and tried to relax, but the man sitting next to her annoyed her by constantly pecking on his keyboard. He noticed her irritation and offered to let her borrow his headphones so that he wouldn't be as distracting, but Nikki declined with a "No, thank you."

"Are you sure?" the gentleman inquired. "I have to finish this report or I won't meet my deadline. I do apologize for the inconvenience."

Nikki sighed and then opened her eyes. She turned to look at her traveling companion and noticed his captivating gray eyes, and although he wasn't smiling, she could see the dimples in his cheeks. For once, she was at a loss for words.

"Uh, yeah, I'm sure," she stammered.

"Well, let me know if you change your mind," he said as he continued to type away on his keyboard.

Nikki couldn't take her eyes off him. When he looked up from his laptop and caught her staring at him, she felt a little embarrassed, but snapped back with a catchy excuse. "Excuse me for staring, but you look familiar," she lied.

He smiled and assumed she was flirting. He didn't mind at all. He'd lost his concentration now that she was finally warming up to him. From the moment Nikki sat down next to him her alluring fragrance had captivated him. The red blouse she wore accented the two things he admired most on a woman, pretty eyes and ample breasts.

"I'm Byron Matthews and you are?" he asked while extending his hand.

"Nicolette Montana, but my friends call me Nikki for short," she replied, extending her hand as well.

They shook hands and in unison they said, "Nice to meet you."

They both felt a jolt of electricity, and since neither knew how to respond to it, they both remained silent. Byron went back to pecking on his laptop and Nikki pretended to be reading one of those airline magazines she had just pulled from the back of the seat in front of her. Several minutes later the stewardess headed down the aisle with the drink cart, offering passengers drinks. When the stewardess got to them, Nikki passed on a drink and Byron appeared to be engulfed in his work and didn't respond to the query.

"The stewardess wants to know if you want something to drink," Nikki said, tapping Byron on the arm.

He looked up. "I'm sorry. Yes, a cup of coffee would be nice."

After the stewardess fulfilled Byron's request, they continued the rest of the flight in silence. Both tried to ignore the feeling of being in such close proximity to one another. Soon they heard the stewardess's voice blaring over the loudspeakers instructing the passengers to turn off all electronic items. As Byron attempted to put away his laptop under the seat in front of him, he'd forgotten that he had set his almost empty cup of coffee on the floor and accidentally splashed the remains on Nikki's shoes. He looked up to apologize, but nothing came out of his mouth. Nikki jumped in her seat and blurted out, "Excuse you."

"I'm so sorry. I forgot that I had put it there," Byron apologized.

"I just got these shoes and now they're ruined." She frowned.

He pulled out his business card and wrote something on the back before handing it to her. "My home number is on the back. I'll buy you another pair, regardless of the cost."

Although she knew she should be upset that he'd ruined a 120-dollar pair of shoes that she had received as a birthday gift, one look into his apologetic eyes almost made her melt in her seat.

"Okay," she said and smiled. "Trust me. I'll be calling you. Let me give you my information, too."

He wrote down her information as she recited it to him.

"Again, Nikki," Byron said as they headed off the plane, "I'm so sorry."

"Apology accepted, but it's Ms. Montana to you," she teased.

2

Byron's brother was always late, and today was no exception. As Byron stood at the curb at pickup outside baggage claim, he took out his cell phone and called to find out why Frederick wasn't at the airport to pick him up. He normally drove himself and parked his car in the secured parking garage, but it was at the dealership for its scheduled maintenance, so instead he had arranged for Frederick to be his means of transportation.

The two brothers were total opposites. Byron prided himself on being punctual and would rather be early than late. Frederick ran on his own clock, the clock of never being on time. Byron was thirty-four and although he was five years younger than Frederick, his six-four frame towered over Frederick by two inches. They both had inherited their mother's honey-brown complexion and their father's alluring gray eyes. Byron chose to wear his hair short, usually an eighth of an inch from his head, while Frederick opted for a clean-shaven bald head.

Byron redialed Frederick's cell phone number, but before it could ring, a charcoal-gray Range Rover pulled up to the curb in front of where he was standing. "Man, where have you been? I've been waiting for almost an hour," Byron scolded as he threw his luggage into the backseat.

Frederick, who was on his cell phone, bobbing his head to the beat of the tune that was playing in his CD changer, ended his phone conversation, and responded, "I'm sorry. I got caught up in construction traffic on 635 and then my phone kept ringing off the hook."

"I've called you twice. I swear our birth orders got mixed up. I should have been the oldest."

Byron settled into the passenger's seat as Frederick drove toward the interstate.

"At least I didn't leave you stranded," Frederick said.

"You would say that."

"Anyway, what are your plans for Memorial Day weekend? A group of us are going to Cancún for the Jazz Festival. If you want to tag along, let me know and I'll get your ticket."

Byron thought about what had happened the last time he hung out with Frederick and his friends and decided to pass. "I'll take my chances on finding something to do around here."

"Whatever, man," Frederick replied, as his cell phone rang again. "It's your loss."

As they rode to Byron's house in Plano, Texas, Frederick updated him on what had been happening with some of their friends. Byron halfway listened because he couldn't seem to get his airline traveling companion off his mind. He couldn't get the softness of her light brown eyes and the smell of her sweet floral fragrance out of his head. He knew he would be calling her the first opportunity he got.

Nikki sat on her camel-colored suede living room couch checking her voice messages at home and at the office. Her mailboxes overflowed with congratulatory messages from people about her nuptials. At the end of her vacation, she thought about the hoax she'd pulled on everyone. She looked at all the gifts she'd received, and a flurry of guilt consumed her. She would send every one of them back once she announced that the marriage had failed. In six months she would announce that she and her invisible husband couldn't work out their differences and were filing for divorce. Yes, that was exactly what she would do. To Nikki's dismay, it still didn't make her feel any less guilty as she knew for the next six months she would be living a lie.

The next morning, she arrived at work ready to play her role. She'd almost forgotten to put the ring she'd purchased back on her finger. She had to make it look authentic. She applied her makeup so she would appear to have a happy newlywed glow. As soon as she entered the lobby door, she ran into some of the office gossipers.

Different coworkers came up to her. "Hi. You look marvelous. We were all wondering if you were going to come back to us after your whirlwind romance."

Nikki smiled and placed her left hand up to her mouth to show off her ring. "Now you know I couldn't leave you guys. I love working here too much," she lied.

One of the ladies spoke out. "You never told us his name."

Nikki began to get nervous. She blurted out the first name that came to mind. "His name is Byron and he's magnificent."

Another lady chimed in and asked, "So what's your new last name?"

Nikki hadn't thought about it, but answered, "Matthews, but I'll still use my maiden name."

After her initial encounter with her coworkers, the day was uneventful for Nikki until Kenneth dropped by her desk with a bouquet of flowers. "Nikki, these came for you and I must admit I was nosy and read your card. So your new hubby's name is Byron?"

Nikki cleared her throat. "Yes, but how many times have

I told you to mind your own business and stay out of mine!" she stated.

"You're the one who's always trying to be secretive. I swear your husband is going to have a time with you."

"Apparently he can deal with me or else he wouldn't have married me."

"Touché," Kenneth said as he walked away.

Nikki picked up the bouquet and inhaled the sweet fragrance of the tropical flowers. She placed the pretty blue vase on the corner of her desk before opening the card that read *Thank you for understanding—Byron*.

She closed her eyes, and for a moment, pretended the sexy man from the airplane really was her husband. The phone rang and interrupted her daydream.

"Hello," she answered.

"May I speak to Nicolette Montana?" the male voice on the other end of the line asked.

"This is Nikki," she responded.

"Sorry, I didn't recognize your voice. This is Byron. You know, the clumsy guy from the plane."

Nikki laughed. "Hi, Byron. Thanks for the flowers," she said, playing with one of the soft petals.

"You're welcome. That's the least I could do for ruining your shoes." Byron took in Nikki's little chuckle, took a deep breath, then got right to his reason for calling. "Are you available this evening for dinner?"

Nikki hesitated, caught off guard by Byron's forwardness. But then she saw Kenneth pass by her desk again. "Sweetie, why don't we meet around seven?" She spoke loud enough for Kenneth to hear.

"Seven is fine. I need to know where I can pick you up."

"That won't be necessary. I can meet you somewhere."

"My mom taught me that a gentleman always picks up a lady."

A big Cheshire cat grin spread across Nikki's face. "This

lady appreciates it, but it'll be rather late when I get off work so it'll be more convenient for me if I meet you there."

"Okay. I know when to give up. Seven it is and I'll meet you at the new Italian restaurant on Second Avenue downtown. Do you know the place I'm talking about?"

"Sure. I'll see you then, Byron," Nikki said as she twirled from left to right in her chair.

Before Nikki could end the call, Kenneth had reported back to the other office gossipers about Nikki's conversation with her new husband. Nikki overheard him exaggerate the truth and laughed. Exaggerating the truth seemed to be on the menu for everybody.

3

Byron spent the rest of the afternoon going over his presentation for his upcoming meeting. As one of the top salesmen at North American Telecom, he had the responsibilities of not only bringing on new customers, but teaching other NAT employees about new products and sales techniques. Although NAT already had a good reputation as one of the leading telecommunications companies in the world, Byron's natural sales ability was what helped him succeed in his current role. He tried to stay focused, yet he couldn't get Nikki Montana's sexy voice out of his head. She had invaded his dreams all night and he couldn't wait to see her. The last time a woman took over both his conscious and his unconscious thoughts, it was nothing but trouble, so he knew that he should probably run in the opposite direction. Besides, his last relationship had also drained him financially and emotionally.

Tara was always full of drama. The final straw came when Byron received a two-thousand-dollar Visa bill for a shopping spree that he later found out included men's clothing and underwear. He knew he hadn't treated himself to a shopping spree. It turned out that not only had Tara been cheating on him for quite some time, but he had been financing her rendezvous.

That was over a year ago and Byron had barely looked at a woman since. Instead, he poured himself into his work and continued to win clients for his company. For the last four quarters, he'd been the top salesman. A few weeks ago his company awarded him with the top honor of salesman of the year.

A huge grin covered Byron's face as he thought about his dinner date. His secretary walked into his oversized office decorated with glossy mahogany wooden furniture, one of the perks of being the company's top salesman, holding several folders.

"Byron, I must say Seattle must have agreed with you. There's something different about you," Joyce Sanders said as she placed the folders on Byron's oval mahogany desk.

Byron twisted his multicolored silk necktie at the collar. "You think so? Let's just say on the way back from Seattle, something brightened my horizons."

"It must be a woman." Joyce laughed. "I'm happy for you and I'm sure everyone else at the office will be too."

"Hold on," Byron said as he held up his hand. "There's nothing to tell yet. It's just dinner."

"Oh, you're having dinner with her?"

"Yes, tonight. But don't broadcast this to the world."

"You know me." She smirked.

"Yes, I do know you. That's why I'm telling you not to broadcast it to the world."

Joyce laughed and walked out of his office.

Byron spent the rest of the afternoon working on his presentation. As he prepared to leave his office, the phone rang. The number displayed on the caller ID didn't look familiar. *It must be her,* he thought. He paused before answering, hoping that Nikki wasn't calling to cancel their date. "Hello," he said, looking at his watch.

"Byron, darling, I'm glad I caught you. How are you?" a female voice said.

After hearing the familiar voice over the phone, Byron regretted that he had answered the phone at all. "I'm fine. To what honor do I owe this call?"

The woman's voice sounded like a cat purring. "Darling, I can't call to check on you?"

"No. It usually means you need money. I've told you before, this well is dry. Tara, you need to move on."

"How can you dismiss what we had?" Tara sounded angry.

Byron tried to control his anger. "Look, Tara. It's been over a year now. You need to forget my number and get a life," he said with authority.

"I don't want you," she lashed back. "I called to see how you were doing. We were together for a couple of years and, unlike you, I don't have any hard feelings."

"I'm doing fine and I'll be doing even better if you forget my number and I never have to talk to you again."

"Oh, you *will* talk to me!" Tara yelled.

She started to continue her rant, but Byron slammed down the phone before she could finish. "The nerve of that woman!" he said to himself.

He turned out the light in his office and left to meet Nikki.

4

After paying for valet parking, Byron entered the restaurant and searched for Nikki. Tara's phone call had him in a foul mood, but when he spotted Nikki sitting at a table and her beautiful smile, a sense of calmness washed over him.

"Have you been waiting long?" he asked as he approached her.

When she looked up, her smile brightened the room. "No. I've only been here for about five minutes."

He quickly apologized. "I had to take a last-minute call." He glanced at his watch. "I'm normally prompt."

As soon as Byron sat down, a waiter walked over and took their drink orders.

They sat in silence until Byron said something to ease the tension. "Can I call you Nikki or do I have to call you Ms. Montana?"

Nikki playfully responded, "It all depends on how fast you are in replacing my shoes."

He flashed her a smile. Before he could respond, a waiter came to their table and took their drink and dinner orders.

"So, Nikki, how did we happen to be on the same flight?" Byron asked.

Nikki told Byron about her vacation, leaving out the part about her invisible husband. Suddenly, it dawned on her that she had used his name as her husband. She became fidgety and decided to steer the conversation around him. "Now that I've told you about my vacation, tell me a little more about you."

Over dinner Byron spoke about his job at North American Telecom, and Nikki gave him a brief overview of her advertising career. They were getting along well until Byron noticed the ring glistening on her finger. *So that's why she was adamant about meeting me here*, he thought, *and not letting me pick her up at her home . . . their home, her and the man who put that wedding ring on her finger.* His tone of voice became dry. "Mrs. Montana, I think I've taken up enough of your time. If you'll wait up front while they bring me my car, we can take care of your shoe problem."

Nikki's smile faded. For the past hour she had thought they were having a good time. But without warning, Byron grew cold. She noticed his eyes wandering down to her ring finger. She started to correct him about her marital status but then thought about the embarrassment of it all. He would think she was crazy or that something was wrong with her, terribly wrong. So wrong that she couldn't get a real husband so she had to make one up. She decided against correcting Byron's assumption.

"Sure. Let me go to the ladies' room and I'll meet you up front," she said, faking a smile.

Byron paid for their dinner and then waited up front for his car and Nikki. *I've been out of the game too long. I should have known that as sexy as she is, she's already taken.*

He felt Nikki's presence as she walked up behind him. The valet attendant pulled up with his car just as Nikki approached him. He went to the passenger side and pulled out a big gift bag. He walked back to the other side of the car and handed it to Nikki. "I think you were waiting on this."

Nikki took the bag and looked inside it. Her mouth dropped open in surprise. "Thank you. I didn't realize you would have the shoes tonight. I hadn't told you what size or where I got them."

He almost forgot that she was already somebody else's woman as he watched her light up while observing the shoes. Her smile was perfect. Her teeth were perfect and her lips were looking delicious. He wanted to reach down and kiss them. "I failed to mention that I worked in ladies' shoes at a department store while I attended college," Byron said.

Another valet attendant pulled Nikki's car up behind Byron's. She was about to thank Byron and leave when she saw one of her coworkers driving up. She quickly reached out and hugged Byron. Before he had a chance to respond, she put her lips against his and they engaged in a passionate kiss. For a moment, they were oblivious of their surroundings. But then Nikki pulled away when her coworker walked up to them. "Nikki, it's good seeing you out. This must be—"

Nikki quickly interrupted. "This is Byron. Byron, this is Mya and her husband, Paul."

Byron, who was still trying to recover from the kiss, reached out and shook their hands.

Mya winked at Nikki and before walking off said, "I'll see you tomorrow."

After Mya and Paul walked away, Byron commented, "She seems nice."

"Yes, but she's one of the biggest gossipers at the office."

Byron was brought back to reality. "Will you be all right? I'd hate for this to get back to your husband. And I sure don't want your reputation ruined on account of an innocent kiss."

"Don't worry. I'm a big girl," Nikki responded, failing to correct her marital status.

Byron sensed an attitude and not being in a good mood

he said, "Look. I know you are. Forget it. You have your shoes. If they're not the right size, the receipt is in the bag. I have an early day tomorrow, so I need to be getting home. Again, I apologize for any inconvenience I may have caused you." He walked to the driver's side of his car, got in, and drove off without looking back at Nikki or giving her a chance to respond.

Nikki stood there with her mouth open. *No, he didn't leave me standing here,* she thought. She took a couple of one-dollar bills out of her purse, handed them to the valet driver, and then drove off.

She dialed Charlotte's number from her cell phone as she drove home. By the time she had updated Charlotte on her trip and Byron, she was relaxing on her couch flipping through stations on the TV. Their conversation was cut short when the battery on her cell phone indicated that it was low.

"Charlotte, I'll talk to you tomorrow. I didn't mean to talk your ear off," Nikki said.

Charlotte yawned. "Girl, it's cool. Keep me updated on your invisible husband and Byron."

"There is nothing to report on Byron."

"That's what your mouth says. Apparently he left a lasting impression for you to use his name with those people at your office." Charlotte laughed.

"I don't think it's funny."

"I'm going to bed," Charlotte said, prepared to end the call. "Oh, I almost forgot. I'm not supposed to tell you, but in this case, I think you need to be prepared. Your sister is planning a surprise dinner to welcome your husband into the family."

Nikki's cell phone went dead at that point. She frantically searched for the cordless phone and immediately called Charlotte back. "I know I didn't hear you say what I thought you said," Nikki gasped.

"You sure did. Now on that note, I'm going to bed. Some

of us need our beauty rest. Not all women are as fortunate as you to already have a husband." Charlotte laughed as she hung up the phone.

Nikki sat there wondering how she was going to get out of going to her family's dinner.

5

Byron spent the next few weeks trying to forget he'd ever met Nikki Montana. On edge and snappy as he was, his co-workers could sense something was bothering him. Joyce even kept asking him about how things went at dinner, but he had managed to ignore her or brush her off. He was so upset that he was on the verge of firing her if she asked him about Nikki one more time. "Can you leave the shoe lady alone?" he snapped.

Joyce completed what she was writing before looking up. "I can, but can you?"

"What do you mean by that?"

"Let's look at this. A week or so ago you were floating. Now you're lighting into your team about insignificant things. It's totally out of your character. This has been going on ever since your dinner with her. So something must have happened."

Byron knew she was right, but still denied it. "Mrs. Nicolette Montana has nothing to do with this. I swear if you weren't my cousin, I would be looking for a new secretary."

Joyce gathered her things and calmly said, "I'm out of

here. When you want to apologize for your attitude, you know how to reach me." She slammed his office door.

Byron placed his face in the palm of his hands while leaning on his desk. *I need to do something about this,* he thought. *I can't go on snapping at folks. I'll call Joyce later and apologize.* He sat down in his chair at his desk and allowed his thoughts to continue. *I've been lusting after a married woman. Maybe if I see her one more time and if she tells me she's happy with her husband, I can then get her out of my system.*

With Nikki's phone number embedded in his memory, Byron picked up the phone and dialed it. As soon as the phone rang, he hung up. "What am I doing? I'm not one to share," he said to himself.

He grabbed his jacket and decided to do something he hadn't done in months, go out to a club. He called Frederick on the way to the club and made arrangements to meet up with him. An hour later he entered the club and found a comfortable spot at the bar. It was a perfect spot for him. He ordered a drink, looked around, and got a perfect view of the front door. Thursday night was karaoke night and the club was packed. A few women flirted with him. He knew he was an attractive man, but he didn't feel like playing the cat-and-mouse game tonight.

The announcer grabbed the microphone and began introducing the karaoke contestants. The first one took the stage. Byron couldn't see the person, but it didn't take long for him to realize that the voice he heard was his brother's. There was a female singing along with him, but Byron had no idea who she could be. He moved around to the other side of the bar so that he could get a good look. He knew Frederick enjoyed attention, and that the woman onstage was probably his brother's next victim. He could tell she had a shapely body from the way her red dress clung to her body. He almost dropped his drink when he saw that the woman was none other than Nikki.

The crowd loved them. When they exited the stage, Byron saw Frederick, Nikki, and some other woman walking in his direction.

Nikki was busy talking to Charlotte, and before Frederick could finish the introductions, Nikki and Byron both blurted out in unison, "What are you doing here?"

Charlotte and Frederick looked from one to the other, and then Frederick intervened.

"I take it you two already know each other?" he asked.

"Yes," they both replied, tension surrounding each of their tones.

"Uh, Charlotte, would you like that drink now?" Frederick made an excuse so his brother and Nikki could be alone.

Charlotte, on the other hand, didn't want to miss out on a thing. She put her hand up, motioning Frederick to wait. "Maybe later," she replied.

Frederick wrapped his arms around Charlotte. "No. I think now is a good time."

"Charlotte, go. I'll be okay," Nikki said, assuring her that everything would be fine.

Frederick and Charlotte left and Byron and Nikki stood still like they were glued to that one spot. The thickening crowd forced Nikki to move closer to Byron.

Byron was the first to break their spell of silence. "Mrs. Montana, I see your husband let you out to play. For a moment I thought you were with my brother."

Nikki couldn't hear everything he was saying because of the thunderous music. "Look, Byron. It's Miss Montana. Contrary to what you think, I'm not married."

He looked down at her finger. He leaned closer to her so she could hear him. "How do you explain this, then?" He pointed at the ring.

"It's a long story. But I'm far from being married."

"I have all night. Do you want to go outside on the patio so we can talk?"

Nikki remembered how he had left her outside the restaurant, so she declined. "I don't think that's a good idea. Besides, I'm about to leave anyway. Bye."

She abruptly turned and walked away. Byron watched her and made a mental note on how graceful her stride was. Some of the other men in the club couldn't keep their eyes off her as she strutted by each one of them. Either she was used to the attention or just didn't care, because she ignored their advances as she headed for the door.

Byron didn't move. He didn't know what to do. But he didn't want to let her get away from him a second time either. The moment she informed him that she wasn't married, he knew that he had to make things right between them. He looked around the club for Frederick and Charlotte and saw them sitting at the other end of the bar and made his way toward them.

"Hey, bro," Frederick said to Byron as he approached them at the bar. "Looks like you lost your best friend."

"Looks like you found one," Byron said, referring to how comfortable Frederick and Charlotte looked with one another.

Frederick looked over at Charlotte. "Charlotte and I work together," he confirmed.

"But speaking of best friends," Charlotte interrupted, "where's mine?" Charlotte began looking over Byron's shoulder for her friend. "What have you done with Nikki?"

"He's harmless," Frederick assured her. "This is my brother. This is Byron."

"Byron?" Charlotte asked with excitement. "*The* Byron, huh?"

"I'm Byron," he confirmed. "I don't know about *the* Byron, but I'm definitely Byron. But anyway, your best friend left."

"Left?" Charlotte said with a puzzled look on her face.

"Yep, headed for the door," Byron informed her.

Charlotte's first thought was to get up and go after her friend, but then she had a second thought. "Byron, as you can see I just started my drink. Would you mind being the designated driver?"

"What do you mean?" Byron asked, confused.

"Nikki, she's going to be needing a ride home, seeing as how she rode with me." Charlotte winked.

Byron hid the grin that was trying its best to take over his lips. He wanted to jump up and click his heels. But instead, he kissed Charlotte on the cheek and exited the club. He felt a surge of confidence at the opportunity to make things right with Nikki.

Nikki rushed out of the club before it dawned on her that Charlotte had driven. She was fuming mad. Byron acted as if they were long-lost friends. Though she was infuriated, at the same time his stare caused a warm sensation to go through her entire body and she felt like poking his eyes out for making her feel uneasy inside.

She had decided that she would head back toward the club when she heard someone call her name. She turned around and came face-to-face with Byron.

"Are you following me?" she asked him.

Byron tried hard not to laugh, because he knew she was stranded. "No, but I do know that unless you plan on waiting all night for Charlotte, you need a ride home."

"Did my ex–bestfriend tell you that?"

Byron was unable to control his laughter. "Yes, and I kindly told her I would take you home, since you were ready to leave and she wasn't."

Nikki didn't find any of what he was saying amusing. "Don't worry. I came here with Charlotte and I'll leave with Charlotte."

Byron pulled her body against his chest and began kissing her intensely. Some onlookers shouted, "You need to take that home."

Byron pulled away first. "You were saying."

Nikki stuttered, "Where are you parked?"

"Now that's more like it." He led her to his car.

Once they were in the car, Byron reached over her to help fasten her seat belt. Unable to hold back his desires, he kissed her again. This time their kisses were more relaxed and they only stopped when Byron accidentally hit the horn.

"Maybe this isn't a good idea," Nikki said, pulling away. "I can still get Charlotte to take me home."

"I promise to behave." Byron smiled. "Now how do we get to your place? There's something I want to talk to you about."

She stared at him. Her eyes revealed she didn't believe talking was all that was on his mind. She gave him directions and they headed toward her place.

Byron maneuvered the car into Nikki's driveway. Before she could make a move, he jumped out and ran around to open the door for her. She got out and he closed it behind her, following her trail as he walked her to her door.

Nikki was confused, but bluntly said, "I hope you don't think I'm indebted to you because you brought me home."

He looked directly into her sparkling, soft brown eyes. "No. I'm indebted to you."

She nervously fumbled with her keys before losing her grip and dropping them at her feet. Byron picked them up and opened the screen door for her. Nikki couldn't understand why this man made her so nervous.

"Would you like to come in for a minute?" She couldn't understand how he made her so weak.

Byron glanced at his watch and contemplated on whether to go in or go home. Nikki unconsciously took out her tongue and licked her lips. At this point, Byron decided to throw caution to the wind. "I'd love to come in," he replied.

Nikki led the way into her home. He watched her as she turned on the lamp.

"Why don't you wait in the living room and I'll get us something to drink?"

Byron sat down on the couch and before he could relax, Nikki walked back into the room carrying a couple of glasses of ice, Sprite, and bottled water on a tray. "I brought out both. Take your pick."

At that moment, as he watched her enter the room like a ray of sunshine seeping from behind a dark cloud, the only thing he wanted to do was drink of her sweet juices. He snapped out of his trance and replied, "Sprite will be fine."

Setting the tray down on the oblong, dark tan coffee table in front of the couch, Nikki sat down next to Byron, and then kicked off her heels and crossed her legs. "Are you ready?" she asked.

He almost choked on his Sprite. "Come again?"

"You said you wanted to hear my long story behind the ring. Are you ready?"

Realizing that he almost made a fool of himself, Byron responded, "Sure, I'm all ears."

Nikki noticed a small diamond stud in his ear. It added another sexy appeal to the man. She decided not to look directly in his eyes, because she needed to concentrate. She hoped after hearing her story he wouldn't think less of her.

While she spoke, she paid close attention to his facial expressions. She went as far as to tell him that her coworkers and family thought he was her invisible husband. "I understand if you don't want to have anything else to do with me, but I was tired of people assuming that there was something wrong with me just because I wasn't married."

For a moment, he didn't say anything. All of a sudden he burst out laughing. "If someone else would have told me this story, I would have said they were kidding. But for some reason I believe you. Either we're crazy or they are. Believe it or not, I can understand why you did what you did."

"You can?"

"Yes, of course. I get the same thing all the time from my family and friends. Frederick is older than me, but because he's always had the reputation as a ladies' man, he doesn't get any flack. I've always been considered the responsible one, so people assume I would be married by now with 2.5 kids."

They both laughed. Nikki wiped her right eyebrow. "I feel so much better getting everything off my chest."

"I do have one question, though."

"What?"

"When do we consummate the marriage?"

She picked up one of the red and gold pillows on the couch and threw it at him. He picked up one and they got into a pillow fight and ended up in each other's arms.

Nikki led him into her master bedroom. They laid back on the lavender-and-cream-colored satin bedding that dressed the king-sized bed. Their kisses intensified as Byron's hands took pleasure in roaming over her voluptuous body. Moans of satisfaction escaped Nikki's lips. The desire for Byron was about to overtake her.

"Byron, nooo . . . stop," she moaned.

Byron looked into her eyes. He saw how frightened she was as they almost took their relationship to another level. He didn't want to rush her.

His voice was hoarse when he responded, "Okay, baby. Let me hold you." Nikki nestled against his chest. He wrapped his arms around her warm body until sleep overtook them.

6

The next morning, Byron did a double take when he opened his eyes to be staring at an eggshell ceiling trimmed with a border of lavender and cream designs. He slowly lowered his chin to his chest and looked down, convincing himself that he wasn't dreaming. The skirt Nikki wore was bundled up around her waist and her legs were entwined in his. His pants were snug in one spot and he needed to move, but he didn't want to wake her up.

Last night while he was listening to her recount her invisible husband story, he felt a need to protect her from everyone. He was drawn into her more than he should be, but couldn't help it. There was something about her that made him want to be everything she needed.

Nikki stirred before opening her eyes. "I'm sorry for falling asleep on you. I felt comfortable being in your arms."

Byron brushed the hair from her forehead. "You can fall asleep on me anytime."

"It's almost eight o'clock," Nikki said after looking at the clock. "I can't believe I overslept. I hate being late. I'd rather not go at all than to walk in late." She thought for a moment. "I think I will call in sick today."

A mischievous look came across Byron's face. "I think I'll play hooky from work too." This would be the first sick day he'd taken in two years. "I don't mean to disturb this very relaxing position, but let me go get my cell phone out of the car. I need to make a couple of calls but then I'll be back to join you in your sickbed."

"Don't be using me," she teased.

He assured her before standing up. "Trust me, I'd never use you. Only love you."

Nikki reached over and took the cordless phone from its cradle and handed it to Byron.

"You can use this. I'll give you some privacy. I need to go jump in the shower," she said as she fumbled for under-garments in her dresser drawers.

Byron walked over and sat down in the chair that was be-side her bed. He watched Nikki as she walked out of the room and into the attached bathroom to go take a shower, his eyes focused on her ample behind.

He was quite tempted to join her in the shower, but opted to remain sitting in the chair. He had been careful about get-ting involved with anyone, but in less than a month, Nikki had him committed to her.

While he waited on Nikki, he made several phone calls. One of the first calls he made was to Joyce. He apologized to her for his behavior. Joyce pretended not to forgive him, but reassured him that she would handle everything while he was out.

"Can you pass me the outfit that's hanging in the closet? Right there to the left," she yelled as she stuck her head out the bathroom door.

He opened the closet door and was amazed at all of the clothes and shoes. It was like her own private boutique. The closet floor was full of shoes in different styles and colors. He shook his head as he thought about her attitude about one pair of shoes. He handed her the outfit. "I couldn't help but notice that you're a shoe freak."

She laughed. "Takes one to know one." She then disappeared back behind the bathroom door.

"Do you mind if I use your guest bathroom? I have some gym clothes out in my car that I can change into," Byron yelled while she got dressed in the bathroom.

"Not at all. It's down the hall and to the right. I'll be out in a minute."

By the time he made it back inside with his gym bag, Nikki was dressed. She showed him where the towels and extra soap were located. While he showered, she cooked breakfast. They spent the entire day talking and laughing. They realized they had more in common than they had originally thought. Both of their last relationships ended when the ones they trusted betrayed them by cheating. They both poured themselves into their work to hide the disappointment. They were equally surprised that they were bonding in such a short time.

Nighttime was closely approaching and they hadn't left Nikki's house. They were deciding on a movie to watch when Nikki's cell phone rang. "Hello," she answered.

Charlotte's voice echoed from the other end. "Are you okay? I called you at work and the receptionist said you were sick and she also added that you were probably somewhere with your handsome husband."

"Oh, she did?" Nikki sighed. "I'm fine, but I have company right now, so I'll have to call you back."

"Oh no, sista, you're not going to drop the bomb on me and then rush off the phone. Is it Byron?"

"Maybe."

"I told Frederick that you two were probably together."

"You talked to Frederick?"

"Yes. He called to see if I had talked to you because he

was trying to reach his brother. He got the same response from Byron's secretary. I can't wait to tell Frederick where he is." Charlotte giggled.

Byron walked behind Nikki and looped his arms around her waist. He planted kisses on the nape of her neck. She could barely concentrate. "I'll tell Byron that Frederick's looking for him."

"I knew it. You just confirmed my suspicions. You go, girl!"

"Bye, Charlotte."

"Looks like your brother and my best friend have been looking for us. Don't worry, she can't wait to call him and let him know that you're safe."

Byron turned Nikki around to face him. "My brother is the last person on my mind right now. Come here."

He took her hand and led her to the oversized living room chair. He sat down first before pulling her onto his lap. "Girl, you're so tantalizing, I could devour you right now."

"Oh, really? Well, you're not too bad yourself."

"Before we take this further, I think we need to discuss where we both want this to go," Byron said.

She ran her hands through her hair, hoping Byron couldn't sense her nervousness. She'd never wanted anyone as much as she wanted Byron. Yes, she wanted him in the physical sense, but she also wanted to share her thoughts and dreams with him. Perhaps her family's and coworkers' past concerns about her living the single life had finally gotten the best of her. She didn't want to do the dating thing anymore. It was a waste of time knowing that the person you were with was no more than a date, a time filler. She wanted more. She wanted Byron. She desired to have him be the person she could be herself with and not worry about being judged. She didn't know what his response was going to be, but she felt like she had nothing to lose by being completely honest.

"I want more than a booty call," Nikki resolved.

"I agree. From the moment I laid eyes on you, I've been

drawn to you. At first I admit it was your physical essence, but your inner spirit has captivated me. I've tried forgetting you, and the more I tried, the worse off I felt," Byron confessed.

"Really?"

"Yes. I needed to see you one more time to get you out of my system. It's too late, because I realize now I can't get you out of my system."

"You're not just saying that, are you?" she asked, feeling like she had won the lottery.

With a stern, yet soft look on his face, Byron answered, "I don't say anything I don't mean. If you don't remember anything else I tell you, remember this—I don't play when it comes to my emotions. I know this may not be an appropriate time to be asking you this, but I'm going to ask anyway. If you're dating other men, will you please stop and allow me the chance to show you that we can have something wonderful? All I'm asking for is a chance, Nikki."

"I'd love to, but there's one problem," Nikki said, looking down.

Byron felt his heart dropping. "What?"

"I'm not dating anyone else." Nikki looked up and smiled.

"You had me worried for a minute." He released his breath.

So that there would be no misunderstandings, she asked for clarification. "Does this mean we're going to exclusively date one another?"

Byron took his hand and placed it on the back of Nikki's neck. He gently pulled her mouth down to his. He kissed her with tenderness before responding, "Yes. That's exactly what it means. After all, I'm already your invisible husband, aren't I?"

Nikki stuttered, "I . . . I . . . I can't believe this is happening."

"Neither can I. Who would've thought that I would be sitting here with a woman who seems to be everything my heart has ever desired?"

"You're definitely a keeper. You know how to make a woman feel special." Nikki laid her head on his chest.

"You are special and don't you ever forget it."

They formed a special bond that day as they sat in the chair talking.

They were so into each other that the night passed and the dawn of a new day found them still awake. They remained in the bed the majority of that Saturday. Between watching movies and talking, nighttime approached once again. Although they had cuddled and done some heavy kissing and panting, they had not yet crossed the realm of physical intimacy.

Nikki hoped Byron understood her reasoning for not wanting to have sex with him this early on in their relationship. But the only way to find out was for her to talk to him about it.

While they cuddled, Nikki brought up the subject. "Byron, how would you feel about us taking *it* slow?"

"*It*," he repeated.

"Sex."

"I told you I don't have a problem with it," he said nonchalantly.

"I don't think you understand." Nikki removed herself from his embrace so they would be facing one another.

"Enlighten me," Byron said with a concerned look on his face.

Nikki looked him directly in the eye. "I'm willing to give us a try, but I don't want sex clouding either one of our judgments. I want to be sure there's more than a physical attraction."

"For me there is," Byron stated.

"Good, because I think waiting to have sex will enhance our relationship. It'll give us a chance to know each other better."

Byron pulled her back into his arms and said, "When we

do have sex, I want it to be because we both know beyond a shadow of a doubt that neither one of us is going anywhere."

"Exactly." Nikki gleamed.

"Don't get me wrong. It'll be hard, because you're a desirable woman, but building a lasting relationship with you is more important to me at this time."

Nikki hugged him tight. "Where have you been all of my life?"

"Waiting on you."

7

Nikki felt guilty about spending the entire weekend being lazy. She didn't go to work on Friday, nor did she take care of any of her weekend errands. But the number-one thing she felt bad about was that she'd overslept and missed church. As she got dressed, she was thankful that God had brought Byron into her life. She made a silent promise to God to attend Wednesday night's Bible study since she missed Sunday service.

After being at her place for the entire weekend, Byron went home to get a change of clothes. After Nikki's telling Byron her dilemma about not having the husband her family expected to see at their monthly Sunday dinner, he suggested that he make his very first appearance as the invisible husband. Nikki told him that he didn't have to do that for her, but he insisted.

"It'll be our little secret," he assured her.

She agreed when he flashed his killer smile. Nikki knew she would never be able to resist those dimples of his.

* * *

They spent the next few weeks getting to know each other better. Nikki hadn't felt this at ease with a man in a long time. With Byron agreeing to attend her family dinner, she was able to relax her nerves.

Nikki was putting on her lipstick when she heard her doorbell. She finished with her lipstick and then messed with a few strands of hair. She made it to the door but then had to go back into her bedroom to retrieve her purse with her keys in it. By the time she made it back to the door, the doorbell had sounded a second time.

"Sorry," she said, answering the door where Byron stood waiting. "I had to get my keys."

He took her hand and led her to his silver SUV. "No problem. I thought you were having second thoughts."

"Oh, you're not getting rid of me that fast, mister."

"That's exactly what I like to hear."

They rode in silence for the majority of the trip except when Nikki blurted out little facts about herself that her family might ask him, and Byron did the same about himself.

Nikki gave him directions to her parents' house. As they pulled into a residential area, she commented, "I thought you were going to change your mind. I wouldn't have blamed you if you did."

Nikki pointed to a dark brick-red split-level house.

"I'm a man of my word," Byron responded as he parked in front of her parents' house.

"I'm sorry. I didn't mean to imply otherwise. It's not every day a woman finds a man who's as caring as you are . . . and willing to do the insane."

Byron interrupted her. "Before we go in, I wanted to give you something."

She remained quiet. Byron reached into his pocket and pulled out a black velvet box. "I know we're still getting to know one another, but I know enough to know that I want you in my life. Please wear this pendant as a symbol of what the future can be. When you feel you're ready to make a commitment, say the word and we can upgrade it to a ring and make this thing legit."

Nikki knew that if a fly flew around her now, it would be able to find a resting spot in her mouth, because she was speechless. "I don't know what to say. I never expected this. Everything is happening so fast. We can take it slow. We don't have to rush it."

"So, Ms. Montana, is that a yes?"

She jokingly responded, "It's Nikki and yes, it is."

Byron removed the necklace from its box and placed it around Nikki's neck. After making sure the clasp was secure, he pulled her into his arms and kissed her. They were caught up in the passion and didn't stop kissing until they were disturbed by a knock on the passenger's window.

"It looks like we've been busted," Nikki said as she straightened her dress before opening the door. "That's my nephew, Jerry Junior, but we call him Junior."

She opened the door and gave Junior a hug. Byron walked around and Nikki introduced them. They followed Junior into the house to the foyer. The entire family was lounging around in the living room waiting on the guests of honor to arrive.

Byron took Nikki's hand and kissed the outside of it before giving her hand a reassuring tug as they headed down the foyer and walked hand in hand to the living room. When they reached it, all eyes were on them. Nikki cleared her throat and announced, "Hi, everyone. I know you all were wondering if we were going to show up." She paused and took a couple of deep breaths before continuing, "I want you all to meet Byron Matthews."

Byron flashed a smile before completing Nikki's sentence. "Her husband."

* * *

Everybody crowded around them. You could tell the family resemblance because all of the Montanas had high cheekbones and some had hazel eyes like Nikki. They ranged from brown-sugar to milk-chocolate complexions. In attendance were Nikki's two brothers, Gerald and Caleb, and their wives, April and Janice. Her two sisters, Pam and Adrienne, were also there with their husbands, Louis and Edward. Nikki's father stayed in the background and observed from his dark green La-Z-Boy chair that sat positioned in the middle of the room. Her nieces and nephews were running throughout the four-bedroom, full-basement dwelling.

Each member of Nikki's family reached out to Byron with open arms. The men gave him a hearty handshake, while the women gave him tight hugs. Finally, Gerald led him to their father. Nikki's mom, Ethel, directed her to the kitchen. Her sisters walked right behind them while her sisters-in-law went to see about the children, who were making their way through almost every room in the spacious house. It was the same house Nikki and her brothers and sisters had grown up in.

Ethel flashed an approving smile. "Nikki, baby, he looks like a winner. Why did you hide him from us?" she said as she walked over to the refrigerator and took out a pitcher of lemonade and then a pitcher of tea, placing them both down on the newly updated black-and-gray marbled kitchen counter.

Nikki cleared her throat. "I was selfish. We don't get to spend much time together, so I wanted him all to myself." She began assisting her mother by gathering glasses from the cupboards.

"I see why, because he is *fine*. He makes Denzel look like mincemeat," Pam said while everyone else laughed.

"I can't put my finger on it, but something doesn't feel right." Adrienne frowned as she sat down at the kitchen table, the table that was now used as the kids' table while the adults dined in the formal dining room.

Nikki ignored her comment and proceeded to get plastic cups for the kids.

Pam, who sometimes instigated the sibling rivalry, asked, "Adrienne, why do you say that?"

A wicked-looking smile spread over Adrienne's face. "Nikki, you've only known him a short while. Nobody in the family has met him until now, and so we're supposed to accept him into the family? Are you sure you really know him? He looks like one of those playboy types. Why did you go to Vegas when everybody knows you've always wanted a church wedding?"

Ethel jumped in before an argument started. "Adrienne, it doesn't matter, he's family now. So please keep your comments to yourself. Byron is part of this family now, and if your sister is happy, then that's all that matters."

Nikki hugged her mom. "Thanks, Mom."

"Now, ladies, I didn't slave over this hot stove for my food to get cold. Pick up one of the bowls or platters and help me get everything on the table," Ethel ordered.

They each filled their hands with glasses, beverages, and platters and headed toward the dining room. Ethel cooked a dinner fit for royalty. She had baked a ham, a roast, made mashed potatoes, macaroni and cheese, fresh green beans, candy yams, with fresh dinner rolls and a peach cobbler for dessert.

"I think you outdid yourself this time," Nikki stated as she placed the glasses down at a setting and headed back to the kitchen.

Adrienne walked back into the kitchen and stood next to Nikki and whispered, "You're hiding something and I'm going to find out what it is."

Even when they were kids, Adrienne had always stayed on the other siblings' heels in an attempt to catch them in the act of something that was sure to land them in punishment or embarrassment. It was clear that she still hadn't grown out of her childhood tactics as a result of sibling rivalry.

"Whatever. Just because your marriage isn't what you want it to be, there's no reason why you should try to find something wrong with mine." Nikki tried to control her anger, but failed.

They were both giving each other the "evil eye" when Byron walked into the kitchen.

"I hope you ladies aren't talking about me with that look on your faces," he joked.

Adrienne reached out and hugged him. "Now don't worry about what we were talking about, brother-in-law. Just make sure you don't remain a stranger." She then turned and walked out of the kitchen.

Byron looked at Nikki. "Are you going to tell me what happened?"

"It's a family affair." Nikki looped her arm around his and they walked out of the kitchen.

8

Napoleon Montana sat proudly at the head of the table. He hadn't said much since Nikki and Byron had arrived. His only concern was his daughter's happiness. Once everyone was seated around the table, he spoke out. "I have to admit I was a little skeptical about meeting my new son-in-law, especially since he didn't ask me for my daughter's hand in marriage."

Everybody remained quiet. All eyes were on Nikki and Byron. Byron squeezed Nikki's hand under the table.

Napoleon continued, "Son, after seeing how happy you've made my daughter, I want to officially welcome you into the Montana family."

Sighs of relief could be heard around the table. Nikki's stomach turned. She felt bad because she knew it was all a charade. She faked a smile and almost squeezed the life out of Byron's hand.

The rest of the dinner went by uneventful. Small talk was made. Most of the questions were directed at Byron. Byron, not sure of what Nikki had already told them about him, was forced to ad-lib on some of the facts they had just discussed in the car on the way over. Nikki remained quiet.

Nikki noticed Adrienne's quizzical look. Each time she caught Adrienne staring, Adrienne flashed that same wicked smile, the same one she'd flash across the dinner table when they were children and she was holding something over one of her brothers' or sisters' heads that would be sure to land them in at least a week of punishment.

After dinner, the men took on the job of clearing away the table. Gerald chimed, "Byron, in this house, since the women do most of the cooking, the men wash the dishes. Well, only if there's not a major game on. Then Mom lets us get by without kitchen duty."

Byron was concerned about Nikki since she hadn't said more than a few sentences. "I'll be in there in a minute, Gerald. I need to talk to Nikki for a minute."

Gerald winked. "I understand. I was like that when April and I first got married." He then vanished into the kitchen.

Byron pulled Nikki to the side and embraced her. He lowered his voice and said, "I can tell something's wrong. You can tell me now or later, but either way, we're going to talk about it."

Nikki felt uneasy about lying and even more so with her nosy sister Adrienne snooping around. "It's nothing I can't handle. Don't worry about it."

"If it affects you, it affects me."

She pulled away and began walking off. "You're taking this a little too far, aren't you?"

"Excuse me." Byron reached out and grabbed her arm.

"This whole thing was a mistake. I'm going to tell them the truth and that's it."

Byron was confused about the sudden change of events. "It's your choice, but do you think your family will forgive you after you've made a fool of them?"

Nikki's eyes filled with tears. Byron picked up a napkin

off the table and wiped the tears as they began falling from her eyes.

"Nikki, please don't cry. It's going to be all right," he comforted her.

"Nikki, what's wrong?" Adrienne asked when she walked into the room.

Nikki straightened herself up and responded, "Nothing." As she looked into Byron's eyes, she said, "Byron informed me he's leaving out of town tonight for a two-week trip."

Byron was caught off guard, but followed Nikki's lead. "Yes, and I waited until the last minute to tell her because I didn't want her to worry about me leaving again."

Adrienne's voice was showered with concern. "Nikki, you know you can always call me or anyone else in this family if you get lonely."

"See, baby, I told you everything would work out."

Nikki felt trapped. "I hate to do this to everyone, but I think I'm ready to go. I don't want to spend the last few hours with my husband around my family."

"I'm sure everyone will understand," Adrienne reassured her.

"Byron, wait right here while I go tell Mom and Dad we're leaving."

As Nikki walked away, Byron looked for a trash can for the tearstained napkin. Adrienne stood right behind him. "If you hurt my sister, you'll have me to answer to," she said out of nowhere and without hesitation.

Startled, Byron responded, "I have no intentions of hurting your sister."

Adrienne still displayed an attitude. "You'd better not. I know about traveling salesmen and the kind of life they live."

"I'm not that type of guy."

"Uh-huh. Just don't do anything you'll regret." Adrienne turned away and quickly left the room.

Byron and Nikki said their good-byes to everyone and were on their way.

"I still don't trust him," Adrienne blurted no sooner than the door closed behind them.

Her remarks made Gerald angry. "Look, why don't you stop being so negative?"

"And mind your own business," her father added.

Adrienne didn't respond to them directly but instead mumbled under her breath, "My sister's business is my business. You can best believe that."

9

Nikki remained quiet on the drive back to her place. Byron was debating whether he should break the ice or let her get herself together before discussing what had happened at her folks' place.

Once they arrived at her house, Byron walked her to her front door. "Nik, we need to talk. What happened back there?"

Rolling her eyes, Nikki responded, "I don't know, you tell me."

"I was doing you a favor, so why are you giving me a funky attitude?"

Nikki rolled her eyes and lashed out. "Don't worry about me."

"Oh, you don't have to worry about that. Right now, I can't stand being around you like this."

Nikki's feelings were hurt, but she didn't let Byron know. "Whatever. Thanks for the favor . . . even though I think it was a mistake. It's all a facade." She reached for the necklace.

"A mistake, huh? Look, you can keep the necklace. Let it

remind you of what we could have had." He stormed away and got into his SUV.

Nikki wanted to call out to him and tell him to stay, but her pride got the best of her.

She watched as he backed up. He stopped for a moment as if contemplating on whether to leave or not. The sound of screeching tires brought tears to Nikki's eyes.

She heard her phone ringing as she fumbled for her keys. Without closing the front door, she rushed to the phone and sounded out of breath when she answered, "Hello."

"How did it go?" the voice on the other end of the phone inquired.

"Charlotte, I thought you were Byron." Nikki sighed as she walked over and shut the front door, threw her purse on the plush living room chair, and plopped down on the matching sofa.

"No. I was anxious to see how the dinner went."

Nikki's hand toyed with the necklace Byron had given her as she gave Charlotte details of the events leading up to Byron's speeding away. "Now what am I supposed to do?"

Charlotte responded by saying, "You should call Byron and apologize and then figure out how to come clean with your family."

"I can't."

"You can't apologize to Byron or you can't tell your family the truth?"

"Both."

Charlotte laughed and then abruptly stopped. "Girl, you have some serious issues. This goes deeper than I thought."

"Whatever!" Nikki said as she found the television remote and flipped from channel to channel.

"I'm serious. You're losing it over there."

"I have everything under control."

"Yeah, right."

Nikki became agitated with her best friend. "Char, I hate

to end our lovely conversation, but I have to go. Bye." Nikki hung up without waiting on Charlotte to respond.

How dare she tell me I have issues! Nikki thought. *Oh, I have one issue and that's everybody is always in my business. If people had stayed out of my business in the first place, it never would have gotten to this. I finally meet a nice guy who could be marriage material, and now he's mad at me. I can't win for losing.*

Nikki turned the TV off and went to her bedroom. She lay across the bed and thought about the events from the past few months: buying that stupid engagement ring, participating in that stupid wedding shower, having that stupid wedding celebration dinner with her family. The only good thing that had happened recently was meeting Byron. If it wasn't for all that stupid made-up stuff about an invisible husband, perhaps she wouldn't have met the man that could very well be her future husband, her *real* future husband . . . one that everybody could see.

Nikki reached over and picked up the phone and dialed Byron's number. She got under the covers as she waited for him to answer. Disappointed that his voice mail picked up, Nikki hung up. She threw the phone on the other side of her bed before closing her eyes.

Byron decided not to answer when he saw Nikki's number pop up on the caller ID. He was still upset with her from earlier. He enjoyed her company and really wanted things to work out between them, but he didn't feel like dealing with her attitude right now.

He sat up on the burgundy leather living room couch where he had lain down and collapsed in thought about what had just transpired between him and Nikki. He then picked up the phone to dial his brother's number, but inadvertently dialed Nikki's instead.

"Hello," Nikki said in a gentle voice.

Byron held his finger over the Disconnect button. He paused. "Nikki?"

"I called to apologize." She sounded more alert.

"I saw that you called and didn't know if it was an emergency," he lied.

"In a way it is. I hate to leave things up in the air."

"Oh, you got your point across loud and clear."

"Look, Byron, I'm sorry for how I acted earlier. Lying to my family took more out of me than I thought it would."

"So why are you doing it? Why don't—"

Nikki interrupted him. "I can't. I have to pull this off or my family will never forgive me."

Byron began to feel sorry for her. "I guess your apology is accepted. I can't understand why you're doing it. But if we're going to make this thing work between us, I guess I'll have to go along with it."

Nikki sounded surprised. "Does it mean we're cool again?"

A smile came across Byron's face. "I guess. But we need to set up some ground rules if I'm going to help you fool your family and friends."

"What kind of rules?"

"Hmmm, let me sleep on it and we can talk about it tomorrow."

"You got me wondering what's going on in that head of yours."

"Miss Montana, you'll find out tomorrow. Until then, get plenty of rest, because you'll need it."

Byron hung up as he heard Nikki ask, "What are you—"

He laid the phone on the cradle and walked up the spiral staircase to his two-room master suite. He couldn't help speaking out loud. "She wants to act, does she? Let the charades begin."

10

Byron woke up the next morning in a chipper mood. He dreamed of him and Nikki in every sexual position imaginable. Although he had agreed to take it slow with her, he knew it was going to be difficult to restrain himself much longer. He woke up with emotions he didn't know existed. It was because of her, he now had something else to occupy his thoughts instead of his next sale.

After getting dressed, he poured himself a glass of orange juice and a bowl of his favorite Captain Crunch cereal. His brother teased him about his choice of cereals. He had been eating Captain Crunch as long as he could remember. He ate and placed the empty bowl and glass into the stainless steel dishwasher that matched the other appliances in his kitchen. He grabbed his black leather briefcase and cell phone before rushing out the door.

He was halfway to work when his cell phone rang. Frederick's name was displayed on the screen. He hit the Speaker button.

"Hello," he answered as he maneuvered between lanes.

"Man, where have you been hiding? Nikki must have really laid it on you," Frederick teased.

"It's not even like that."

"All I know is my little bro used to call me every day and now I barely hear from him."

"Like you really care."

"I do care."

They both laughed.

Byron slammed on his brakes after the car in front of him abruptly stopped.

"Damn!" Byron exclaimed.

"Man, you okay over there?"

"Yes, but somebody decided to go 1.5 miles an hour in the fast lane. Now every lane's jacked up."

"You must be on 635."

"You know it."

"So what's the 411 on Nikki?" Frederick asked, getting back to the topic of conversation.

Byron took the phone off speaker and put in his earpiece. *It's a long story,* he thought, *but since it looks like I'm going to be stuck in traffic, I might as well get a second opinion.*

"Before I go into details, promise me this conversation will stay between us," Byron said.

Frederick was silent for a second. "I promise. Now what's the deal, man?"

Byron updated Frederick on his and Nikki's situation.

Frederick laughed uncontrollably throughout the entire conversation.

"Man, it's not even that funny."

"Yes, it is. Now I know why Lifetime is television for women, because, man, what you just explained to me sounds like the making of a Lifetime movie. And on top of that, I can't believe you're going along with it, and her family and friends must be crazy not to see through her game."

"Man, I told you it's complicated."

"I wouldn't touch that situation with a ten-foot pole or with my remote control." Frederick laughed.

"I know I just met her, but I really think she's the one," Byron said over his brother's laughter.

"Man, you got it bad."

Someone blew their horn at Byron as he jumped in front of them. "I don't know what it is about her, but I'll do whatever I can to keep a smile on her face."

"I'll have to talk to Charlotte about her girl."

Byron took the Hillcrest Road exit. "I have a plan, but I hope it doesn't backfire on me."

"Before you say any more, are you sure she's worth it?"

"I know she is."

"Whatever you decide to do, man, I'm behind you one hundred percent."

"Thanks. I'll let you know when I work some of the details out."

"You know there's a bright spot to all of this, don't you?"

"What?" Byron asked curiously.

"Since you're pretending to be her husband, you should take advantage of her wifely duties."

Byron laughed. "Don't even go there, man."

"I'm just trying to help a brother out. Let me go. Tell my *not-really-my-sister-in-law* I said hi," Frederick teased.

"Bye," Byron said as he ran a yellow light.

"Peace."

The day at work was typical for Nikki, except for the fact that she couldn't get thoughts of Byron out of her mind. She checked her voice mail at home, on her cell phone, and at work, and she had yet to receive a call or message from him.

Did I dream our whole conversation? she thought. When he had called last night, she was dosing off. She was happy to hear his voice and glad they were now speaking again. She was curious to find out what he meant by setting up some ground rules. *At least, he's willing to help me with my dilemma. So what's a few rules?*

Nikki was startled when Kenneth walked up to her desk and said, "A penny for your thoughts."

"Nonya," she replied.

With a puzzled look on his face, Kenneth asked, "Nonya?"

"It means none of your business."

"I was only concerned. You don't seem like your normal self." Kenneth sat down in her extra chair.

"It's nothing. I'm tired. I haven't adjusted to juggling work and marriage yet."

He leaned in closer as if he didn't want to miss anything. "Tell me more."

Nikki looked down at her notepad. "I've said enough." She looked directly at him with a frown. "Don't you have work to do?"

Kenneth stood up. "I guess so, since it doesn't seem like I'll get anything else out of you."

Nikki's mouth went from a frown to a smile. "Now you know I don't tell you anything I don't want repeated."

He took his hand and placed it across his chest. "I'm appalled that you think I would break your confidentiality."

With a bit of sarcasm Nikki said, "Now why would I think that?"

Kenneth pushed the chair back and before walking away said, "Don't come running to me when you feel like talking. I'll probably be too busy."

"Bye, Kenneth."

Five o'clock arrived and Nikki still hadn't heard from Byron. *Oh well. I guess I was dreaming.*

She was surprised when she spotted Byron's SUV parked

in her driveway when she pulled up. He opened her door before she could get her seat belt off.

"What a pleasant surprise," she said.

Byron helped her with her briefcase. "I didn't get a chance to call because of meetings all day, but thought I would meet you here and possibly cook you dinner."

Two double beeps were heard as she turned on her car alarm. "I'm always game for a free meal."

"Let me get the bag out of the truck and I'll meet you inside."

Nikki felt like skipping to her front door, but refrained. She was barely through the door when Byron came from behind her.

"That was quick."

"I only had one bag." He laid her briefcase by the front door and carried the grocery bag to the kitchen.

Nikki yelled, "Let me get freshened up and I'll help you."

"I got it. Take your time," he responded.

Nikki began humming a song by Alicia Keys, one of her favorite singers.

She opted for a quick shower instead of a bubble bath. She sprayed on her favorite perfume by Issey Miyake and put on a comfortable pair of jeans and a Dallas Cowboys T-shirt.

She smelled an aroma of oregano and garlic as she made her way to the kitchen. "A girl can get used to this," she said upon entering the kitchen.

Byron turned around and was wearing one of her aprons. She tried not to laugh, but couldn't hold it. "You look so cute."

He poured a cup of chopped vegetables into a pot and stirred. "Don't go there."

"If you could see yourself in my apron, you'd say the same thing."

"Keep joking like that and you'll starve."

Still laughing, Nikki said, "Seriously, everything smells good." She walked over to the stove.

Byron placed the spoon close to her mouth. "Taste this."

"Mmm, this is good," she said after taking a taste of the sauce he spoon-fed her.

With a splash of spaghetti sauce still on her lips, Byron leaned down and kissed her. The sound of the stove's timer going off broke their kiss.

"I agree. It's very good," Byron said as he turned off one of the burners. "Dinner will be ready in a minute."

"Did I tell you Italian food is my favorite?"

"Yes, among other things."

Nikki's heartbeat accelerated. She had to get her hormones under control. "I'll set the table while you finish up."

Byron responded, "Okay."

They worked in silence. Nikki sneaked a look at Byron, only to catch him looking in her direction.

By the time she placed the silverware, plates, and glasses on the table, Byron was bringing in the food.

As he set two plates of spaghetti on the table, he commented, "It's a little hot, but by the time we eat our salad, it should be ready for consumption. Have a seat."

He pulled out her chair.

"Thanks. You're really spoiling me."

He walked to the refrigerator to take out the salad and said, "I plan on doing more than that."

He placed the bowl of salad directly in front of her before taking a seat at the glass kitchen table with a seating for four, directly across from her.

He reached for her hand. "Precious Lord, we thank you for this food we're about to eat. Thank you for allowing our paths to cross. Amen."

Nikki, teary eyed, said, "Amen." He had prayed over his food the first dinner they had together, but he had done it in silence. Now he was praying out loud for them both.

The only sound heard between the two at first was the clinking of silverware.

"Nikki, after we eat, there's some things I want to discuss with you," Byron stated.

Nikki went back and forth in her mind on what to say, but decided to see what was weighing heavily on Byron's mind first.

11

After clearing the dishes from the table, they lounged around in the living room on the couch as Nikki turned on the television where a movie with Patty Duke was playing.

Byron took his hand and gently rubbed it against Nikki's face. "You're beautiful," he said almost in a whisper.

She stared into his eyes. "You're not too bad looking yourself."

He continued to hold her hand as he talked. "Our relationship is far from conventional."

"To say the least," she said, turning her attention back to the television.

"Listen, Nikki, if I'm going to help you fool your family, some things will have to change."

"Like what?" Nikki asked with a puzzled look on her face, now looking back up at Byron.

"Number one, if we're pretending to be husband and wife, we need to be under one roof."

She removed her hand. "I vowed not to just live with a man, not unless . . ."

"I'm not just any man, I'm your husband. Remember?"

"No, you're a man I'm dating. Living together is out of the question."

Byron pulled out his cell phone. "I guess we can call your folks now and tell them the marriage is a hoax." He pretended to be dialing some numbers.

Nikki grabbed the phone out of his hands. "Maybe we can come up with an alternative solution."

He held out his hand. "Give me my phone back."

"Only if you promise not to make that call."

"Okay."

She placed the phone back in his hand and said, "Why don't you move some of your stuff over here? So if someone stops by, they'll see your clothes or something. It'll look like you live here."

"I have a better idea. Pack up some of your things and move over to my place. I have a four-bedroom home and it needs a woman's touch."

"Why don't you just do what I asked and we'll both be happy?"

"Ms. Montana, you don't get off that easy. You roped me into your little scheme, so now it's either my way or deal with it on your own." Byron stood up and walked toward the door.

Nikki yelled, "Byron, wait. Maybe we can work something out."

"Now that's more like it." He turned around with a wide smile on his face.

He walked back to the couch. "Now on to rule number two."

"You sure have a lot of rules."

"Only a few." He removed a box from his pocket. "Instead of the ring you're wearing, I would like for you to wear this one."

Nikki's mouth dropped open when she saw the two-carat pear-shaped diamond. "This is gorgeous but I can't wear this."

"Don't you like it?" Byron asked, not sure what to make of her reaction.

Nikki turned her hand in several different directions. admiring the ring. "Like it? I love it. But I can't."

Byron held her hand. "But you will. Rule number three."

"Not another one." She stood up.

"Please sit. I promise this is the last one." Byron kissed the back of her hand. "We already said we would date exclusively, so this last one shouldn't be too hard."

Nikki held her breath. "This must be a doozy."

"Rule number three. You have to tell everyone you come in contact with that you're Mrs. Matthews. Even if you meet another man you might be interested in."

"But I—" Nikki couldn't finish without Byron interrupting her.

"Take it or leave it."

"Before I got interrupted, I was going to say, I don't have any intentions of talking to another man. I can tell you're going to be a handfull."

"One last thing."

"I thought you were finished."

Byron leaned closer to her. "If at any time you feel the need to consummate our relationship, please let me know. I'm ready, willing, and able."

Nikki felt like slapping the smirk off his face. "I have a feeling I'm getting more than I bargained for."

"Isn't this what you wanted? We get to learn more about each other and you get to look good in front of your family."

Their closeness had Nikki's hormones jumping through hoops.

Byron devoured her mouth and they became one with a kiss. Moans seeped out of her throat. Before realizing it, Byron was on top of her. She felt the hardness of his manhood.

She was quickly losing control. She used her free hand to get his attention. "I think we should slow it down."

Byron sat up. "I think you're right. Sorry, I got caught up in the moment, Mrs. Matthews."

Nikki pulled down her T-shirt. "I did too, Mr. Matthews."

Byron stood up and reached for her hand. He pulled her up and they walked toward the front door.

Byron stopped at the door and turned around and looked directly into her eyes. He kissed her one last time before walking through the door. "By the way, I wasn't going to call your parents, because I don't have the number."

She stood with her hand on her hip. "You tricked me."

He turned around and winked. "No, dear, I would never do that."

She watched him walk to his car.

"Call me later if you feel like it."

"I'm just going to go back in there and finish watching that movie. They show the best movies on that channel."

"What channel is that?" Byron asked just out of curiosity.

"Lifetime," Nikki replied before shutting the door.

12

Charlotte screamed through the phone, "He did what?"

"I'm not repeating myself. People are beginning to come into the office and I don't need Kenneth or anybody else in my business," Nikki said as she logged on to her computer.

"Girl, you're a trip."

"We only have to do it for a few more months."

"What if you guys really do work out? What then?"

People walked by Nikki's desk with their morning coffee. "Girl, I'll cross that bridge when I come to it. For now, I'm going with the flow."

"Okay, Ms. Going with the Flow. I think you've bitten off more than you can chew with those lying teeth of yours."

Nikki skimmed through her e-mail. "You know, Char, I don't know why I even tell you anything. You're always so negative."

"Not negative, just realistic."

"Whatever. Here comes Kenneth. Let me get off this phone."

After hanging up with Charlotte, she pretended to be busy. Kenneth made a beeline straight toward her.

"Good morning, Nikki."

She looked up from her computer and smiled. "Good morning, Kenneth."

"Did you have a good evening?"

Nikki waved her hand in the air and in her most proper voice said, "Oh, I had a lovely evening."

Kenneth ran up and grabbed her hand. "Let me see that rock."

"You like?"

"Yes, but what happened to your other ring?"

With a smug look on her face, she responded, "He wanted to upgrade."

Kenneth wouldn't let go of her hand. "You have a good man. Don't mess up."

"You can let go of my hand now."

Kenneth took her hand and placed it on her desk. "You're a lucky woman," he said as he walked away.

"Yes, I am."

Her e-mail indicator beeped to inform her of incoming mail. It was a message from her boss. *What does he want?* she thought. She clicked on it and skimmed through it.

Another meeting? How many meetings will we have on the same issue? I swear these people up here like to meet just for the sake of having a meeting.

Nikki grabbed her pen and pad and headed to the meeting.

Byron watched Joyce as she closed his office door behind her and sat in the chair across from his desk.

"Uh-oh. Whenever you shut the door, I know I'm in trouble," he teased.

"I spoke with Frederick while you were at lunch. He told me to keep an eye on you. I asked him a few questions."

"I bet you did."

She sat on the edge of her chair. "All I want to know is, when will I get to meet this Nikki?"

"Soon. Everybody will meet her real soon."

"I hope she's not like Tara. Tara was a gold-digging—"

"Don't even go there," Byron interrupted.

"She was and you know it. You were blind to her evilness at first. I don't believe in voodoo, but I was about to do something to get rid of her."

Byron laughed. "She was definitely a character. Nicolette is nothing like Tara. They are totally opposite."

"As long as you're happy."

"I am."

Joyce stood up. "I'll let you get back to work, then. You know I have to keep tabs on you."

"Between you and Frederick, I'm surprised I have any privacy."

"You don't," Joyce said as she walked out the door.

Byron was no longer able to concentrate on work. He tried to prepare a presentation, but the only thing he could visualize was Nikki sandwiched between him and the couch.

He shifted in his seat at the thought. *I don't know if I made the right decision about insisting we live under the same roof. I only wanted to prove how silly her scheme to fool her family was, and it might have backfired.*

"How was your day?" Byron's sexy baritone voice vibrated through Nikki's cell phone.

"Busy. I had back-to-back meetings," Nikki said as she pulled into her driveway and turned off the ignition.

"When do you want to move your stuff?"

"You don't waste time, do you?" She got out of her car with her laptop and purse. She almost dropped her phone. "Oops."

"Did I catch you at a bad time?"

"I just got home."

"Call me on my cell phone when you get settled in and we can discuss your move date."

"Bye." She hit the End button on the phone. Her keys fell to the ground. "Darn it."

When she got inside she dropped her keys and purse on the couch. After washing up and changing into a jogging suit, she made herself a turkey sandwich.

She sat down at the kitchen table. *I didn't think he was really serious about us living together,* she thought. *I was just playing along with him.* The doorbell rang before she could take the first bite.

"This better not be Byron!" she shouted.

13

Nikki opened the door without looking through the peephole. She was shocked to see her sisters Pam and Adrienne standing there.

Pam was the first to speak. "Do you always open the door without looking to see who's on the other side?"

"I thought y'all were somebody else," Nikki replied as she hugged her sisters while they each walked through the doorway.

Adrienne walked toward the living room and said, "Obviously."

After closing the door, Nikki followed them to the living room. "Why are y'all here?"

Adrienne and Pam exchanged glances. Pam asked, "When do we need an invitation?"

Adrienne added, "Oh, I forgot, since she married her invisible husband."

"He's not invisible anymore. You've seen him with your own two eyes. Remember?" Nikki reminded her sister.

"Ummm-hmmm," Adrienne moaned.

"Whatever. You normally call and I was eating."

"Don't let us stop you," Adrienne said.

"Sis, we were only concerned," Pam said as she rolled her eyes at Adrienne. "No one in the family has heard from you since our Sunday dinner."

"Let's continue this conversation in the kitchen," Nikki said as she led her sisters into the kitchen. "Would you ladies like a sandwich?"

They both responded, "No."

Nikki grabbed a Sprite from the refrigerator, then sat down and took a few bites out of her sandwich as her sisters sat watching her.

Adrienne cleared her throat a couple of times, stood up, and said, "I'll be back. I need to use the bathroom."

After she left the room, Pam started talking. "What's going on, Nikki?"

She took a sip of her Sprite. "Nothing at all. I've been working late."

"Are you sure? Adrienne insists that something isn't right with your relationship."

"Adrienne needs to mind her own business."

"Did I hear my name?" Adrienne asked as she took a seat.

Nikki took the last bite of her sandwich. "That was quick."

"It was a false alarm."

Pam intervened. "I was telling her our concerns about her relationship."

"And I was telling Pam, y'all need to stay out of my business," Nikki said.

Adrienne stood up. "If everything was fine, you wouldn't be on the defensive."

"Sit down, Adrienne. I'm with Nikki, you need to chill."

Adrienne frowned, but sat down. Nikki felt bad about lying to them. After seeing how they acted, she knew it was too late to tell them the truth.

"Look, Byron and I are fine. I'm missing him. He's hardly ever here."

Pam got up and took a Sprite out of the refrigerator. "Do y'all want one?"

Adrienne responded, "Sure."

Nikki held her can up.

Pam passed a drink to Adrienne. "Nikki, Gerald said Byron has a four-bedroom house in Plano," Pam said.

"How does he know that?" Nikki said, feeling a knot form in the pit of her stomach.

Between sips, Adrienne added, "You know Gerald thinks he's Inspector Gadget."

Nikki remained quiet. She felt her world crashing in on her.

Pam continued, "When will we be invited over for dinner?"

She wanted to crawl under the table. "I'll have to check with Byron. He's in and out of town, so it'll have to be a weekend he's here."

Adrienne stood up and threw her can in the trash. "We all want to get to know our new brother-in-law, so the sooner, the better."

Nikki was losing her patience. "It'll be soon. I'll call him tonight and then let everyone know."

Pam looked at her watch. "It's getting late and I have to drop off Ms. Thing." Pointing at Adrienne, she continued to say, "At the other end of town."

They all stood up. They hugged each other. Nikki walked them to the front door. Adrienne lagged behind.

"Pam, I'll meet you at the car," Adrienne said as she turned around and faced Nikki. "Why isn't any of his stuff in your bedroom?"

Nikki was livid. "Why were you going through my stuff?"

"I wasn't. I only wanted to see your reaction." She turned and headed out the door. "Bye, sis."

Nikki didn't respond. She could only imagine what was going through Adrienne's mind.

I need to do something quick, Nikki thought. *That sister of mine is relentless.*

14

As he lay across his California king-sized mattress layered in navy blue linen, Byron decided to put his plan into effect. He planned on spending most of his free time with Nikki. He sat up and picked up the phone from his nightstand and dialed her number. He lay on his back, waiting for her to answer.

"Hello," she said.

"Hi, sweetie. Are you all settled in?" he asked her.

"I sure am. Actually, I was about to call you."

"Perfect timing." His stomach had butterflies.

"I need to move some of my stuff over there as soon as possible."

"Woooo. Your attitude sure changed quick."

"I had some unexpected visitors yesterday and let's just say they convinced me you were right."

"Good. How about this weekend? That'll give you a few days to get your things together."

"Sounds like a plan."

Byron sat straight up in bed. "What are you wearing?"

Nikki laughed. "Don't even try going there with me."

"Now whose mind is in the gutter? I was only looking out for you."

"Uh-huh. Tell me anything."

Byron dropped the bass in his voice. "Did you miss me?" He could hear her giggle and it turned him on.

"Did you miss me?" Nikki teased.

"Yes. I thought about your kisses and the way your body felt under mine *all day long*."

"Prove it."

"Nikki, don't play. I'll be over there before you can hang up the phone."

They both laughed.

"All you have to do is answer one question and you'll be off the hook."

Byron smiled. "What, dear?"

"What are you wearing?"

He sang, "I have my T-shirt and my boxers on."

Neither could stop laughing.

"I need to get some sleep. I'll talk to you tomorrow."

"I knew you couldn't hang. The T-shirt did it to you, didn't it?"

"No, it was imagining you in those boxers. Bye." She hung up.

Byron placed the phone on the nightstand, turned over, and went to bed with a smile on his face and his manhood at attention.

Nikki showered and as she got dressed, she couldn't stop singing. "Could this be love at first sight?" She sang the words to a song by Mary J. Blige. "This is going to be a great day," she said as she grabbed her purse and laptop and headed out the door.

Traffic was much, much lighter than usual as she drove to work. And today she seemed to make it without getting caught by a single red light, so it only took her thirty minutes instead of the usual hour to get to her job.

Few people were in the office when she arrived. She went into the lunchroom and started the coffeepot to make a fresh pot of coffee. While she waited, she attempted to get a Nutri-grain bar out of the vending machine, but it got caught on one of the claws and wouldn't drop. She tried beating on the machine to release the bar.

"Do you need some help with that?" Kenneth asked as he entered the lunchroom.

Frustrated, Nikki grunted and responded, "If you don't mind. It took all of my change."

Together they shoved the machine in different directions until the bar fell down.

Kenneth wiped the sweat from his forehead. "Girl, that better be the best bar you've ever eaten."

"Thanks. I owe you one. I'll treat you to lunch next week."

She poured them both a cup of coffee and they walked to their desks. Kenneth looked around the room. "I guess we're the only ones here."

Nikki looked at the clock. "It's only seven thirty. People will start piling in here soon."

Kenneth acted as if he wanted to linger, but instead he said, "I have a report to finish before nine and I didn't get all of the information I needed until last night."

"I hate when that happens. Then they get upset when you don't have it ready for their weekly meeting."

"I know. When I win the lottery, everybody up here can kiss my . . ." He took his right hand and patted his right butt cheek as he walked away.

"Kenneth, you don't have it all," she said out of his ear-shot.

Nikki went through her e-mails. She had an e-greeting from Byron. After opening it, she picked up the phone and dialed his office number.

"Hello," he answered.

He barely got his words out before she blurted out, "You're the sweetest man I know."

"I see you got my e-mail."

"Yes, and it made my day. I can meet you around one for lunch," she responded to the question in his e-greeting. She picked up her pen and doodled on her yellow steno pad.

"Okay. I'll swing by and pick you up."

"Then I'll see you at one o'clock."

"Okay. Bye, sweetie."

"Bye."

Nikki was still holding the phone with a glazed look in her eyes when Mya stopped by her desk.

"I remember those days," Mya said, gazing off as if reminiscing.

"Oh. Hi, Mya," Nikki said.

Mya sat on the edge of Nikki's desk. "Kenneth told us about the ring."

A smile crossed Nikki's face. "I knew he couldn't hold it for long."

Mya reached for her hand so she could get a good view. "Girl, I know my diamonds, and old boy spent a mint on this one."

Nikki looked at her hand at different angles as the sparkle from her ring radiated. "You think so?"

"I know so." Mya stood up. "I'm running late for a meeting, so I better go."

After Mya walked away, Nikki admired the ring Byron had given her, and for the first time really felt as if she was actually married.

Girl, you need to snap out of it. You're beginning to believe the hype you've been dishing out.

15

The rest of the morning went by fast. Byron met with his clients and sealed a multimillion-dollar sale. Because of the signed contract he now possessed, North American Telecom would be handling all of the fast food chains' phone communication in several states. His commission check for next month would be huge. He smiled as he drove to Nikki's job.

While waiting at a red light, he reached over to the passenger's seat and took a CD out of its case. He was feeling upbeat, but he wanted to set a romantic mood when he picked her up. He put on the latest Gerald Levert CD. He knew if Gerald couldn't set the mood, no one could.

He picked up his cell phone and dialed her number. Nikki picked up on the second ring. "Hi, I'm parked in the front," he told her.

"I'll be right down." She grabbed her purse and sprinted toward the elevator. She couldn't wait to see Byron. After hanging up with her, he got out of his SUV and put his briefcase and some other items in the backseat. As he closed the back door, a beautiful petite caramel-skinned woman with flowing auburn hair walked over to him. He almost closed the door on his hand.

"Byron, fancy meeting you here," she said.

Byron's mouth stood wide open. "Tara?"

"In the flesh, baby." She twirled so he could observe how her two-piece navy blue suit accented the curves of her body.

"What are you doing here?"

"I have an interview for a management position at a company in this building. What are you doing here?"

"I'm meeting someone for lunch."

"Whoever she is, she's one lucky lady."

The last thing Byron needed was for Nikki to walk up and see him this close with one of his ex-girlfriends. "I'm the lucky one," he commented. He glanced at the door several times to see if Nikki was coming. "I don't want to make you late for your interview."

Tara winked. "Oh, I won't be. I'm always early. Good thing too, or I would have missed seeing you." She handed him a card. "Here's my number if you ever want to catch up."

"Tara, like I told you before, we don't have anything else to talk about."

"Oh, but we do." She looked down at her watch. "I'll be in touch."

Byron watched her as she twisted toward the front door. She and Nikki almost bumped into each other. Byron let out a breath of air when he saw Nikki smiling as she walked toward him. He gave her a tight hug.

"Hi, sexy," he said as he held the door open for her.

"Hi yourself," she said, being careful to pull her skirt down when she sat. After he was behind the driver's seat pulling off, she continued to talk. "I couldn't wait to get out here to see you. I almost didn't make it when this woman almost ran smack into me when I was coming out to meet you."

"Really? You're okay, right?" he asked.

"Oh, I'm fine. Sad part about it, she didn't even say excuse me."

"Some people are rude like that."

"Anyway, how did your meeting go?"

"Let's just say, celebrations are in order."

"Cool. That's my man."

"What would you like to eat for lunch?" He turned into what was known as restaurant row.

"So many choices. How about Outback Steakhouse?"

"Steak it is."

After pulling into the parking lot, he found a spot near the door. Before getting out of the vehicle, Nikki commented, "I love me some Gerald Levert. Is this his latest?"

"Yes, I picked it up last week."

Byron walked around and opened her door. "And you're just now letting me know about it. Tsk-tsk."

As they walked toward the restaurant, he said, "I'll make you a copy."

"I want the original." Nikki batted her eyes at him as he opened the door.

"I'll think about it."

Before she could respond, a hostess said, "How many in your party?"

"Two," Byron answered.

They followed one of the waiters to a table. As they sat, Nikki commented, "This place is still crowded. I thought by going to lunch at one, it wouldn't be."

"Seems like everybody else had the same idea."

They enjoyed the rest of their lunch, taking time to flirt in between bites. On the ride back to Nikki's job, Byron turned up the music. As he drove, he watched Nikki sway to the smooth sound of Gerald Levert's voice.

When he dropped her off, it was hard saying good-bye. They stood outside the passenger door. He cornered her in. "I wish you could play hooky for the rest of the day."

Glazing into his eyes, Nikki didn't say anything. Instead, she took her hand and put it on the back of his neck and pulled his mouth onto hers. "That should hold you until tonight."

Byron was left standing, watching her sashay into her office building. He readjusted his pants and got in his SUV.

16

Nikki glanced at the clock. It was after six and she had been trying to decide on an outfit for at least an hour. She finally decided on a pair of red slacks, a white satin blouse, and a matching red jacket. She threw on her red pumps and made sure her Mac makeup was intact.

She was putting on her lip gloss when the doorbell rang.

"I'm coming," she yelled.

Byron stood with a bouquet of red roses when she opened the door. "These are for you," he said.

"Thanks. How lovely," she said while taking them and smelling the fragrance.

"Red is your color," Byron said as they walked to the living room.

Nikki placed the roses in the center of her coffee table. "These roses are perfect."

"Just like you."

She nervously laughed. "I wish."

"Come here." Byron wrapped his arms around her waist. "To me, you are."

Nikki was nervous. She could feel the sweat under her

armpits. "Hey, we better get going. My stomach's been growling for the last hour."

He hesitated before releasing his embrace. "I'm hungry too, but not for food."

She picked up her keys and her Louis Vuitton miniloop bag. "You can stand in that one spot if you want to, but Pappadeaux is calling my name."

Byron followed her out the door.

On the ride to the restaurant there was light conversation as the Oasis, a Dallas radio station, played in the background. About fifteen minutes later they arrived at their destination. For a weekday, the popular seafood restaurant was packed. They were immediately seated, but had to wait a few minutes before a waitress came to their table to take their orders.

"Have you decided what you want to order?" Byron asked.

Without looking up, she replied, "I should know what I want, since me and my friends come here all of the time."

"I know. Frederick and I used to hang out here every Sunday after church."

Nikki lowered her menu. "I bet y'all did."

"What do you mean by that?" Byron asked, trying to sound innocent.

"Everybody knows that Friday nights and Sunday evenings, men and women come to scout out the opposite sex."

"Is that why you and your friends hung out here?"

"Of course." Nikki grinned and lifted the menu to hide her face.

Before Byron could retort, a waitress stopped at the table. "Would you like to order an appetizer first?"

Byron looked in Nikki's direction. She put her menu down and ordered. "I would like the blackened oyster and shrimp fondeaux."

"Good choice," the waitress responded. "And you, sir?"

"I'll have an order of your Louisiana seafood gumbo," Byron ordered.

After writing down Byron's order the waitress asked, "Would you like to order your dinner now or do you need a few more minutes?"

Byron and Nikki said in unison, "I'm ready."

They all chuckled. Byron spoke first. "Ladies first."

Nikki picked up her menu. "For dinner, I would like the shrimp etoufée, and can you bring some extra garlic bread?"

"I sure can," the waitress cheerfully said before looking in Byron's direction.

"I'll have what the lady is having and can you bring us a pitcher of iced tea?" he said.

"Your tea and appetizers will be right out."

They handed their menus to her. After the waitress walked away, Nikki stated, "I told you I was hungry."

Byron laughed. "Yes, you did. I thought I could put away some food."

"I need to go to the ladies' room. I'll be right back."

"I'll be right here."

The waitress brought the appetizers and tea while Nikki was gone. Byron was busy looking in the direction of the restroom and was caught off guard when someone came up behind him and put their hands over his eyes.

"Guess who?" asked a familiar voice.

Byron removed a soft pair of lady's hands from his eyes. Tara walked around and took a seat at the table. "We have to stop meeting like this."

"I'm on a date, so you might want to remove yourself from that chair."

"Oh, I saw your date. That's the same lady I saw earlier at the place I interviewed. I should have known when she almost ran into me without even bothering to say excuse me that she was racing out to see you. I don't blame her, though. I'd knock down a woman or two to get to your fine self as well."

Byron glanced in the direction of the ladies' room. "She'll be back in a minute, so please leave."

"Not without a proper introduction, I won't."

"Tara, why are you doing this? I'm beginning to think I'm being stalked."

"No, I'm not stalking you." She laughed. "You're full of yourself, aren't you?"

Byron moved around in his chair. "Either you leave now or I'll have them escort you out of here."

Tara shook her head. "You wouldn't want to make a scene, would you?"

Irritated, Byron responded, "I want you to leave me the hell alone."

Tara stood up, reached in her purse, and dropped an envelope on the table. "When you get a chance, take a look at these. Trust me, you'll be calling me." She bent down and kissed him on the cheek. "Ta-tah."

She walked away as Nikki was walking back toward the table.

Before Byron could say anything, Nikki asked as she sat, "Who was that woman I saw kissing you on the cheek?"

Byron stuttered, "She was no one."

Nikki had a concerned look on her face. "Really now?"

"She's someone I dated in the past."

"She looks familiar too," she said with a puzzled look on her face.

"She has one of those faces," Byron stated as he lifted the hot gumbo to his mouth.

"This is bitter," Nikki commented before opening two packages of Equal and adding it to her tea. She took another sip. "Now that's better."

"I'm surprised you're dropping the subject without asking questions," Byron commented.

Nikki took a bite of her appetizer. In between bites, she responded, "I'm waiting to see if you'll willingly volunteer additional information."

"She's not worth discussing."

She wiped her mouth with her napkin. "I hear you."

"Seriously."

The waitress brought out their food. "I can take those if you're through."

"Put this in a to-go plate if you don't mind," Nikki said.

"Okay," the waitress said as she took her half-eaten plate. The waitress placed the main course in front of them.

Nikki could tell Byron was doing his best to avoid making eye contact with her. *Byron is acting guilty about something,* she thought. *There's more going on here. I'll give him until the end of the night to tell me about Ms. Thing.*

Nikki tried to ignore the dryness of her and Byron's conversation as her patience wore thin. She couldn't enjoy her meal. "Byron. You have two minutes to tell me who she was or I'll leave you sitting here by yourself."

"And how would you get home?" he replied.

"Oh, it's like that." Nikki stood up.

"Sit," Byron demanded as some of the restaurant patrons sitting next to them looked on. "Please."

She sat and tapped her fingers on the table. "I'm waiting."

Byron reached across the table for her hands. She ignored his gesture. "Where should I start?"

"The beginning," she remarked as she crossed her arms.

"To make a long story short, Tara and I dated for about two years. I was blinded by lust for a minute. My family and friends saw right through her from day one. She was a drama queen to the fifth power."

"And what else?"

He took a drink of tea before continuing. "She tried her best to manipulate me into buying her everything she could get her hands on."

"Did it work?"

"At first it did, because I wanted her to be happy. After a while, it became draining emotionally and financially."

"I can imagine."

"She stayed in the stores so much that I felt like I had stock in the galleria. But anyway, that's not what broke us up."

"It sounds like enough to me," Nikki said, rolling her eyes, not at Byron, at the situation.

"What broke us up is the way she treated people and her dishonesty. In my face, she would pretend to be sweet, but behind my back, she'd say nasty things to my family and friends. When Frederick told me how she acted toward him, I thought he was jealous, but then I began to see things for myself."

"She had you whipped."

"No. I was naive."

Nikki poured herself another glass of tea. "Whipped," she confirmed.

"Do you want to hear the rest?"

"Sure." She shrugged her shoulders.

"I began having suspicions that I wasn't the only one in her life when she went from calling me all of the time to only calling me when she needed some money."

"A red flag," Nikki said sarcastically.

Byron ignored her comment. "I didn't get proof she was seeing someone else until after we broke up and I got my credit card bill."

"Bummer," Nikki threw in there, shaking her head.

"You're really not making this easy for me."

Nikki set her glass down and looked him directly in the eye. "Why should I?"

"Touché. My suspicions and her attitude were enough for me to end the relationship. She cried, begged, and even lied and told me she was pregnant to stop me from ending the relationship."

"She had some serious issues."

"And she still does."

Nikki paused for a moment as Byron awaited her response. "Thanks for telling me everything. I'm sure it was hard."

Byron smiled and felt relieved. "It wasn't hard. I just like leaving the past in the past."

The waitress came over and gave them empty cartons to put their uneaten food into. Byron paid for their meal. When they were getting ready to leave, the waitress came up behind them.

"Sir, you left this envelope on the table." She handed him a small brown envelope.

"Thanks. I forgot all about it." He took it and put it in his jacket pocket.

"What is it?" Nikki asked.

"Nothing. It's something I need to look at later."

Nikki didn't say a word. She walked out the door, with Byron right behind her.

17

"I would stay, but I have an early meeting," Byron said as he bent down and kissed Nikki good-bye.

She was stuffed from all the food she had eaten at Pappadeux. All the food weighing her down made her want to do nothing more than go lie down. "I do too. Good night," she said, closing the door and locking it behind her.

She changed into a pair of red satin pajamas before getting into bed. She saw the red light on her cordless phone blinking, indicating she had messages. After checking her messages, she dialed Charlotte's number.

Charlotte picked up on the third ring. "Girl, I've been calling you all evening."

"I had a date with Byron," Nikki said as she crossed her legs. "I got your message."

"You guys are really getting cozy. I told Frederick he had nothing to worry about."

Frustrated, Nikki blurted, "I wish people would stay out of my business."

"Don't be getting an attitude with me."

"I'm sorry. Everything's been going great with us, but tonight I saw one of his exes and it went downhill from there."

Nikki conveyed the entire evening, not letting Charlotte get in a word. Finally, Charlotte found an opening and interrupted. "What do you think is in the envelope?"

"It's probably business related, but he acted suspicious."

"Or you're being paranoid."

"Probably."

Charlotte yawned. "I need to go. Oh, before I forget. What are you doing Friday?"

"Nothing. Why?"

"I bought some of your favorite DVDs, so stop by the house when you get off. Let's have a girls' night in."

"I'll have to let you know. I'm moving some of my stuff this weekend."

"I forgot about the move. But let's make a deal. If you come over Friday, I'll help you move."

"Now that's a deal I can't refuse. I'll be over around seven."

"Make it eight."

"Eight it is." Nikki yawned. "Girl, I'll let you go. You got me yawning too."

Nikki hung up with Charlotte and climbed under the covers.

I'm surprised Byron hasn't called me, she thought as she lay there. *I guess I am getting a little paranoid. If he doesn't call me tonight, I'll call him tomorrow.*

She closed her eyes and went to sleep.

The next morning Byron stayed in bed longer than usual.

I know I should have called Nikki last night, but after telling her about Tara and the awkwardness between us, it's probably best that I didn't, he thought.

After slowpoking around, he got dressed. As he looked

for his car keys, he spotted the unopened brown envelope he had laid on the counter the night before.

A shocked expression crossed his face as he stared at a picture of a one-year-old boy with jet-black hair and a radiant smile. "I wonder if . . ." he said to himself. He continued to stare at the picture. "No, it can't be."

He turned the picture over and read Tara's handwriting on the back: *Christopher Matthews Spain.*

He dropped the picture and envelope. "This can't be. Why now?"

He picked up the picture and put it back in the envelope. He tucked the envelope inside his brown leather briefcase and walked out the door.

After getting to the office, he informed Joyce to hold all his calls. He closed his door and contemplated on how to handle the situation. Hardly getting any work done anyway, he got up from his desk and walked over to the window. After he'd been staring out of it for a few minutes, Joyce knocked on the door. "Can I come in?"

"Sure," Byron said as he walked back over to his desk and sat down.

"I know it's none of my business, but something seems wrong. Nikki called," Joyce said and then added, "And Tara has called you about four times."

Byron dropped his head. "Thanks, Joyce. I'll call Nikki back shortly."

Joyce walked closer toward him. "Is there something you want to talk about?"

"Nothing I can't handle."

"If this has anything to do with Tara, you know I want to whip her behind anyway. Say the word and I'll give her a beat-down she'll never forget."

A smile flashed across Byron's face for the first time that day. He laughed. "Let's hope it doesn't come down to that."

"I'm serious," Joyce said before walking out and closing the door.

He leaned back in his chair. "The problem is not going to disappear. I better deal with it," he told himself.

He dialed Frederick's cell phone and got his voice mail. "Call me ASAP. I need to talk to you about a situation with Tara."

He hung up and then dialed Nikki's work number. After three rings he thought her phone was going to voice mail when she answered. "Nicolette Montana. How may I help you?"

"I'm so glad you answered." He sounded relieved.

"What's wrong?" Nikki asked.

"It's been one of those days." He rubbed his head nervously. "I called to apologize for not calling last night."

"No problem. I figured you were tired."

"I was, but I still should have called."

"Don't worry about it."

"How has your day been thus far?"

"Great, but I'm running late for a meeting, so I'll have to call you back."

"Call me on my cell," Byron said, disappointed, before hanging up.

His private line rang. He hit the Speaker button. "Hello."

"My man, what's up? I got your message," Frederick said, sounding worried.

Byron picked up the receiver. "Guess who's back and trying to wreak havoc in my life?"

"Is Tara up to her no-good antics again?"

"This time a child's involved."

"What the—"

"I told you about her calling. As big as Dallas is, I keep running into her. I saw her last night at Pappadeaux and she handed me a picture of a baby." Byron pulled out the picture of the baby and began to stare at it.

"Aw, man. Is the kid yours?"

"I don't know. I guess I should show it to Mama and see if he looks like one of us when we were babies."

"I don't envy you at all."

"I finally meet a woman that I want to spend my life with and now this."

"You sure Nikki's the one? Anybody who will lie to her family probably can't be trusted too much either. You sure know how to pick 'em," Frederick said critically.

"Trust me. Nikki is nothing like Tara."

"For your sake, man, I hope it works out."

"Me too."

They talked for a few more minutes until one of Byron's other lines rang.

"I have another call I need to take. I'll call you later." Byron clicked over to his other line. "This is Byron."

Tara's screeching voice was on the other end. "Daddy, how are you?"

Byron tried hard to control his temper. "What kind of game are you trying to play?"

"This is no game, sugar. You're a daddy and I'm back to collect."

"We haven't been together in almost two years."

Tara seemed to ignore his comment and said, "Christopher recently celebrated his first birthday. He's the reason why I moved back to Dallas. I decided he needed to have a relationship with his papa."

"It's taking a lot for me not to call you the female dog that you are. Until a blood test is done, I'm not claiming Christopher, or whatever his name is, as my child."

"You can fight it all you want, but when the test results come back, be prepared to pay out of your pockets."

Byron balled up his fist. "It's always about the money with you, isn't it? If he is my child, I'll make sure you never see a dime, or him either for that matter." He slammed the phone down.

I promised myself I wouldn't lose control, he thought as he stood up and paced the floor. *What am I going to do? I guess I'll do like the rest of the grown men in America do, run home to Mama.*

He picked up the picture and placed it in his jacket pocket. He then briskly exited his office.

"Joyce, I'll be leaving for the rest of the day. Take messages," he said before leaving. "And if anything urgent comes up, call me on my cell."

18

Nikki's mind was elsewhere during the entire team meeting. Eddie Bates, the director of her department, walked in with a petite African-American woman. Nikki paid attention when she looked up into the face of the woman she had almost clashed with a few days before.

Eddie smiled before making the introduction. "Good afternoon. I want to introduce you to one of the newest members of the team. This is Tara Spain and she'll be taking Jack Patterson's spot. She has over five years of marketing and management experience."

Nikki sat expressionless. *I can't believe this mess,* she thought. *How in the world am I supposed to work for Byron's ex? It's time to look for another job.*

Nikki watched Tara as she gave more of her background. Tara's eyes found Nikki and their eyes locked. Nikki could tell she was thrown off balance for a minute. Nikki smiled. Tara rolled her eyes and then went back to her professional mode.

I wonder if anyone else noticed how she rolled her eyes at me. Nikki looked up and noticed Kenneth looking between her and Tara. *The king of gossip would see that.*

The meeting ended after Tara's introduction. Nikki tried to leave the room without having to come face-to-face with Tara. It didn't work, because Eddie pointed to her and called her name. "Nikki, come here please."

Nikki regrettably stayed behind. Tara extended her right hand. Nikki had no choice but to shake it. "It's nice to meet you, Nikki. Eddie tells me you're the best in your area."

"I try to be," Nikki said, forcing a smile.

"Put me on your calendar for lunch next week. I'll e-mail you and we can coordinate the time," Tara said with a fake smile.

"Sure."

Eddie placed his hand on Tara's back. "Tara, I want to introduce you to one more team."

"Okay," Tara said as they walked out. She looked back at Nikki with the fake smile still plastered across her face.

Nikki wanted to slam the conference door. Before she could head out the door, Kenneth rushed in and shut it.

"What was that all about?" he asked.

"I don't have time for this." Her voice shook as she spoke.

"I saw how she rolled her eyes at you. She acts like you stole her man."

Nikki used her left hand to move Kenneth out of the way. "I will not entertain this."

She opened the door and left Kenneth standing in the conference room by himself. She made her way to her desk and immediately picked up the phone. She dialed Byron's number as soon as she got to her desk. Joyce informed her that he would be out for the rest of the evening. She tried calling him on his cell phone several times, but his voice mail picked up each time.

"Byron, this is urgent. Call me at my desk," Nikki said into the receiver. "If I'm not here, call me on my cell phone."

She logged on to her e-mail and shot Charlotte a quick message about the new chain of events. She looked around to make sure no one was looking and logged on to Monster. com and updated her resume.

I'm serious about finding me another job, she thought. *There is no way I can work with one of his exes. I won't work with one of his exes!*

Byron saw Nikki's number on the display but decided not to answer the call. He pulled into his parents' driveway. He needed to talk to his mother before talking to Nikki, or anyone else for that matter.

He rang the doorbell, although he had a spare key. He didn't want his mom to have a heart attack because of his surprise visit.

A beautiful caramel-brown, five-six elderly woman wearing glasses opened the door.

"Dear, what are you doing here?" his mother asked.

They hugged and he kissed her on the cheek. "I thought being your favorite son I didn't need a reason."

"Don't let your brother hear you say that." His mom blushed.

Byron walked toward the kitchen. "Something sure does smell good." He picked up the top of one of the boilers.

His mom lightly slapped the back of his hand. "Now you know I don't like people over my food while I'm cooking."

Sounding like a little boy, Byron said, "Yes, Mom."

"Have a seat and I'll cut you a piece of cake, and then we can talk."

He poured two glasses of milk while she cut two thick slices of the lemon pound cake.

"Where's Dad?" Byron said as he set the glasses down at the kitchen table.

"He's out playing golf. I hope he wins, because when he loses, I have to hear about how such and such cheated."

Byron tried to hide his anxiety with laughter as his sat down at the table.

"You didn't come over here to talk about the family," his mom said, joining him. She looked him straight in the eye and asked, "What's going on with you?"

He reached into his jacket pocket and handed her the picture.

"This is a cute little baby." She stared at the photo. "Is this your child?"

Byron let out a deep breath. "I was hoping you could shed some light on it for me."

"Now I can do a lot of things, but paternity tests aren't one of them," she said, shaking her head while staring at the baby in the photo.

"Does he look anything like us when we were kids?"

She studied the photo before answering. "He's cute, but not as cute as my babies were. I can't see any resemblance, but that doesn't mean anything."

"That's what I was afraid of."

She turned the photo over and saw the name on the back. "Don't tell me Tara is this poor child's mother."

"I'm afraid so."

His mom raised her hand up in the air. "Lord, I told him messing around with her would be a big mistake."

"I'm sorry, Mom. I hadn't planned on telling you like this. I didn't know where else to turn."

His mom rubbed the top of his hand. "Dear, you can always come to me. Have you gotten a blood test done?"

"Not yet. I'll contact her and get it done as soon as possible."

"If this is your child, you know you must do right by him."

Byron looked away. "I will, if it's mine."

She got up from the table and walked over to Byron and put her arm around his neck. "I know my baby will do the right thing. If it's yours, you don't have to worry about a thing. We'll make sure he grows up loved."

"Thanks, Mom. I do have something else I want to talk to you about."

"I'm listening. I need to check on my food." She took one of her cooking utensils and stirred in one pot.

"I've fallen in love. I think she's the one."

His mom looked over the rims of her glasses. "Is this the one I heard Frederick telling your cousin about?"

"Who doesn't know about Nikki?" Byron said, throwing his hands up.

"You know how your brother is."

"Mom, she's good for me. I never thought I could feel so strongly about someone after all the stuff Tara put me through."

"Have you talked to her about your situation?"

"No." He took the last bite of his cake.

She cut him another slice and placed it on his saucer. "Don't let her find out from anyone else."

"I'll tell her. But only after I find out whether or not he's my son."

"When do we get a chance to meet her?" she asked as she poured yellow flour meal and other ingredients into a bowl.

"Let me check with her and I'll let you know."

After talking with his mom for another half hour, Byron knew what he had to do.

"Mom, I'll call you this weekend."

"You better," she said as she walked him to the door. He hugged her and kissed her on the cheek before leaving.

19

Nikki left work early after the Tara bombshell. She talked to Charlotte via cell phone as she drove home. "I know I might be overreacting, but if that cow rolls her eyes one more time, I'm going to stick my foot straight up her behind."

Charlotte laughed. "Calm down. Like I said in my e-mail, you don't report to her, so you probably will only see her in passing."

"With all I have going on, this is the last thing I need."

"I know, girl," Charlotte sighed with sympathy.

"And Kenneth is so nosy. There's no telling what kind of rumor he'll start."

"Give him some credit."

"I do. I know he loves to get stuff started and play the innocent role." Nikki's phone beeped. "Char, hold on."

She clicked over. "Hello."

"Nik, it's me. Sorry it took me so long to return your call," Byron said.

She had an attitude when she responded. "Hold on." She clicked back over to the other line. "Girl, this is Byron, who's been MIA, missing in action, for the last few hours."

"Calm down, girl. What did our mamas tell us? Never let them see you sweat."

"Whatever. Bye." She clicked over. "Hello." She heard nothing but silence. "Byron!"

"I'm here. I was adjusting my earpiece," he said.

She raised her voice. "I've been trying to reach you all evening. Something happened and I need to tell you about it."

"Calm down. I'm on I-35 right now. I can jump on LBJ Expressway and be over your way in about thirty minutes."

"Please do, because we need to talk."

"Will you give me a hint?"

"You'll see when you get here." She turned into her driveway. "I'm at home, so I'll see you in a few."

"Bye."

She rushed through the door because she had to use the restroom. Afterward, she decided to take a quick shower to relax her nerves. She put on a pair of white shorts and a white Las Vegas T-shirt. She threw on her slippers and waited in the living room for Byron to arrive.

I know he has no control over his ex, she thought, *but he may be able to shed some light on this situation for me. I'm not prepared to leave my job right now.*

Byron waited outside for almost five minutes before making his way up the walkway.

I need to tell her about Tara and the baby, he thought to himself, *but she seemed like she has a lot going on. Okay . . . I'll tell her after she tells me her problem.*

He was surprised to get a long, tantalizing kiss from Nikki when she opened the door.

"Oh, wifey. I can get used to this," Byron joked.

She grabbed his hand and led him to the couch. "I know you can. Have a seat."

"You're working those shorts," Byron said, followed by a whistle.

"Get your mind out of the gutter, because we need to talk."

"I heard the urgency in your voice when I called."

Byron's cell phone rang, but he didn't answer it.

"You're not going to answer it?" Nikki asked.

"No. Whoever it is can wait. I'm more concerned about you right now."

"I need a hug." She leaned in as they hugged each other.

"What's wrong, baby?" Byron asked as he brushed her hair back.

"They hired a new manager and she's your ex."

Neither spoke for a moment. Byron broke the silence. "Which ex?"

Nikki removed herself from his embrace and looked him in the eye. "Tara. Who else?"

"Is she your manager?" There were other questions he wanted to fire out, but he refrained from doing so.

"Not directly, but we'll be in some of the same meetings and she'll be my manager's backup."

A sign of relief washed across his face. "What are you worried about?"

"I forgot to tell you, she rolled her eyes at me during the meeting."

"She what?"

"Yes, and it wasn't my imagination, because one of my coworkers noticed it too," she said, pouting.

"I don't know what to tell you."

"You don't have to say anything. I went on Monster dot com and updated my resume. I guess I'll be looking for another job."

"Don't you think that's a little drastic?"

"Answer this. If she got a job at your company, would you want to work with her?"

"Hell no!" Byron was quick to say.

"Then why should I?"

Byron knew this was the perfect time to tell her about Christopher. That way everything would be out in the open and she would know exactly what she was dealing with.

Looking at Nikki and her vulnerable state made Byron want to do everything he could to protect her. He decided to wait until after the paternity test and prayed that Tara would be on her best behavior in the meantime.

"I can't change the situation, but I'm here. If she does anything to disrespect you, let me know and we'll deal with it together."

He wrapped his arms around her and they fell asleep on the couch.

20

The sound of Nikki's telephone ringing the next morning woke Byron. Nikki still slept. He carefully moved her before getting up to answer the phone.

"Hello," Byron whispered.

"Hi. Sorry to wake you. This is Adrienne. Is my sister awake?" she said.

"Hold on. She's asleep, but I'll try to wake her for you," he said sluggishly. He shook Nikki several times before she woke up. "Telephone." He held the phone out to her.

She wiped the sleep out of her eyes. "Who is it?"

"Adrienne."

She stretched before taking the phone from him. "Girl, why are you calling here so early?"

"Because I had this bad dream last night and I needed to make sure you were okay."

"I'm fine."

"I see your husband is in town this week."

"Yes, and I'm enjoying every minute of it."

"That explains why you're still sleeping at seven in the morning."

"Seven? I'm really running late. I'll call you from my car."

Byron waited for her to finish her conversation and hang up the phone. "I guess we were both worn out," he said. He bent down to kiss her.

She held her hand over her mouth. "I'm warning you. I have dragon breath."

"Come here, girl," Byron said. "I couldn't care less. Give me some sugar."

After rushing to get ready for work and seeing Byron off, Nikki couldn't find her car keys. It took her fifteen minutes to realize that she had left them in the bathroom when she had rushed in the evening before.

While driving to work, she switched the radio station between Skip Murphy and the *Morning Team* and the *Steve Harvey Show*. She was laughing at one of Steve's jokes when her cell phone rang.

"I forgot to call Adrienne," she said out loud when she saw her sister's number on the display. She clicked the Speaker button. "Hey, sis."

"Don't be heying me. Ever since you got married you don't call anymore," Adrienne said.

Nikki blew her horn at the motorist in a blue sedan that cut her off. "Remind me to hire a chauffeur when I get rich."

"You better slow down. Don't be getting mad at them because you overslept."

"Did you want something?" she asked, trying not to sound irritated.

"I'm just worried about you."

"Girl, I'm fine. I had some shocking news at work yesterday. Byron and I talked and everything is going to be fine now."

Adrienne cleared her throat. "Speaking of Byron, when will you be selling your place?"

"Who said I was?"

"It doesn't make sense for you to have two places."

"Look. I have too much stuff to deal with at work to worry about my busybody sister." She clicked the End button on her cell phone.

Her phone rang again. She saw it was Adrienne, turned up the radio, and continued her drive to work.

Byron picked up the phone several times to dial Tara's number, but before he could dial the last digit, he hung up. *I have to deal with her sometime, so I might as well get it over with.*

This time, he let the phone ring. Tara answered in her annoying voice. "Hello."

"Tara, this is Byron."

"I knew you would come around. When do you want to meet your son?" she asked in a victorious tone.

"I'll meet Christopher after it's been determined I'm his father."

"Don't fight the obvious."

"Obviously, you've lost your mind if you think I would accept your words as fact." He scrolled through the yellow pages online.

"I can bring him by this weekend."

He found his doctor's number and wrote it on his notepad. "Look, Tara. I need to call and make an appointment for the paternity test."

"I already know who his parents are," she said sharply.

"I don't."

"Do what you have to do."

"I'll call you back with the date and time."

"Byron?"

"What?"

"Does your girlfriend know about your son?"

"Frankly, that's none of your business and I'd appreciate you staying out of it."

"Don't worry." Tara hung up.

Byron held the receiver. "I hope she doesn't do something stupid," he said to himself.

He called the doctor's office and made an appointment and then he dialed Tara's number again.

"Hello," she answered.

"I called you back to give you the appointment info," Byron told her.

"Nikki, can I borrow your pen? For the life of me, I can never keep up with one," Tara said.

Byron's mouth dropped. "What kind of game are you playing?"

"Dear, I am at work. Now give me the info so we both can get back to work."

He wiped the sweat from his forehead as he gave her the information. "I need you both to be there on time."

"We'll be there and your son can't wait to see you."

After hanging up, Byron didn't know if he should call Nikki and tell her everything.

This is one of Tara's games. She's playing with my mind and I will not let her win, he told himself in thought. *I'll stand my ground and wait until after the test results before telling Nikki.*

Nikki pretended to be reading over some notes while Tara was on the phone. She overheard her mention something about a son.

I feel sorry for her child, she thought. *I couldn't even imagine having a mother like her. Listen to me. I need to stop. I should give her a fair chance. I need to approach this situation differently. We're both grown and professional women, so there's no reason why we can't be cordial on the job.*

"Sorry about that. My baby's daddy is tripping," Tara said to Nikki.

"I hear you."

Tara picked up a picture frame and handed it to Nikki. "This is my heart. Isn't he the cutest little thing?"

Nikki smiled and had to agree. "He's adorable. What's his name?"

"Christopher. He's one going on one hundred."

Nikki handed the picture back to Tara. "I have to admit, I never pictured you as a mother."

Tara laughed. "Neither could I. But my little bundle of joy has changed my life."

They spent the next thirty minutes going over some technical specifications for an upcoming project. Nikki noticed how Tara seemed to be on point on various things.

When the meeting ended, Tara stood up and closed her office door. "There's something else I need to talk to you about."

Nikki uncrossed her legs. "Work related, I hope."

Tara sat on the corner of her desk. "I think you know who it's about."

"To keep the peace, I think conversing about Byron is off-limits."

Tara picked up an object on her desk and swirled it around. "You're not the least bit curious as to why we broke up?"

"What does that have to do with our work relationship?"

"Nothing. I know if it was me, I would want to know details."

Nikki had to restrain herself. "But you're not me."

"Look, Nicolette, I'm not trying to start anything."

Before Nikki could respond, someone knocked and opened the door.

"I hate to interrupt, but, Tara, I have an important call I need you to be on," Eddie stated without acknowledging Nikki.

"Give me one minute, Eddie, and I'll be right there," Tara told him.

Nikki interrupted. "No need. We're through here."

Tara addressed her. "We'll continue this conversation next week at lunch."

As Nikki walked past Eddie, she said under her breath, "Not if I can help it."

21

Nikki tried to avoid Tara the remainder of the week as much as possible. She ended up taking work home and only spoke with Byron by phone or via e-mail. She was e-mailing him when Kenneth snuck up behind her.

"Boo," Kenneth said.

She almost jumped out of her seat. She hit him with her hand. "Don't you ever do that again," Nikki said.

"Sorry. You've been in your own little world. I was wondering if you were available to go with us to happy hour."

"I'll pass. I'm hanging out with my best friend tonight."

"What does Charlotte have that I don't have?"

"Free food and my favorite movies," she said in a serious tone.

"Can I tag along?"

"No, silly, this is ladies' night. Meaning no men."

"Your loss, baby." He tugged on his collar.

She laughed. "I'll get over it."

"See you on Monday." He turned to walk away.

Nikki looked at the clock. "You're leaving already?"

"Yeah, I need to run to the bank and the post office before-hand."

"Be safe. Have a good weekend."

"You too."

Soon after Kenneth left, Mya passed by her desk carrying her purse and laptop. Nikki asked her, "Are you going to happy hour too?"

"No. Didn't Kenneth tell you?"

"Tell me what?" Nikki asked.

"Me and some friends are going to Las Vegas for the weekend."

"Have fun."

"I plan on it," Mya said before walking away.

Nikki turned her attention back toward the computer and read Byron's response:

> *We've only known each other a short time, but I will do whatever I can to make you happy. I know you're an independent woman and you're not accustomed to depending on a man for anything, but I'm here for you. You're becoming my best friend and I hope one day to be your REAL husband. I love you and there's no turning back from this journey we're on. Have fun with Charlotte. I'll be over tomorrow to help you move. I can't wait (smile).*

She read it several times before responding:

> *Byron, you always know the right things to say. Thank you again for being my "knight in shining armor." I wouldn't be able to get through this or-deal without you. As I mentioned in my previous e-mail, work is work. I'll deal with it. I'm on my way out the door now. You know how bad Friday traffic can be. I'll see you bright and early tomor-*

*row morning. I don't have much stuff to bring be-
cause I know it's only temporary. I wish . . . well, I
won't say what I wish, but know that I care about
you too (smile).*
    Nikki

After hitting the Send button, she logged off her computer, locked her desk, and grabbed her purse. She stood up
to leave and accidentally bumped into Tara.

"Oh, I'm sorry," Nikki said while catching her balance.

Tara said, "No problem. I came over to say congratulations."

"For what?"

"I found out you and Byron are married."

Nikki stuttered, "Who told you that?"

"A little birdie."

"People need to mind their own business."

Looking down at her ring, Tara commented, "I don't know
why I didn't figure it out earlier. Your ring does sparkle."

Nikki moved the hand with the ring out of view. "This is
nothing."

"I see why you wouldn't want to talk about Byron now."

Nikki tapped her foot on the carpeted floor. "I don't mean
to be rude, but I need to get out of here."

Tara moved out of her way. "By all means, I don't want to
hold you up."

As Nikki walked out the door toward the elevator, she
heard Tara say, "Have a good weekend."

She is getting on my last nerve, Nikki thought. *Now I
wonder who's been discussing my personal life with her. All
I need is for her to blow my cover.*

Byron walked straight to the bar. He ordered a Heineken
and waited for his brother to show up. He watched the inter-
change between the women and men. He laughed to himself

as he saw men being turned down by provocatively dressed women.

Now, brother man, you know if you don't have a platinum card, these women are not even trying to hear you, he thought to himself.

"Excuse me," said a tall, curvaceous woman as she accidentally bumped into him, spilling some of her drink on his shirt.

"You're excused," he replied.

"Why don't I buy you a drink to make up for it?" she asked as she flirted.

"That's okay. Thanks for offering, though."

She batted her eyes and got close enough to him so he could see her cleavage. "You sure?"

He cleared his throat and stepped back. "I'm sure."

"Okay, *papi.*" She twisted away.

He was watching her walk away when Frederick came up behind him. "I see you're not dead. She was hot."

He gave Frederick a brotherly hug. "What's up? I'm cool on that. I have a woman."

"That's right, you're an old married man," he joked.

"Hey, man, I didn't see you standing there," Byron said to his friend Steven, who was standing behind Frederick.

Steven was short and athletically built. He had a cute baby face and was often mistaken to be younger than his thirty-three years. They gave each other a tight handshake.

"Man, I've been doing my thing. I heard you were tied down now," Steven said.

Byron looked at Frederick. "I'm enjoying life. How's the force been treating you?"

"I'm a sergeant now. I saw your brother speeding on Central Expressway earlier today and he invited me to join y'all."

Frederick jumped in. "Yeah. I thought pipsqueak was going to give me a ticket for a minute."

"You better watch how you talk to me. I have my hand-cuffs on me," Steven joked.

"Don't say that too loud, one of these honeys might take it the wrong way." They all laughed.

They continued to laugh, order drinks, and talk over the loud music.

22

Nikki went straight home from work, showered, and changed into a comfortable pair of black jeans and a T-shirt. She put on her black Nikes and headed to Charlotte's.

"Somebody must be having a party. I can't find a parking place anywhere," she said to herself as she parked several houses down.

She rang the doorbell and turned her back toward the door, waiting on Charlotte to answer.

"Hey, girl, you're a little late," Charlotte said.

Looking back at the crowded street, Nikki said, "Girl, I had the hardest time finding a parking place."

Charlotte hugged her. "Come on in." She grabbed Nikki's hand and led her to the living room.

"It's awfully dark in here. You having a séance or something?" Nikki joked.

"Girl, you're crazy. Wait here and I'll turn the light on."

When the lights came on, all Nikki could hear was thunderous voices yelling, "Surprise!"

A shocked expression went across her face. "What is this?" she said.

Adrienne and Pam hugged her. "We didn't get a chance to give you a shower before you got married, so we decided to give it to you now."

She stuttered, "But . . . but . . . you didn't have to."

April, her sister-in-law, walked over and hugged her. "But we did. I remember the lovely gifts you gave me when I got ready to marry your brother, so of course I had to return the favor."

Emotions swamped Nikki and tears fell down her cheeks. "I don't know what to say."

Janice spoke. "Don't say anything. Enjoy being the lady of the hour."

Nikki needed to get some space. "Char, come with me for a minute." She looked back in the room at her sisters and her sisters-in-law and a few friends from school. "Y'all, I'll be right back. I need to pull myself together. I love y'all."

She heard them say, "We love you too." She grabbed Charlotte's arm and pulled her into the kitchen.

"Girl, why didn't you warn me?" she whispered.

Charlotte tried to remove her arm, but Nikki had a tight grip. "I couldn't or it would have ruined the surprise."

"No kidding, Sherlock. You and I both know this isn't right."

She jerked her arm away. "Look. You wanted me to help fool everybody, and that's what I'm doing. What was I supposed to do when your sisters asked me to help them plan this?"

"You could have told them no."

"How would that have looked if your best friend didn't want to throw you a shower?"

"Any excuse would have done." Nikki turned away and pouted.

"Look. For two hours pretend to be overjoyed and enjoy the attention."

"It's easy for you to say."

Charlotte crossed her arms and leaned back. "I did warn you about lying."

She rolled her eyes. "Now is not the time to remind me."

Pam walked into the kitchen. "Are you okay? We didn't mean to make you cry."

"I'm fine. Just overwhelmed at what you ladies have done for me."

"Come give your big sister a hug."

She hugged Pam and glanced over her shoulder at Charlotte with a "what am I going to do?" look.

When they walked back into the living room, Adrienne said, "Let's get this party started. Let's play a few games, eat, and then open some presents."

Janice placed a tiara on Nikki's head. "You get to wear this."

Nikki smiled. *I've pretended thus far, so I might as well enjoy it,* she thought.

Adrienne tried to get everyone's attention. "What game do y'all want to play first? We have charades, taboo, and Pictionary."

"How about charades? Nikki's good at that game," Charlotte said with a smirk on her face.

Nikki cut her eyes at Charlotte. She stood up and asked, "Who's on my team?"

The ladies teamed up and started up a game of charades. As they were winding down from playing, the doorbell rang. Charlotte was gone a few minutes and walked back into the living room. "Ladies, the food is here. I've set everything up in the dining room."

All ten of them walked toward the dining room with Nikki and Charlotte lagging behind.

"Char, I'm sorry for earlier," Nikki told her best friend.

She wrapped her arms through Nikki's. "You're forgiven. I know you're under a lot of pressure."

"That's an understatement."

"Are you having fun?"

Nikki laughed. "Believe it or not, I am. It's weird."

"Good. Now don't ask me to do this for you again."

As they ate, the women asked Nikki about Byron. She tried to sound enthusiastic, like she was head over heels in love.

Who am I fooling? I am in love with him, she reminded herself.

She tried to dodge some of the questions, but Adrienne wouldn't let her drop them.

"When are you selling your place?" Adrienne asked.

"We haven't decided. For now, we're living between the two," Nikki responded.

April commented, "If I were you, I would rent it out. Never know when you might need something to fall back on."

"Y'all need to stay out of her business. If she wants to sell or keep it, that's her business," Pam said as she sipped on her frozen strawberry daiquiri.

"Thanks, Pam," Nikki said.

Charlotte rang a bell. "Ladies, we're going to move this party back into the living room. It's time to open up the presents."

"Come on, girl, this is the fun part," Janice said to Nikki, hurrying her along.

Charlotte pointed for Nikki to sit in the chair surrounded by gifts. Teary-eyed, Nikki sat and said, "Before I open these gifts, I want to thank you all for everything. I don't know how I'll ever repay you."

Adrienne wiped tears from her eyes. "Girl, open up these gifts."

"Okay," she said as Pam handed her the first one.

Nikki read the card. "This is from April." She carefully opened the beautiful floral-wrapped box. She held up a black-laced teddy with some garter belts. She blushed. "Oh my."

"Now that's what I'm talking about," Charlotte said.

Every gift she opened was either a piece of lingerie or a couple's bath set.

"Chocolate body paint. Now what am I supposed to do with this?" Nikki asked.

"If you don't know, give me my gift back," Janice said.

"Ugh. I can't imagine you and my brother," Adrienne said, shaking her head.

They all laughed.

The doorbell rang. "I wonder who that is," Charlotte commented.

"The party's almost over," Pam said with a sneaky smile on her face.

Charlotte left to answer the door. She walked back in, just as they finished placing the gifts in the corner.

"Ladies, I have another announcement to make," Charlotte said. All eyes were on her. She hit the button on her stereo and yelled, "Let's get this party started."

A song by Usher and Lil' John began to play and two handsome, well-built men dressed in fireman uniforms walked in.

One of them spoke out. "I heard there was a fire in this room."

Adrienne fanned herself and said, "Yes, and it's right here, baby."

In beat with the music, the dancers removed pieces of their uniforms. Each of the ladies took turns dancing with them.

The tallest one made his way to Nikki. "Can your man put your fire out like this?" he asked her.

He took off his g-string and swung it around. Nikki shrieked and put her hand to her mouth. "Oh my goodness."

Charlotte laughed. "Girl, enjoy yourself. I told you I'm only doing this once."

Nikki got up and danced as they sandwiched her in. "If you tell anybody about this, I'll deny it," she yelled.

The ladies gave away some dollars and then sent the dancers on their way.

"This was so much fun," Nikki commented as everyone helped her put all the nice gifts in her car.

"I'm glad you had a good time," Charlotte said.

She hugged everybody before getting in her car. "Thank y'all again."

She drove home feeling elated, yet sad.

23

Byron woke up Saturday morning feeling refreshed. He made a fresh cup of coffee before taking a shower. He put on a black Sean John jogging suit and a pair of black Air Jordans.

"Nikki, what are we getting ourselves into?" he asked himself out loud. He got in his car and dialed her number from his cell. "Wake up, sleepyhead," he said into the phone receiver.

"I'm not asleep," she responded.

"I'll be there shortly. Have you eaten breakfast?"

"No, not yet."

"Do you want something from I-Hop or the Waffle House?"

"Surprise me."

"Okay. See you soon. Bye."

Byron went by the Waffle House and ordered two big breakfasts. The food was still warm when he made it over to Nikki's. He walked up to her door and rang the doorbell. "Good morning," he said when she opened the door. He leaned down and kissed her on the lips.

"Let me help you with this," she said, taking one bag. "What all did you get?"

"Enough to carry us until later," he said as he noticed some gift bags and boxes on the table.

"I'll be back. Let me get some real silverware," Nikki said as she exited into the kitchen.

"I'm not going anywhere," he said.

While she was getting the silverware, he caught a glimpse of some lace in one of the bags. He pulled it out and a wide grin crossed his face. He held it up in front of him.

Nikki walked back in. "I don't think that's your size," she joked.

"But it's yours."

"Last night my best friend and my sisters decided to throw me a surprise bridal shower."

He continued to look at the lingerie. "Really now? I wish I could have seen the expression on your face."

"I'm glad you weren't there. It was already awkward enough." She snatched the lingerie out of his hands and placed it back in the bag. "Your waffles are getting cold."

They ate breakfast and Nikki shared with Byron the events from the previous night.

After drinking his orange juice, Byron asked, "I'm curious. Did you have any strippers?"

Nikki slipped and said, "They're dancers."

"I knew it." Byron laughed. "You conveniently left that part out."

"I was going to tell you."

"Sure."

They finished eating and packed up Byron's SUV with a few of her items. Nikki made sure he had everything that she had packed. "That's it. I guess I'm officially moving in," she said, brushing her hands together.

He pulled her to him. "And you're making me a very happy man."

Her eyes gleamed. "Don't be getting any ideas. Remember this is only for about four more months."

"That's what your mouth says."

"We'll see."

They stared into each other's eyes and the trance was broken by Byron's cell phone vibrating.

"I guess that means it's time for me to let you go," Byron said as he headed for the door, ignoring his vibrating phone. "You're not going to follow me."

"I want to stay here for one more night," Nikki whined. She still couldn't believe she was actually moving in with this man.

"When will you start informing me of your decisions?"

"When I feel like it's something you need to know."

"I know the marriage isn't real, Nikki, but we are in a relationship."

"Everything is happening so fast. I need more time," she continued whining.

"It's your own fault, so don't be taking it out on me."

"I'm not. Give me one more day." She batted her eyes at him. "Please. With sugar on top."

"Now that was the magic word." He smiled and kissed her lightly on the lips. "Pull yourself together, girl. I'll call you later. If you're not at my place by noon on Sunday, I'll personally come drag you out of this house."

"You wouldn't."

"Dare me."

He jumped in his car and sped away.

It didn't take Byron long to carry Nikki's stuff inside his house. He decided to put her things in the spare bedroom across from his and let her unpack herself.

I guess I'll have to share my office with her, he thought to himself. *This is going to be an adjustment.*

His cell phone rang again but by the time he got to it, whoever it was had to leave a message.

He hit SEND and his phone dialed the last missed call.

"Hello," Tara said.

"Why are you calling me?" Byron asked.

"I'm at Wal-Mart buying some Pampers and I thought of you."

"Oh, how sweet."

"By the way, you failed to mention you were *married*."

"Excuse me." Byron remained calm, although his instincts told him to hang up.

"I saw the ring you gave Nikki. Beautiful, I might add. It looks like it cost a pretty penny."

"What's it to you?"

"I have one question. How does she feel about your son?"

"We're adjusting."

"Really? She didn't seem to know anything about it when I showed her his picture."

"Why would she be discussing anything with you?"

"You know how women talk. Besides, we work together, so we're bound to find out personal things about each other."

Byron heard a cry in the background. "Sounds like Christopher needs you more than I do right now, so take care of him. I'll see you at the doctor's office. And, Tara?"

"What?" she snapped.

"Please don't call me again."

Lord, please don't let that child be mine, Byron prayed. *I love kids, but I never imagined having one out of wedlock. I know. I should have kept my zipper up, so it's my fault. I promise if you get me out of this one, I'll wait until I'm married.*

Byron laughed at himself.

I must be desperate to be making promises to God about not having sex.

II

TWISTER

Round and Round We Go. Where Life Stops, Nobody Knows.

24

Nikki spent Sunday morning relaxing and avoiding phone calls from her family, especially from her mom, who wasn't too happy about her missing yet another church service. Nikki forwarded her home phone to her cell phone, grabbed her Louis Vuitton backpack, and then turned on the alarm before making her way to Byron's.

Nikki stood impatiently outside the door after knocking. "I thought you'd changed your mind," she said when Byron opened the door.

"Let me take that," he said, reaching for the bag.

She walked in like she owned the place. "Where's my stuff?"

He walked up the stairs with Nikki on his heels. "I put your things in the bedroom across from mine."

"How convenient," she stated, following him into a spacious bedroom.

She walked around the room. "I don't like these colors."

"Feel free to decorate any way you like."

"Now don't get mad at me when I change the whole place around."

"I won't. What's mine is yours," Byron said with a wink.

"Music to a woman's ears," Nikki said as they both laughed.

"I'll leave you alone to get settled. I'll be downstairs if you need anything."

"Thanks."

After Byron left the room, Nikki lay across the queen-sized canopy bed.

This is perfect, she thought. She hugged herself and fell back on the bed.

I've died and gone to heaven. This bed feels almost as good as mine. She sat up.

A thought crossed her mind. *I know he cares about me, so between now and then, I have to convince him that I can be the perfect little wifey.* She laughed at her last thought. *What am I doing? This is a temporary situation. In another four months, it'll be six months and we can go our separate ways . . . or not.*

She unpacked her stuff. When she went downstairs, Byron was nowhere in sight. She yelled, "Byron!"

"I'm in here," he shouted from the kitchen.

The table was set with platters of fish, shrimp, potato salad, and biscuits.

"I was going to cook for you," Nikki said as she entered the kitchen and noticed the spread.

"You can cook for me tomorrow." He walked around and pulled out her chair.

After fixing their plates, Byron said grace. "Lord, thank you for this food we're about to eat. Nikki and I might not be together under the best of circumstances, but, Lord, you know our hearts and please allow our time together to manifest itself into something special for both of us. Amen."

"Amen," Nikki bashfully said as she took her napkin and draped it across her lap.

In between bites, Byron asked, "Do you think you'll find the bed comfortable? If not, we can go tomorrow and get you a new one."

"It's perfect," Nikki assured him.

They made small talk the rest of the meal.

"Don't worry about the dishes. Go relax," Byron said.

Nikki wiped her mouth. "I told you not to start something and not keep it up."

Flirting back with her, he said, "I don't start anything I can't finish."

She left and went to the den. She took off her shoes, found the remote, and began watching a movie on the Sci-Fi station.

"Ugh, that's gross," she shouted after watching a movie about insects for about thirty minutes.

"You're the one who put it on that channel," Byron said as he took a seat next to her. "Let me see your feet." He began massaging her toes after obliging his request. She leaned back and momentarily forgot about the movie she was watching.

"Mmm. That feels good," she moaned.

"I'm glad."

She looked at him and smiled. "You'd make a great husband. You cook, you clean, and you do toes."

He laughed. "There are a lot of other things I do too."

"I can imagine," she said as he delicately handled each toe. With each rub, she could feel her insides getting moist. She moved her foot. "Byron, I think my feet are okay now."

"What about the other parts of your body?"

She stood up and pushed him back playfully on the shoulder. "You would have to make this difficult."

With a boyish grin on his face, he asked, "What did I do?"

"You know what you did." She walked toward the stairs. "I think I'll finish unpacking."

"You said you were through."

"I lied." She left him downstairs.

* * *

That didn't go exactly like I had planned it. It's still early and she's gone to bed, Byron thought. He waited to see if she was coming back downstairs. When she didn't, he retreated up the stairs. He knocked on her door and when he didn't get an answer, he began to walk back downstairs.

"I'm sorry," she said after opening the door.

"No. I'm the one who should be apologizing. I can't resist touching you."

"I guess you need to pull out your rule book and add no touching." Nikki smirked.

"Oh, you got jokes?"

"Plenty."

25

The next morning Byron woke up to the smell of bacon and coffee. He whisked out of bed, took a shower, and got dressed.

When he entered the kitchen, Nikki was wearing a robe and a head wrap and was seated at the table reading the morning paper and drinking coffee. She put the paper down. He felt like wrapping his arms around her when she smiled at him.

"Good morning," he said as he leaned down and kissed her on the forehead.

She pulled away from the table. "I hope you don't mind, but I felt like cooking a big breakfast for some reason."

"Don't spoil me now," he said, using Nikki's own words.

"Have a seat and I'll bring everything to the table." She filled his plate with bacon, scrambled eggs with cheese, grits, and toast.

"If you cook like this every day, I know I'll need to put in extra time in the gym," he commented as he buttered his toast.

Nikki fixed her plate and after Byron said grace, they ate, making small talk.

"Don't worry about those dishes. Finish getting ready for work and I'll throw them in the dishwasher," Byron said as he got up and cleared the table.

"Yes, I can't go to work looking like this," she said, rubbing her hand down her yellow terry cloth robe that matched her Tweety Bird slippers. She then headed upstairs to get ready for work.

Byron was turning the dishwasher on when Nikki came back downstairs fully dressed. He did a double take. There was not a strand of hair out of place. Her makeup was immaculate. He licked his lips as he imagined kissing the ruby-red lipstick off her.

"Byron, are you ready?" Nikki asked, forcing him back to reality.

"I'll be leaving in a minute. I'll walk you to the door."

She needs to stop wearing that fragrance. It's intoxicating, he thought.

Before walking out the door, Nikki asked, "Do I get a key or will you be here by six?"

"I'm sorry. With everything going on, I forgot to give you a copy. Wait right here."

He rushed upstairs and came back with a couple of keys on a heart-shaped key ring.

"Thanks." She took them and added them to her key chain.

He handed her a slip of paper. "This is the code for the alarm."

She tucked it in her bra. He wished he could be where the paper was.

"It's in a safe place now," she said as she glanced at her watch. "I better get going. I have to deal with rush-hour traffic."

Although he wanted to kiss her, he gave her a tight hug instead. "Have a good day."

"You too," she said as she walked to her car.

He closed the door and spoke out loud. "Lord, the promise I made to you about refraining from sex, can I take it back?"

Tara is the last person I want to see, Nikki thought as she headed toward her desk. *Why is she camping out near my desk?* Nikki decided to detour to the break room, secretly hoping Tara would be gone by the time she got to her desk.

She fixed herself a cup of coffee. After adding two packets of Sweet 'N Low, she poured a small container of cream into her cup, then took a sip. After a couple more sips she decided to head back toward her desk. On her way she noticed that Tara was no longer standing there. As she approached her desk, Nikki noticed a yellow sticky note attached to her computer screen. She set her coffee down on the coaster on her desk, removed the sticky note, and read it.

I forgot about lunch, Nikki thought to herself after reading the note. *She's the last person I need to be having lunch with.*

She logged on to her computer and returned e-mails she had failed to acknowledge on Friday. Just as she hit the Send key on the last e-mail, her phone rang. She looked at the display and saw Kenneth's five-digit extension and name displayed.

"What, Kenneth?" she answered.

"See, if I had a customer on the line, you would be in trouble," Kenneth said.

"You only call me when you want to gossip. I don't know why I entertain you by listening."

"What are you doing for lunch?"

She looked at the sticky note again, balled it up, and threw it in the trash. "I'm going to lunch with Tara, but I'm trying my best to get out of it."

"You still haven't told me why she rolled her eyes at you."

"Kenneth, you're paranoid. Anyway, what's so hot that you can't tell me over the phone?"

"It's actually about the person you're going to lunch with."

She sat up in her chair and contemplated whether to inquire for more information, but decided to take the high road. "Whatever it is, I don't want to know about it."

"Are you sure?"

She paused and whispered, "Yes."

"I guess I'll have to find somebody else to tell, Ms. Looks Like She's Got Herself Together is really falling apart at the seams."

"I won't ask how you know this," Nikki said, fighting back the urge to just make Kenneth spit it out.

"Let's just say, we both see the same therapist."

"Everybody who gets counseling is not crazy."

Kenneth laughed. "Thank you. That's what I've been trying to tell y'all."

"I'm hanging up on you now." And she did just that.

After getting off the phone, Nikki was curious as to why Tara was seeing a therapist.

Don't I have enough issues on my own than to be worried about somebody who's not even one of my favorite people? she asked herself.

Just then Nikki heard her computer signaling her that she had a new e-mail. Her manager had just sent her an e-mail congratulating her on saving an account. At the bottom of the e-mail he asked her to bill him for today's lunch with Tara.

Dang it. I hate that he even knew about it. Now I have no choice but to go.

She typed up a quick e-mail to Tara, informing her to meet her by the elevator at one o'clock.

They sent several e-mails between each other on where to eat. Nikki decided on the Olive Garden.

If I have to go with her, it might as well be somewhere I like.

* * *

As Byron paced back and forth in front of his desk, Joyce walked in with a concerned look on her face.

"We need to talk," Joyce said. "You're on an emotional roller coaster. You've been a wreck."

"But—" Byron started.

"But nothing. I'm your coworker, friend, and most importantly, I'm your cousin. Do I need to call your mama?"

"Sit down. I don't need you calling my mama, worrying her." He closed the door and then sat in the chair next to hers. "I need another woman's point of view."

"You know I'll be honest with you," Joyce said sincerely, as she listened to Byron tell her about Tara and the claim of Christopher being his child. "I knew that heifer was up to something!" she exclaimed.

"Calm down."

"Why did she wait over a year to tell you?"

"I remember her claiming she was pregnant when I broke up with her, but I thought it was a ploy to keep me."

Almost in a whisper, she asked, "When is the test?"

"July first, but in the meantime, I have to decide on whether to tell Nikki about it."

"She needs to know."

"Yes, but if it's not my child, I don't want to burden her with it." His cell phone rang. He answered and after hanging up, he looked up at Joyce. "That was Nikki."

"Then why are you looking so sad?"

"She told me that she's having lunch with Tara."

Shocked, Joyce asked, "What? How did this come about?"

He explained that Tara now worked at the same company as Nikki and they both knew about each other. "If it wasn't for bad luck, I wouldn't have any luck," he stated as he sat down behind the desk.

"You better tell Nikki about the baby before the Wicked Witch of the South does. I don't trust Tara and you best believe Ms. Thing has a hidden agenda."

"I will."

"Don't wait until it's too late," Joyce said as she stood up.

They hugged. "Thanks, cousin," he said.

"Thank me by giving me a raise," she joked as she headed toward the door.

"Ha-ha," he said.

26

One o'clock came too soon for Nikki. She turned on the screen saver on her computer, grabbed her purse, and walked to the elevator. She decided to check her voice mail on her cell phone while she waited. As she was hanging up, Tara walked out the door.

"Sorry I'm late," Tara apologized. "The conference call I was on lasted longer than I expected."

"No problem," Nikki said, placing her cell phone back in her purse and pressing the Down button on the elevator.

The elevator door opened immediately. Tara took out her car keys. "Why don't we go in my car?"

"Sure," Nikki said, trying not to sound standoffish.

Neither said anything else while the elevator took them to the lobby.

Tara walked fast and Nikki had to almost run to catch up with her. "People always say I walk fast," Tara stated.

"I don't see why," Nikki mouthed under her breath.

When they reached the parking garage, Tara pointed to a four-door gray Lexus. "That's my car over there." She clicked off the alarm.

Nikki spotted the car seat along with toys strewn around inside the car.

"How old is your son again?" Nikki asked as Tara swirled the Lexus into the oncoming traffic.

"He recently turned one."

"I admire you," Nikki said, not knowing if she really meant it, but it felt like the right thing to say.

Tara looked in her direction with a stunned look on her face. "You do?"

"Yes. Being a single mother has to be hard. I don't know if I could do it." Nikki held up her hand and her wedding ring glistened as the sunlight hit it.

"I wish his father would do more."

Looking out the window and absentminded, Nikki said, "Men who make babies should be held responsible to take care of them, and not just with money either."

"Fortunately, you don't have to worry about it since you're married," Tara said sarcastically.

"Excuse me," Nikki responded.

"If you get pregnant, you have Byron. I don't have any-one."

"I'm sorry. I didn't mean to sound so heartless," Nikki said apologetically. "I simply can't imagine what type of man would leave a woman to raise a child alone."

A devious smirk came across Tara's lips as she drove them to their destination.

Joyce placed a memo on Byron's desk. "Staring at the phone won't make it ring," she said.

"It's that obvious?" Byron asked as he looked up into Joyce's concerned face.

"Yes. Now according to this memo, you got some work to do, so I suggest you concentrate on your work and deal with everything else later."

"Yes, ma'am."

His phone rang as Joyce exited his office. "This is Byron."

"Byron, we need you to fly to Miami as soon as possible to hand-deliver a contract," said Michael Bates, one of the only African-Americans in upper management at his company.

Byron looked at his calendar. "Sir, can't we use FedEx or UPS?"

"No, we can't. This account is worth millions and their board is hesitant on a few things. I thought sending my best employee would make sure we sealed the deal."

He played with his stress-relief balls in one hand while doodling on his notepad with the other. "Anything special I need to know?"

Michael went over details about the customer. Byron took notes when needed. After filling him in, Michael added, "My secretary is making your travel arrangements. She'll call Joyce and give her the details."

"I'll call you tomorrow and let you know how everything goes," Byron stated.

"I'll be looking forward to the call."

After hanging up the phone, Byron called Joyce and informed her of the change of events. "Call me at home or on my cell with my flight info," he said before hanging up the phone and exhaling a deep sigh.

The first part of lunch was filled with frivolous conversation. Nikki decided to play it cool because she couldn't figure Tara out. One minute she was professional and wanted to talk about business, and the next it was as if she was prying into her and Byron's life.

"How long have you known Byron?" Tara asked as she drank her raspberry lemonade.

"Almost a year," Nikki lied.

"I still can't believe you guys are married. Marriage was the last thing on his mind when we were together."

Trying to sound nonchalant, Nikki said, "It was love at first sight. We met on the plane. He spilled some coffee on my favorite pumps and the rest, as they say, is history." A smile swept across her face.

"Oh, I see."

"We had a fairy-tale wedding," she added.

"I heard you guys got married in Vegas." Tara stared at her.

"Yes, we did. Everything was so beautiful. I can remember it as if it was yesterday. We wed at the Venetian Hotel. You would have thought we were royalty. Everyone treated us like a king and queen." She drank from her iced tea.

"Do you have any wedding pictures?"

Nikki almost strangled. "Funny thing happened. The pictures were in my suitcase and the airlines still haven't found them."

"I know you were pissed."

"I still am. I wish now I would have put them in my carry-on, but Byron insisted nothing would happen to them."

The waiter brought over Nikki's order of lasagna with extra shredded Parmesan and Tara's shrimp fettuccine. While eating, Nikki decided to turn the tables on Tara and pry into her life.

"So what are you going to do about your son's father?" she asked, taking a bite into the moist seasoned bread stick.

"I'm taking him to court so I can get child support."

"Is he spending time with the child?"

Tara put her fork down and looked like she was about to cry. "This is hard for me. Especially to be discussing this with my ex-boyfriend's wife."

Nikki felt sympathetic. "I know this is awkward, but if you need someone to talk to, I'm all ears." *Why in the world did I say that? Maybe I need to see the shrink she and Kenneth are seeing.*

After taking the napkin and wiping her teary eyes, Tara

said, "Sometimes I don't know what I'm going to do. Like last weekend, I was buying Pampers and when I called my son's father, he was so rude to me."

Nikki, unsure of what to say, responded, "Maybe he'll come around soon."

"I hope so. The first word out of my son's mouth was 'Da-da.' And it breaks my heart to tell him Da-da won't be around."

"Is your family helping out in any way?"

"I wish. My sisters all have kids by different men. My mom is disappointed in me because she thought I would do better."

Tara went on to tell Nikki about her dysfunctional childhood and the nonexistent relationship she currently had with her mother and siblings. Nikki couldn't imagine not having the support of her family.

"Having a child out of wedlock is hard, but I don't see why she's disappointed. You're a very successful woman. There aren't too many people who have your credentials. You haven't done too badly for yourself."

With a coy smile Tara said, "Thanks. You're too kind. I see why Byron fell in love with you."

Nikki glanced away. A waiter came over to the table. "Would you ladies like dessert?" he asked.

Both declined. Nikki pulled out the company credit card to pay for lunch. "I'll take care of it," Tara stated as she pulled out her own credit card.

"No, this is on the boss," Nikki said. "He e-mailed me to congratulate me on saving an account and insisted we bill today's lunch to the company."

Tara put her card back in her purse and said, "In that case, I should order dessert to go."

They both laughed.

While they were driving back to the office, Nikki's cell phone rang.

"Hello," she answered.

Tara turned down the radio. Nikki could tell Tara was trying to figure out who she was talking to.

"Baby, I haven't made it back to the office yet." Nikki emphasized the word "baby."

"How did lunch go?" Byron asked.

"Just lovely," Nikki said.

"Is she right there?"

"Of course."

"I have to make an emergency trip to Miami. I'll be back tomorrow night if all works out."

"I'll miss you."

"Are you saying it because Tara's sitting there?"

"No."

"I'll call you when I get settled in."

"I love you."

"Do you mean it?"

"Yes, dear."

"I'm going to hold you to it. Let me get out of here. Oh . . . love you too." He hung up.

Nikki put the phone back in her purse.

They pulled into the parking garage and before exiting the car Tara said, "I really appreciate you having lunch with me. We must do this again."

"Anytime," Nikki said, hoping she sounded convincing.

27

Byron's flight to Miami went smoothly. After checking into his hotel, he had dinner at one of the restaurants on South Beach. While he was watching the skimpily dressed women, his thoughts were on Nikki. These women were beautiful, but none could hold a match for the inner and outer beauty Nikki possessed. A few flirted with him in passing. He smiled and continued to eat by himself.

He dialed his home number as soon as he got back to his hotel room. He got voice mail. He hung up and dialed Nikki's cell phone.

"Hello," Nikki said.

"Hi. Where are you?" he asked.

"I'm at the house."

"Your house or my house?"

"Your house."

"Then why didn't you answer the phone?"

"I didn't know if it was for you or me."

"I told you to make yourself at home."

"I'm not used to being here yet."

"How did lunch go?"

Nikki reiterated everything that had happened during her lunch with Tara.

Byron laughed. "She almost got you when she asked about the wedding pictures."

"I know, didn't she, though?"

"Not to be a spoilsport, but I'm surprised your family hasn't asked to see pictures."

"Me too. I guess the shock of me being married and not really knowing you has them dumbfounded."

"I would be too if the baby of the family up and married a stranger."

"Ha-ha. Oh, before I forget, Adrienne says the family wants to come over for a family dinner."

"You plan it, and I'll be there."

"I know you will be. What day should I tell them?"

"How about the second of July? We can have a barbecue."

"I hate to tell you, but I don't know anything about barbecuing."

"You don't have to. Let me worry about that. I only need two things from you."

"What?" she asked.

"For you to do the grocery shopping and cook the side items and I'll take care of the rest."

"Sounds like fun."

"Nikki?"

"What?"

"You realize this will be our first event as a couple," Byron said as he removed his shirt.

"I didn't know you were sentimental."

"Normally I'm not. You bring out the best in me," he said with a smile.

"Can I talk to you about something?" Nikki asked.

He sat on the edge of the bed and took off his shoes and then his pants. "What's wrong?"

"I know we're pretending and all, but do you think our relationship is actually going anywhere?"

He was caught off guard by her question. He paused before answering. "Granted, I hate pretending, but I did agree to help you out."

"Yes, you did," Nikki said, sounding disappointed.

"Before you say anything, let me finish. I hate pretending that we're married. A part of me wishes we really were." He turned off the overhead light and lay across the covers on the bed.

"Really?" she questioned.

"Why wouldn't I? You're everything I've ever wanted. I would be a fool to let you out of my life now."

She sighed. "What a relief."

"What prompted you to ask?"

"Byron, we've been living a lie for over a month and I don't want our *entire* relationship to be based on a lie."

"Nicolette Montana, I, Byron Matthews, honestly, truthfully, without a doubt, am glad to have you in my life. I love you and will do *anything* to keep a smile on your face." Nikki became quiet. Byron asked, "Nikki, are you still there?"

She sniffled. "You're too good to be true." She hung up the phone.

Now did I miss something? Byron thought to himself while he looked at the phone in confusion. *I told her how I felt and she hung up on me. This can't be happening.*

Nikki couldn't stop crying. She didn't mean to hang up, but before she knew it, she had pressed the End button on her cell phone. She realized she had not gotten any of his hotel information. She was about to dial his cell phone number when the house phone rang.

She rushed to answer it. "Hello."

"What happened?" Byron asked.

"The cell phone accidentally disconnected," she lied.

"Oh, okay."

"I owe you an apology for being so emotional. It's that time of the month and—"

"No need to go into it any further," Byron said, cutting her off.

"I don't know why every time a woman starts talking about her period, men clam up."

"Because, number one, we're pissed because that means we won't be getting any loving for at least a week."

"Is that all men think about?"

He ignored her question and added, "Number two, some of y'all become like a . . . let's see . . . what is another way to say female dog?"

She laughed. "Oh, I can be, but I'll pretend you didn't say it."

They talked and joked for the next couple of hours. Nikki saw that it was getting late. "Byron, you have an important meeting tomorrow, so I'm going to let you get some sleep."

"Did you set the alarm?" Byron asked with a voice of concern.

"I sure did. I have to admit, it feels funny being in this big house without you here."

"If you need anything, call me on my cell phone. I'll have it on the nightstand."

"I will. Hope everything goes well tomorrow."

"Thanks, dear."

"Good night."

28

"It's weird, but a part of me feels sorry for her," Nikki whispered into the phone.

"Keep your guard up. Women like her can't be trusted," Charlotte commented.

Nikki felt someone's eyes on her. She turned around to see Kenneth standing behind her. "Char, let me get back with you." She hung up and turned around. "I don't know why you like to sneak up on people."

Kenneth sat in Nikki's spare chair at her desk. "If you weren't doing anything you shouldn't, you wouldn't say I was sneaking."

"Whatever. What do you want now?"

"Dang. I stopped by to see how your lunch went yesterday."

"It went fine. Why wouldn't it have?"

Kenneth leaned in to whisper, "According to her secretary, she's not wound too tight. I thought I would warn you."

Nikki couldn't help but laugh. "Yesterday, you called and told me she's seeing a shrink. Now you're telling me something about what her secretary said. You need to get a life."

"I'm only looking out for you. Just be careful."

Nikki picked up a piece of paper off her desk, stood up, and walked away. "I got work to do."

He followed behind her. "What's wrong with you?"

"What's wrong with me?" She stopped and looked him directly in the eye. "I'm sick and tired of people getting in my business." Her voice was getting loud and people began staring.

"Calm down. I'm sorry. You must be on your period. I'll talk to you later," Kenneth said before walking away.

Nikki stood and stared at the few people who were looking. They quickly looked away. She continued her walk to the copy room, talking under her breath. She made a copy of the piece of paper she had in her hand, and as she was walking out, Tara walked in.

"Hey, Nikki, I was looking for you," Tara said as if the two were the best of friends.

Nikki halted and replied, "What can I do for you?"

Tara walked closer to her. "I need a favor."

Nikki hesitated. "It depends on what it is."

"My babysitter is sick and I have this dinner tonight with the VPs and I normally wouldn't ask, but can you please do me this one favor and keep Christopher for me?"

Nikki couldn't believe what she heard. "I don't know if that's a good idea."

"I know it's awkward, but I'm desperate."

"Oh, thanks," Nikki blurted out.

Tara reached for her arm. "No, I don't mean it like that. I'm new and it's not every day you get invited to dinner with the vice president and other bigwigs."

"Let me think about it and I'll get back with you."

"Please. If you do me this one favor, I'll owe you one."

"I'll let you know by noon." Nikki walked away, confused on what to do, thinking that perhaps she should call Byron and ask his opinion.

* * *

"Thank you so much for hand-delivering this contract and making sure my team understands what the changes to our communication network will entail," Johnson Mason said as he took the folder from Byron.

"We're here to serve you in any way necessary," Byron commented.

"Let me share a little secret with you," Johnson said, taking his tone down to a whisper. "This was actually a test, and if anyone would go to this extreme to get our business, then I'm more than happy to sign the ten-year deal."

Byron smiled. Although he wouldn't get a commission off this deal, he was sure he would get some type of bonus. "If you have any other questions, I'll be here for the majority of the day."

"I'll have our attorneys look this over once more and you should be able to take your signed copy back with you."

Byron extended his hand. "Thanks. Here's my cell phone number." He handed him his business card.

Johnson walked him to the door and addressed his secretary. "Find Mr. Matthews a vacant office and see that he gets everything he needs."

"Thank you," Byron said.

He followed Johnson's secretary to an office at the end of the hall. "I hope this is sufficient," she said.

He looked around the plush office. "More than enough. Thanks."

"If you need anything, and I do mean anything, press one and it'll ring my extension," the secretary flirted.

"I think I'll manage. But thanks." He ignored her advances.

She twisted out of the room, turned around, and winked at him.

You're fine, but you're not worth risking my relationship or my job over, Byron thought with a smirk.

He sat behind the desk and dialed his office. After telling them the good news, he tried calling Nikki. He got her voice mail and decided to leave a message.

"I'll be home tonight," Byron said through the phone receiver. "Everything here is going great. If I don't talk to you beforehand, I'll see you tonight. Love you."

He hung up. He opened his briefcase, and Christopher's picture fell out. He stared at it for a few minutes. *You're a beautiful child and if you're mine, I will make sure you have the best.*

He began fantasizing about being a father. *What am I doing? Having a child with Tara would cause nothing but complications. I could possibly lose Nikki,* he thought to himself. He was in deep thought, when his cell phone rang.

"Hello," he answered.

"Where are you?" Frederick asked from the other end.

"I'm in Miami."

"Did you find out about the baby yet?"

"No, the test will be done on the first."

Johnson's secretary knocked on the door before walking in. "I'm ordering lunch. Would you like for me to order you something?"

"Hold on, Frederick." Byron hit the Hold button.

She handed him a menu. "Circle what you want and I'll be back in a few minutes to pick it up."

"Thanks." He viewed the menu and picked up his phone and continued talking to Frederick. "I'm back."

"How did Nikki take it?"

"I haven't told her yet."

"Man, you're playing with fire. I would be pulling my hair out if my woman worked with my ex."

"You don't have any hair."

They both laughed.

"What are y'all doing this weekend?" Frederick asked.

"The same thing other newlyweds are doing."

"She got you living in a fantasy world. Oh, Mama really wants to meet her too."

"I know. I'm throwing a barbecue on the second of July for Nikki's family. They insist on getting to know me better."

"What about your other family?"

"I don't think it's a good idea. I can't chance somebody mentioning our fake marriage."

"I might drop by, though. I would love to see you two in action."

Johnson's secretary walked back in. Byron handed her the menu. "Frederick, I need to work on a few things. I'll call you later this week?"

"What are you doing Friday? Want to meet me for happy hour?"

"I need to check with Nikki."

Frederick laughed. "It's starting already."

"What's so funny?"

"She's already got you henpecked and y'all aren't even really married." He hung up without giving Byron a chance to respond.

Nikki reluctantly agreed to babysit for Tara. She tried calling Byron, leaving him a message when she didn't get an answer, but he never returned her call. She was going to call Charlotte and ask her what she thought, but she felt that she was already the queen of negativity and would only make her decision that much more difficult.

After Nikki informed Tara that she would babysit, Tara gave her instructions on where to pick him up. Because of the unique situation, they both had agreed Nikki would drop him off at Tara's after dinner.

Nikki was amazed at how much fun she was having with Christopher. He was cute as a button and had a beautiful smile. Although Tara was a pretty woman, he must have taken after his father, because Nikki didn't see much resemblance to his mother.

"Smells like somebody needs their diaper changed," Nikki said to Christopher as she sniffed the air. She sat him on the bed and carefully changed his diaper. "Stinky booty," she said as she used the baby wipes to clean him up.

"Da-da," he said.

"No, sport, I'm Nikki." She picked him up. He giggled. "I wonder if you're hungry." She carried him downstairs and went to the kitchen and began going through his bag. "Let's see what your mama packed for you. We have sweet peas." He frowned. Nikki added, "I don't blame you. Sweet peas don't sound too appetizing." She continued to say, "How about some chicken?" She attempted to open up the jar of baby food while holding him with one arm. "This is a little hard, but I'm going to do it," she said as she found a bowl and spoon.

After warming the food, she was sitting at the kitchen table feeding Christopher when she heard the front door open.

"Nikki, I'm home. Where are you?" she heard Byron shout.

"I'm in the kitchen," she yelled.

"I'm so glad to be back," he said as he entered the kitchen, stopping in midsentence at the sight of Nikki holding a baby. "What in the world?" Byron asked, shocked.

"Hey, Boo. Isn't he adorable?" she asked as she wiped Christopher's mouth with a napkin.

"He is cute, but whose baby is it?"

"Tara was in a bind, so I told her I would babysit."

"You what?" he said, overreacting.

Christopher started crying. "See what you did?" Nikki placed Christopher across her shoulder and patted him on the back.

"When did you and Tara become so chummy?" he snapped.

"First of all, you need to watch your tone, and to answer your question, we're not chummy. It's just one coworker looking out for another."

"This is ridiculous. I thought I was coming home to treat you to a nice dinner and I walk in on this."

"If I didn't know better, I would swear you don't like kids."

Christopher was calm by now. Nikki turned him around on her lap. He reached one of his hands out to Byron and said, "Da-da."

"See, he likes you. He's probably wondering why the big old man has a frown on his face."

"Look, it's not like I don't like kids. But after a long flight, I didn't expect to come home to this." He stared at Christopher.

"I'll be taking him home in another thirty minutes anyway, so you won't have to deal with 'this' too much longer."

"Good. I'm going to go unpack." He walked out of the room.

I don't know what's wrong with Byron, Nikki thought, *but as soon as I get back we're going to talk.*

Byron picked up his overnight bag and briefcase that he had left by the door and stormed upstairs.

Have they both lost their minds? he thought to himself. *What kind of game is Tara playing? What is Nikki thinking bringing that woman's child into my home?*

He started unpacking. *He is a cute lil' fella. A part of me wanted to pick him up and hold him. I can see why Nikki's smitten by him. But I can't get emotionally attached to the kid. I know Tara, even if he's mine, she'll give me hell if I want to see him. I feel like the walls are crashing in on me. I know I should have told Nikki right then and there, that he could be mine. I have no choice now but to wait until I get the test results back.*

"Nikki, I'm sorry," he said aloud as he walked down the stairs. He didn't get a response.

After checking all of the rooms, he realized she and Christopher were gone.

"Now what?"

* * *

Nikki couldn't wait to leave the house after encountering Byron's attitude. She cleaned Christopher up. He went to sleep in her arms. After laying him on the couch, she went upstairs and got his diaper bag and her car keys. She paused outside Byron's door but decided to deal with him later.

She turned on the inside car light to read over the directions to get to Tara's place. She missed her exit the first time, so she had to go to the next exit a mile away and turn around. Nikki was not familiar with Irving like she was other parts of the Dallas metroplex.

She glanced in the backseat and Christopher was sleeping soundly.

"I think this is your street," she said.

She pulled up to the gate of the apartment complex and punched in Tara's apartment number. "This is Nikki," she said before being buzzed in.

She had a time juggling the baby and his stuff. "Your mama should have come down to help me," she added as she tried to press her car alarm key.

Tara met Nikki at the door. "Here's Mama's baby," she said, looking at Nikki. "How did it go? He didn't give you any trouble, did he?"

"No, he was a good little boy," Nikki replied.

"Thanks. Come on in. I'll put him in his bed and I'll be right back."

Nikki noticed how spacious Tara's town house was. She could tell she had expensive taste. She walked around the living room and looked at the pictures above the fireplace. She noticed a picture of what must have been Tara's sisters and mom. She paused when she saw a picture of Tara and Byron. She picked it up.

She noticed how cozy and happy they looked. A part of her was jealous. Tara cleared her throat as she entered the room.

Nikki was caught off guard. She placed the picture back on the mantel. "I'm admiring your family pictures."

"I love taking pictures. If I wasn't so short, I would have been a model." Tara asked after a brief silence, "Would you like something to drink?"

Nikki headed toward the door. "No. I think I'll be going. I have to drive all the way back to Plano."

"Thanks again. I *really* do appreciate this."

"No problem. See you at work tomorrow," she said before walking out the door.

29

Nikki was sleepy when she pulled up to the house. She went in and headed straight up the stairs. Byron was waiting at the head of the stairway.

"Glad to see you made it back safely," he said.

"I don't feel like arguing. I'm tired and it's been a long day." She attempted to brush him to the side.

"We need to talk."

With an attitude, she said, "You must have a hearing problem."

"I owe you an apology."

"You sure do, but save it for the morning." She stormed past him and slammed the bedroom door, locking it behind her.

"Men, I can never figure them out," she said, as she got undressed. She changed into a pair of purple satin sleepers and got under the covers.

Although she was tired, she was unable to go to sleep right away. When she did sleep, she tossed and turned the entire night. When the alarm went off the next morning, she felt as if she had been up all night.

She was still upset at Byron, but she wouldn't let him get to her. She took a long shower. After lotioning her body and spraying on some Escape, she put on her money-green power suit. The skirt was cut right above the knee and accented her legs. She curled her hair and added some flair to it. "This stuff is getting long. It's time for me to make a trip to the beauty shop," she said, making a mental note.

She needed to avoid Byron, but luck wasn't on her side. He met her at the bottom of the stairway.

"I wasn't sure if you were up or not," he said.

"Thanks for your concern."

"I made us breakfast." He pointed toward the kitchen.

She moved to the right of him. "Thanks, but I'll get something on the way in."

He gently grabbed her by the arm as she was walking away. "Nikki, I'm sorry. Eat breakfast with me and we can talk."

Nikki's stomach growled, reminding her that she was hungry. "It would save me money." She put her purse and laptop by the door.

She followed Byron toward the kitchen.

"Have a seat. I'll bring everything to you." He pulled out her chair.

He watched her eat and tried to figure out a way to bring up his actions from last night.

"Why aren't you eating?" she said, taking a bite of her toast.

He picked up the crisp bacon. "I'm not too hungry. Since neither one of us has time this morning for idle chitchat, let me get straight to the point." Nikki continued to eat without saying a word. "I apologize for going off on you last night. I don't see why or how you and Tara could get so chummy all of a sudden, especially after I told you what happened."

She took a drink of orange juice and in a sedate manner, responded, "Believe me, she's far from being my friend."

"Then why were you babysitting?"

"She had an important meeting last night and couldn't find a babysitter. I tried to call you and get your input, but I never did hear from you."

"I didn't get your message until I landed at the airport last night."

"Sounds like you need a new cell phone provider."

"That's beside the point."

"This is silly. I'm not going to argue about something that's already over." She stood up to walk out. Byron blocked her.

He took her in his arms and laid a big wet kiss on her lips. They held on to each other to keep their balance.

"You're forgiven," she said as she released herself from his embrace.

"I'll walk out with you."

They held hands as they walked down the walkway to their cars.

"Don't make any plans for tonight," Byron stated.

"I need to swing by my place and pick up a few items, so I probably won't make it here until about seven or so."

"Perfect. Have a good day and I'll call you later." He kissed her after holding her door open for her.

"See you." She started the engine and backed out of the driveway.

He waved and got in his car as the two went their separate ways.

30

Byron was speeding, but so was everybody else who was driving down Central Expressway. It was too late to slow down when he saw the flashing red lights behind him.

"This is the last thing I need," he hissed.

He pulled over to the shoulder, reached over into the glove compartment, and pulled out his license and registration. He looked in his rearview mirror and saw the cop walking toward his car. He couldn't see his face.

"I should lock you up," the stern voice said.

Byron panicked. "Officer, I was only speeding."

He heard the officer laugh and saw Steven's face when he leaned down.

"Man, you know a brother is scared of jail. Don't ever play with me like that again. If you weren't in that uniform, I would give you a beat-down."

"I'm only upholding the law."

"Well, uphold this," Byron said with a smile on his face as he held up his middle finger.

"So where are you headed to in such a hurry?" Steven asked.

"Work. Some of us have a real job."

"Don't hate because you're not one of Dallas's finest."

They laughed. Byron spoke with him for a couple more minutes before heading to his destination.

As he pulled into his job's parking lot he took out his cell phone and called his brother. "Frederick, I'm back in town. I still don't know if I'll make happy hour on Friday, though," he said as he left a message in his voice mail. "Call me when you get this message. Bye."

He lucked out and got a parking place in front of the building. He spoke to everyone as he made his way to his office. Joyce was sitting at her desk.

"Hey, boss, glad you're back," she said.

"Glad to be back," Byron replied.

Joyce followed him into his office and shut the door behind them.

"If you weren't my cousin, people would swear we were having an affair as much as you've been coming in here and shutting my door lately."

She turned the knob to open it. "I could leave it open and let everybody hear your business." She smiled and retreated.

He hung up his jacket, took his laptop out of the case, and began hooking it up to his monitor.

"Anything interesting happen while I was out?" he asked.

"Same old stuff. But you did get quite a few phone calls from Tara."

"I'm so sick and tired of hearing about her."

"What's going on now?"

"When I got back in last night, Nikki was babysitting Tara's son."

Joyce's mouth dropped. "What? I know you almost peed in your pants."

He logged on to his PC as he continued to talk to Joyce. "I was pissed. She'll be getting a phone call from me later on. I don't feel like dealing with her right now."

With her hands on her hips, Joyce said, "I told you she is up to something. No woman in her right mind would have her ex-boyfriend's wife keep her child. Especially when she and the ex are not getting along."

"Did you say wife?"

"Forget I said anything." She headed out the door.

"Joyce, I know I heard you correctly. Come back here." She continued out as if she didn't hear him say, "Frederick."

He dialed Frederick's number. "May I speak to Frederick Matthews?" He picked up the stress-relief ball and squeezed it as he waited.

"This is Frederick, how may I help you?" his brother said.

"You can help me by not telling my business. Especially to the Mouth of the South," he blurted out.

"Calm down. I assumed she knew everything. I called you before I knew you were out of town and she mentioned Tara and the baby and I—"

"Look. I don't want to hear it. As for happy hour on Friday, I have other plans." He hung up the phone.

Nikki was not having the best of mornings. She almost wrecked on the way into work. Her phone rang all morning with irate customers who hadn't paid their bills but were upset that their commercials didn't air during the NBA finals, and Tara kept e-mailing her as if they were chat buddies.

As she was ending a call, the receptionist from downstairs tapped her on the shoulder. She was holding a beautifully decorated candy jar filled with jellybeans.

"These are for you," the receptionist said. "I tried calling, but your phone kept going to voice mail."

"Thanks. I was on both lines," Nikki said as she took the jar and placed it on her desk.

She assumed they were from Byron and was dialing his number as she took the card out to read it.

"I was calling to say thanks for the candy," Nikki said to Byron through the phone receiver.

"I didn't send you any candy," he said.

"Please, let me finish. I know that after reading the card."

"Who are they from?"

"Tara, of all people. The card says 'Thanks for keeping Christopher. It means more than you know.'"

"Tell her thank you and be through with it. I don't feel comfortable with you keeping her son."

"It won't be a habit. I told you that I was only doing a coworker a favor. I would have done it for anyone."

"Be careful. You might want to test the candy on one of your coworkers. What's the guy's name you say is always in your business?"

"Kenneth."

"Yes, that's the one. If he doesn't fall over, then you know it's safe to eat."

They both laughed.

"Let me get off this phone, my other line is ringing. See you tonight." She chuckled before clicking over.

"Things might work out after all. Nikki, you keep turning my world upside down, but I wouldn't trade you for the world, girl," Byron stated, as he hung up the phone. He sat with a huge smile plastered on his face.

His smile quickly faded when Joyce came in and told him Tara was on the phone.

"You might as well take the call or else she'll keep calling," Joyce said before returning to her desk.

He took a deep breath and picked up the line. "Byron speaking."

"You don't have to be formal. I'm sure your cousin told you it was me on the phone," Tara said with an attitude.

"What do you want?"

"Testy, aren't we? I'm surprised you didn't call me and let me know how much fun you had with your son."

"I was out of town, and I don't appreciate you using your son to get next to Nikki."

"It was sweet of her to help me out in my situation. See, women understand other women."

"Was there another reason for your call?" He tapped his pen on the desk.

"Now that I know she doesn't know about Christopher being your son, you better change your tone."

He sat straight up in his chair. "Don't go doing anything stupid."

"I'll do whatever it takes to get what I want." When he didn't respond to her comment, she continued to say, "I want you to acknowledge your son and pay child support like you're supposed to. My attorney will be contacting you."

This time she hung up on him without giving him a chance to respond.

He slammed the phone down.

Nikki couldn't concentrate the rest of the day. She fantasized about Byron and how he would be in the bedroom. She held a secret that not even her best friend knew. She knew in her heart that Byron was the man she wanted to give her love to and spend the rest of her life with.

After work, she went by her place and picked up her mail and some more clothes. She took her time driving over to Byron's. Once she arrived there, she pulled up into the driveway, but waited a few minutes before getting out of her car.

I don't know how much longer I'll be able to hold out. Byron's kisses melt me, she thought on her way to the door with bags of her things in hand. *Just the thought of him touching me in any way makes me want to explode.*

Before she could put the key in the door, Byron opened it and greeted her. He reached down for one of her bags.

"Here, let me help you," he said to her.

"Why is it so dark in here?" she asked.

"Trying to save on electricity," he joked.

As they passed the living room, she saw light flickering from candles. "You're so cheap." She played along with him.

She followed him up the stairs. He placed her bags down next to the bed. "I ran some bathwater. I see that you like Temple Bath and Body Products. I hope you like the Peach Blossoms bubble bath I used. I'll be waiting for you downstairs."

Nikki lifted her arms and sniffed. "Am I funky?"

"You always smell like fresh flowers to me."

She opened up one of the dresser drawers and pulled out a pink-laced bra and matching bikinis. "I could swear I saw you blush." She looked up at Byron.

"I better get going. Meet me downstairs when you finish." He walked out without waiting for her to respond.

A huge smile formed on her face.

Byron fixed a tray of fresh fruit consisting of grapes, strawberries, and slices of cantaloupe and melon. He placed some cream cheese and crackers on the same tray. After placing it on the table in the living room along with a bowl of chocolate, he checked on the roast he had in the oven.

After making sure the roast was done, he removed the apron that he was wearing and threw it on the counter. Before he could do anything else, the doorbell interrupted him. He wasn't expecting anyone, so he was surprised when he opened the door and Frederick was on the other side.

"What's up, bro?" Frederick said as he walked in without waiting on a response.

"I'm surprised to see you here," Byron huffed.

"My date for the evening lives a few streets over. Thought

I would check in on you and my new sister-in-law," he said in a sarcastic manner.

"We're kind of busy right now."

Frederick walked toward the living room. "Something sure smells good." He reached down and took some grapes off the tray and plopped one in his mouth.

"I thought you had a date."

"I do, but I might stay here and eat with y'all." He sat down in the chair near the tray.

"You're already on my bad side, so you might want to leave the tray alone."

Frederick looked around. "Looks like you two are really taking this marriage thing seriously."

"What Nikki and I do is none of your business," Byron said matter-of-factly.

"Where is Nikki, by the way?" Frederick said as he looked around.

"She's upstairs and will be down shortly, that's why you need to go."

"First you hang up on me, now you're kicking me to the curb. Where is the brotherly love?"

"There's a thin line between love and hate," Byron said while holding a smile.

"On that note, I'll catch you later. I see why happy hour is out now. I'm not mad at you. Have fun." Frederick opened the door and walked out.

"Later," Byron yelled to him.

"Who was that?" Nikki said as she stood on the edge of the stairway dressed in a pink terry cloth short set with the word, *delicious* written across the back of the shorts and the top.

Byron turned around, startled, as he closed the door. "That was Frederick. He had a date in the area and dropped by to say hi."

"I hate that I missed him," Nikki said, snapping her fingers.

"He told me to tell you hi."

Nikki headed to the living room. Byron followed her. She stopped and admired the fruit tray.

"This looks good," she said, reaching down and taking a stem of green grapes from the tray.

"It sure does."

She turned around and caught Byron staring at her butt. "Byron."

"I'm sorry. I couldn't help myself."

They sat down. He dipped a strawberry in some chocolate and placed it to her mouth. She took a bite. "Umm. This is delicious."

"Just like you." He kissed the chocolate from her mouth.

"Mmm. A woman can get used to this star treatment."

"In my eyes, you are a star."

Nikki felt queasy. The heat between them sizzled. She felt that if she didn't move soon, she would be at the point of no return. She jumped up without warning. "Whoa, let's see what's in the kitchen."

Byron reached for her. "Hold up, Nikki."

"Hmm. What?"

"Sit." She paused, and before sitting back down, Byron placed his hand over hers. "Every time we get to a certain point, you pull back. You act like you're scared of me sometimes."

"If you only knew."

"I'll only bite if you want me to," he joked.

"There is something I want to tell you, but you have to promise not to laugh."

He fed her some grapes. "I promise."

She picked up a napkin and wiped some of the juice off her mouth. "You're a very sexy man."

"Thanks."

"I'm serious. I don't think you realize how you make me feel whenever you're in the room. Shoot, your presence is still felt when you're not in the room."

"I'm flattered."

Her eyes darted away. Byron reached up and gently ran his hand across her cheek. "What's wrong?"

"I'm not who I pretend to be."

"Duh. Remember, I know all about the fake marriage. I'm the invisible husband, remember?" He shrugged his shoulders.

"There's something else I haven't told you."

The timer on the stove went off. "Hold that thought," he said. "Let's continue this conversation over dinner."

Nikki followed Byron into the dining room. There were gold-trimmed plates and champagne goblets sitting across from one another. The centerpiece had gold ribbons and was made out of gold-spray-painted pinecones. "This is a lovely arrangement," she said out loud. When she turned around, Byron was nowhere in sight. She sat down and waited for his return.

I don't know if telling him about my condition is such a good idea after all, she thought as she waited.

Byron walked in with two plates. Both were piled with slices of roast beef and baked potatoes. The steam was still coming from her plate as he placed it down in front of her.

"I hope you have an appetite," he said as he walked around to the other side of the table and sat down.

"Do I! I didn't have time for lunch today." She reached for her napkin and placed it across her lap.

They said grace and Nikki devoured her roast beef.

"Any room for dessert?" he asked after they finished eating.

Nikki rubbed her stomach. "I couldn't fit anything else in here."

"Not even one little slice of pound cake?"

"My, my. I didn't know you baked."

"I stopped by my mom's and she sent it over."

He walked to the kitchen and came back with two slices. He handed her the smaller slice of the two.

"I need to get this recipe," she said after taking a few bites. "I thought my mom's pound cake was good, but this here is the bomb."

"You can ask her for it when I take you to meet her."

With a serious look on her face, she asked, "You want me to meet your mom?"

"Of course. I've told my mom all about you and she can't wait to meet the woman who's got me lying for her," he stated with a serious look on his face.

"You didn't?"

He burst out laughing. "No. But seriously she does want to meet you."

"I want to meet her too, but I wish it was under different circumstances." She continued to eat her cake.

"We're together, so that should be all that matters."

"Honestly, do you think we would be together if I hadn't convinced you to go along with plans to fool my family?"

He looked at her with caring eyes. "I have no doubt that we would be together. Granted, we wouldn't be living to-gether, but we would still be together."

"Living together was your idea."

"Selfish, I know." He smiled, showing both dimples.

"I guess now is as good a time as any," Nikki said. Byron remained quiet, so she continued. "I need to tell you some-thing and I don't know if you will look at me differently once I do."

"There's nothing you can say that would change my mind about you. Don't worry. You can tell me anything."

"I'm a virgin," she blurted out.

"Yeah, right. Not Ms. Nikki." He tried not to laugh, but failed.

Nikki threw her napkin on the table as tears flowed down her face. "I tried to be honest with you and you laugh in my face." She stormed upstairs.

She's serious. She really is a virgin, Byron thought to

himself. *I never would have guessed. No wonder she clams up every time things get heated up.*

He went after her. By the time he got upstairs, her door was closed. He knocked and said, "Nikki, open up."

"No!" she shouted back.

"Please. I'm sorry. I didn't mean to make light of your situation. I never would have thought in a million years you were a . . ." He paused. "A virgin."

"That's okay. I should have kept it to myself."

He leaned on the door. "No, you shouldn't have. I would have found out eventually anyway."

"I wouldn't be too sure of that."

"Open the door, Nikki. Pleassse," Byron begged.

He heard her unlock the door. He slowly opened it and found her standing there, with red eyes and all. He took her in his arms and gave her a tight, reassuring hug.

Nikki pulled away and asked, "So you're okay with me being a virgin?"

"Baby, it only makes you more special to me."

They walked and then sat on the edge of the bed. "Most men run after I tell them."

"I'm glad. I don't plan on going anywhere any time soon."

"You wouldn't, because this is your place," she joked.

"Glad to see you're smiling again."

"It's getting late and I need to be out of here around six instead of seven tomorrow, because I'm taking Friday off."

"Really, any special plans?" he asked.

"I'm meeting my sisters at the spa and after that, nothing."

"I have a lot to do on Friday, but afterward, let's get together for a movie or something."

"It's a date."

"Ms. Montana, I'll let you get some sleep. I'll try to get up in time to make you breakfast."

She stood up and hugged him. "Don't. I'll grab something at Mickey D's."

"Good night."

"Good night," she said before closing the door behind him. She stood with her back against the door for a moment, then sighed and headed to the bed, where she fell fast asleep.

31

Byron enjoyed the quiet evenings at home with Nikki. They were becoming closer with each passing day. Today was July first and it was also the day that he dreaded. But after the paternity test, there would be no doubt whether the innocent little child was his or not.

Nikki was still asleep when he left home. He was looking forward to their Friday night plans. He would let her choose the movie she wanted to see. He went to the office for a few hours before leaving for the doctor's office.

Byron hoped when he saw Tara at the doctor's office that she wouldn't make a scene. The parking lot was full when he arrived, so he parked on the street.

The receptionist had him sign in. He grabbed a magazine off a table in the waiting room and waited for Tara to show up. After thirty minutes he was beginning to think she had stood him up. He was in the process of dialing her number when she came through the door holding Christopher in one arm and a bag on the other arm.

"Sorry I'm late. There was construction traffic on LBJ," Tara said, sounding out of breath.

"Do you need some help?" Byron asked.

"I got it. Are they ready for us?"

"They were ready ten minutes ago. I'll go let them know you're here."

He walked to the window and informed them of Tara's arrival. When he walked back, Christopher was crawling on the floor. He picked him up.

"Don't you think there's too many germs on the floor for him to be crawling?" Byron asked and handed him to Tara.

"You sound concerned," Tara said.

"I'm not heartless."

She smiled and was about to comment, but didn't.

A nurse came to the door and said, "Byron Matthews."

He looked at Tara. "Are you ready?" he asked her.

They walked to one of the offices. The doctor walked in and explained the procedure.

"It's real simple," the doctor said. "We'll take a swab sample from all three of your mouths."

"When will the results be back?" Byron asked.

"It can take up to a few weeks, but we can always rush them and possibly get them back in a few days."

"Don't rush," Tara said. "We want to make sure it's done right."

"Trust me. The lab we're sending it to will handle everything with care," the doctor assured her.

"I don't want there to be any mistakes—" Tara reiterated.

"Dr. Phillips, have the office call me when it's done," Byron said interrupting her.

The doctor took samples and handed them to the nurse and she carefully labeled each one.

"That's it," Dr. Phillips said as he handed Christopher a lollipop. "This is for being a good little boy."

Christopher giggled.

As Dr. Phillips walked them out, he stated, "I hope it turns out the way you want it to."

Byron shook his hand and replied, "Thanks, Doc."

After paying the receptionist, Byron walked out. Tara was already at the elevator. "What now?" she asked him.

"We wait," he replied.

"Have you gotten the papers from my attorney yet?"

"No, but I'll be handing them directly to mine when they come."

Christopher looked at him and waved. "Bye, little Christopher," Byron said before pinching Christopher's chubby cheeks.

"See, he really likes you. He looks exactly like you, Byron."

"Funny, you're the only one who can see any type of resemblance."

"Soon we'll both know for sure, won't we?" Tara snapped.

The elevator opened. Tara stepped in. Byron stated, "I'll wait on the next one."

"Fine," she said as the elevator door closed.

Nikki and her sisters decided to jump-start their Fourth of July weekend by going to the spa. They tried to get their mother to join them for a day of massages, manicures, and pedicures, but she declined. Their mom didn't want anyone touching her toes. Nikki giggled as she remembered how her mom's face cringed at the thought.

The Relax Mode Spa was located on the outskirts of town. After a full body massage, they sat in the steam room. They were waiting their turn to get a spa manicure and pedicure.

"Pass me the bottle, because my glass is getting low," Adrienne said as she pointed to the bottle of Chardonnay.

Nikki poured some into Adrienne's glass and then stated, "I think this should be your last glass. You know you can't handle your liquor."

"Missy, respect your elders."

"You're right. I should, because you are *ollld*."

Adrienne set the glass down on the table. "I might be old,

but I still look good." She took her hands and outlined her body.

Pam and Nikki laughed.

"You'll never change," Nikki said.

"Why should I? You both know I got it going on."

Pam chuckled and said, "Like a chicken bone."

An attendant walked in. "Sorry for the wait. We're short-staffed. Some of our nail techs are out today," she apologized. "Is everything okay?"

Nikki spoke up. "We're fine."

"The wait shouldn't be too much longer," she assured them.

After the attendant left, Adrienne asked, "So, Nikki, how's married life treating you?"

"Must be pretty good, since she doesn't call anymore," Pam added.

"Darn. You too?" Nikki asked. "I knew Adrienne felt that way. I didn't realize it was such a big deal."

"Since you've been married, you barely call or visit any of us." Pam frowned.

"I'm sorry. I promise to do better."

"Byron must be putting it on her." Adrienne took a sip of her drink.

Nikki avoided responding.

"So do you guys plan on having kids any time soon?" Pam asked.

"We're not supposed to be talking about our mates, re-member?" Nikki tried to divert the conversation.

"Normally we wouldn't. But we're trying to figure out what kind of hold this man has on you," Pam said.

"What kind of man would not allow his wife to keep in contact with her family?" Adrienne snapped.

Pam looked at Adrienne disapprovingly. "Nik, you know I work with battered women, and some men try to dissuade their women from seeing family and friends." Nikki stared at her as Pam continued. "Once they feel they have control over them mentally, physical abuse is not far behind."

Nikki held her hand up. "Hold up. I need to nip something in the bud right now. Byron is the sweetest, kindest man I've ever met. He would never stop me from seeing my family." She paused. "And besides, if he ever laid a hand on me, you guys would be visiting me in the pen, because he would be six feet under."

They all laughed.

"Now that everything's cleared up, do you need us to bring anything with us tomorrow for the barbecue?" Pam asked.

"If you can bake a cake." She addressed Pam and then turned her attention back to Adrienne. "And I would love it if you would make some of your baked beans."

"I don't know," Adrienne said. "What's in it for me?"

"A bowl of my banana pudding." Nikki smiled.

"You got a deal, because your banana pudding is to die for," Adrienne said. "If you're over there whipping it up for that husband of yours, no wonder he got you on lock. Y'all gon' be together forever."

Out of the blue, Pam started crying. Nikki and Adrienne walked over and put their arms around her. "What's wrong?" Nikki was the first to ask.

"Louis has been acting funny with me lately and I'm afraid there's another woman," Pam answered.

Adrienne wiped her face with a towel. "Now, don't go saying things you're not sure of. Have you tried talking to him about your suspicions?"

"Yes, but he's so evasive in his responses. I'm confused. We've been married for fifteen years and I never thought he would . . ." She choked from the tears.

Nikki held her tight. "It might not be what you think."

"If she's thinking it, it might be true," Adrienne stated with conviction.

"I don't even see why Edward married you with your negative attitude," Nikki snapped.

"Ed loves me just the way I am, so stay out of my business," Adrienne said, rolling her eyes.

"Like you stay out of mine?" was Nikki's comeback.

"If you wouldn't have married somebody the family didn't know, I wouldn't have to—"

"If you would have stopped pressuring me about when I was getting married, I probably would have waited," Nikki snapped.

"Stop it!" Pam yelled. "I would have kept my suspicions to myself if I knew it was going to cause all of this."

An attendant opened the door and asked, "Ladies, is everything all right in here?"

"Yes!" they snapped in unison.

The attendant had a doubtful look on her face, but closed the door.

"See, I can't take y'all anywhere," Adrienne said.

"Talk to the hand," Nikki said as she held her right hand up in Adrienne's face.

Pam whined, "Ladies, I'm the one with the problem, remember?"

"Pam, I think you should come straight out and ask him," Nikki stated.

"If you ask, he'll lie. Monitor his e-mail and phone calls for the next few weeks," Adrienne said.

Before Pam could respond, Nikki jumped in. "Believe it or not, I actually agree with Adrienne."

Pam looked from one to the other, as if soaking in information.

"Has he been less intimate?" Adrienne asked.

"Adrienne!" Nikki exclaimed.

"Hey, I'm trying to diagnose the whole problem," Adrienne said.

Pam laughed. "Everything has been copacetic in that department."

"Just checking. Because that's one sure sign. Go ahead and monitor his calls and e-mails, and we pray he's not doing anything stupid," Adrienne stated.

"I'd hate to have to hurt my brother-in-law." Nikki balled up her fists.

"You know we would," Adrienne chimed in.

"And don't let Jerry and Gerald find out, because not even the president could stop them from doing Louis some bodily harm."

"I know," Pam said as the attendant knocked on the door and walked in.

"Ladies, we're ready for you," the attendant said.

After receiving their manicures and pedicures, they got dressed and said their good-byes.

Nikki stopped by the grocery store to buy items for the barbecue before heading home.

After leaving the doctor's office, Byron decided to take a personal day. He went walking in the mall and bought a few items before heading to the gym. He worked out to release his built-up frustrations. When he got home, Nikki was still out with her sisters.

He took a short nap. When he woke, he heard someone moving around downstairs. For a moment, he was disoriented.

He went to the bathroom and wet a hand towel and wiped his face. He stared at himself in the mirror and thought, *This has been the longest day in my life. I don't know how I'm going to hold up between now and the time I get the test results back. My sweet Nikki, how can I convince you to marry me if Christopher's mine?*

He heard his name being called. Nikki walked in and put her arms around his waist as he faced the mirror.

"Hi, sexy," she said.

"You seem so relaxed," he stated.

"I'm floating. A good massage does it to me every time."

He removed her hands from his waist, turned around, and kissed her. "I love you so much, Nikki."

"I love you too."

They held each other. Byron broke the embrace. He took her hand and they walked downstairs together.

He saw the bags of groceries near the front door.

"You should have woken me up. I would have gotten these," he told her.

"With your car parked in the garage, I didn't even know you were here until I came to put something in my bedroom and I heard the water running."

He released her hands and carried the bags to the kitchen.

"You got enough to feed an army," he said.

"You don't know my family, do you?" She laughed.

They held light conversation as they unpacked the groceries.

"Did you get any charcoal and fluid?" he asked.

"No. They weren't on my list."

"It's my fault. I should have reminded you."

"I got them. I was only teasing. They're still out in the trunk of my car."

"Where are your keys? I'll bring them into the garage."

She walked to the counter and handed him the keys.

"Press the left button to turn off the alarm. The right button will pop open the trunk," she told him.

"Yes, ma'am," Byron said as he headed out to get what he would need in order to get the fire started tomorrow.

Nikki peeled potatoes as Byron seasoned the meat.

Nikki commented, "This is fun. Our first event as a couple."

"Are you nervous about tomorrow?" he asked.

"I was, but everything between us seems so real."

Byron stopped what he was doing and looked her directly in the eye. "It is real."

"I wish," Nikki said under her breath.

"It could be. It's all up to you."

Nikki opened her mouth to ask him what he meant, but didn't. Instead she started talking about her family members. "Word is probably out to my cousins too, so don't be surprised if we have more people here than we planned."

"I can handle it. Don't worry. We're in this together." He winked.

She put the potatoes on to boil. "I'm going upstairs to take a bubble bath. Can you watch this for me?"

"Sure. Take your time."

She felt his eyes on her as she left the room.

Her plans changed from a bath to a shower. The water was soothing. She thought of Byron as she lathered the Temple Bath & Body Strawberry Delight shower gel onto her sponge.

If only you were my real husband, she thought. *I wouldn't be taking a shower alone, for one thing.*

She turned the water off and reached for her towel. It was on the other side of the sink, so she stepped out, dripping water on the rug.

She sprayed on some Strawberry Delight body mist before drying off completely. She closed her eyes and imagined Byron rubbing her body in the places she rubbed her lotion. She was putting on her clothes when she heard a knock at the door.

"Your mother's on the phone," Byron yelled.

She opened the door slightly and reached her hand out for the phone. "Thanks." She closed the door back. "Hi, Mom."

"I had a nice long conversation with your husband. For the life of me, I can't figure out why you two rushed to Vegas. He told me you weren't pregnant, so that's reassuring."

"Mom!"

"I asked him because I knew you weren't going to tell me anything."

"I can't believe you asked him that."

"I sure did and anything else I wanted to know."

"Like what else?"

"Our conversation is between him and me. I called to see if you needed me to bring anything tomorrow, but he told me what you were cooking, so I'll bring my appetite."

"Ask Dad to be on his best behavior." She pulled up the legs of her jogging pants.

"Now you know I can't control him. Never have. Never will." Her mother's voice sounded muffled as she continued to talk. "Let me go. Napoleon's trying to fix the sink, and apparently something didn't work, because I hear him in there cussing."

Nikki laughed. "He needs to call the plumber."

"We're talking about your father." Ethel laughed.

"Bye, Mom."

"See you tomorrow." Ethel hung up.

Byron laughed as Nikki did her best to find out what he and her mother had talked about. He sat at the table and watched her make potato salad, pasta salad, and some other dish he wasn't familiar with.

"You can bat your eyes and unzip your jogging suit . . . well, don't do that." He paused before continuing to say, "I'm not telling you what we talked about."

"I'm calling your mom and telling her a few things about you."

"Go right ahead. She knows me like a book."

"Does she know her son is an egotistical, hardheaded, uncooperative jerk?" Nikki pouted.

"She should. She raised me." He laughed.

Nikki bubbled over with laughter. "You're really not going to tell me?"

"Nope."

She opened up a can of evaporated milk and then began measuring sugar. She looked up. "I guess you won't be sampling any of my banana pudding either."

A wicked thought crossed his mind. "It's probably best that I don't sample. Knowing me, I would want the entire bowl."

Nikki almost dropped the bowl she had gotten out of the cabinet.

"What's wrong, Nikki?"

She paused before saying, "Uh, nothing."

He smiled because now he knew he had her. "If I tell you what we talked about, will you allow me to *taste* your pudding?"

"Never mind."

He walked behind her and planted small kisses on her neck. "Are you sure? I'm willing to tell you everything."

Stuttering, Nikki replied, "Some things are best left unknown."

"Exactly." He stopped and began walking out of the kitchen. He felt a dish towel on his back. He stopped, turned around, and picked it up. He then threw it on the table, laughed, and continued out the door.

32

The next morning, Nikki was awakened by the sound of chirping birds outside her window. She smelled the aroma of meat being cooked on a grill. She stretched. Normally she hated getting up early on Saturday mornings, but today she felt refreshed. Her last memory of the previous night included the warmth of Byron's arms. They had been watching one of her favorite movies starring Vivica Fox and Morris Chestnut prior to her falling asleep.

She ran some bathwater and soaked in the tub for almost thirty minutes.

After going through the closet and her unpacked suitcase, she couldn't find anything she wanted to wear. She threw on a pair of jeans and one of her sorority T-shirts. She couldn't find her tennis shoes, so she wore her slippers instead.

Byron was in the kitchen when she walked downstairs.

"Good morning, sleepyhead," he said to her.

"Good morning. How did I get upstairs?" she asked, admiring how fine he looked in his T-shirt that showed off his bulging muscles.

"You fell asleep, so I carried you upstairs."

"Oh." She poured a glass of orange juice.

"I got a surprise for you."

She perked up. "What?"

"I bought us matching outfits yesterday."

"You're going a little too far with this husband and wife thing, aren't you?" She leaned on the cabinet.

"I can always tell them that we're pretending if that's going to be a problem," he threatened.

"You wouldn't." She stood straight.

"Not if you continue to cooperate." He winked.

"I'll wear the stupid outfit. Where is it?" She placed the cup on the cabinet.

"It's lying across my bed. After I put this other meat on, I'll go shower and change." He walked out the back door. "Shut the door for me."

"I could really get used to this. If only it was the real thing," she said as she walked out.

The doorbell rang before she could reach the top of the stairway.

She ran back downstairs and yelled, "Who is it?"

"Frederick," she heard him yell from the other side of the door.

She opened the door and Frederick stood there wearing a Mavericks jersey and jeans. He leaned down and hugged her and kissed her on the cheek. "Hey, sister-in-law."

"Now you know better," Nikki said, hitting him on the arm.

"I'm practicing, so that when the family gets here I won't be caught off guard." Frederick chuckled.

"Thanks."

"I still don't see what the big deal is. But hey, if my brother is going along with it, who am I to mess up what y'all got going?"

"Your brother's out back." Nikki pointed.

"Somebody lied and told him he could throw down on the grill. Let me go show him how it's really done."

She watched Frederick walk out.

"This is going to be a long day." She sighed as Frederick made his way to his brother.

Byron was surprised to see Frederick. "Man, what are you doing here?" he said.

"I told you I wasn't about to miss out on some free food," Frederick answered.

"I take it you saw Nikki."

"Yep. She seemed cool. Did she understand the Tara situation?"

They were startled when Nikki asked, "What situation?"

Byron looked at Frederick. He looked away. "Nothing. We were discussing how awkward the entire situation has turned out."

"I'm no longer worried about Tara and neither should you be." She reached up and kissed him on the lips. "Do you need anything from the store? I need to run out and get a few things."

"Do you have any brew?" Frederick asked.

"There's some in the fridge. Bottom right," Byron intervened. He then turned to Nikki and said, "Sweetie, bring back a couple bags of ice."

"I will. I need to change clothes and I'll be back shortly." She walked away.

Byron sighed. "Whew, that was close."

Frederick whispered, "I can tell you guys really care about each other. I would hate to see you get hurt because you weren't being completely honest."

"If she can't understand, then it's her problem." He pretended not to care. "She's the one going around lying."

"So are you, my man. So are you," Frederick said as he patted Byron on the back.

"Do I look all right?" Byron asked.

"You look perfect," Nikki replied, licking her lips.

"Ms. Montana, let's go do this."

She frowned. "You mean Mrs. Matthews."

"Sorry. I guess I'm nervous."

She looped her arm around his neck and kissed him. "Now you have something else to be nervous about."

She sashayed out of his bedroom. He followed her. When they made it downstairs, her brothers were out back.

They hugged her. "How's my favorite little sister?" Gerald asked.

"I'm doing great, big brother," she responded.

"What's up, man?" Gerald asked before shaking Byron's hand.

Nikki turned to Byron and said, "I'll be back."

He watched her walk away.

"If you weren't already married to my lil' sister, I would have to break your neck," Jerry joked as he walked up and shook Byron's hand.

"How're you doing? Y'all didn't have any trouble finding us, did you?" Byron asked.

"No. We found it just fine," Jerry said as they all walked toward the grill. "How long have you been living here?"

"A little over a year. Everything's not like I want it, but I told Nikki she could decorate the inside. I want to make a few more changes out here."

"I like the deck," Gerald said.

"I had it added on after I moved in. We have enough land back here for me to get a hot tub installed."

"Now that would be nice. Me and the wifey might have to drop by more often," Jerry commented.

Gerald shook his head. "How are you going to invite yourself over to somebody else's house? Welcome to the family, man." He reached out and placed his hand on Byron's shoulder.

Nikki's entire family showed up within the hour. The men and kids were outside and most of the women were inside the kitchen and dining room area. Nikki walked outside and whispered in Byron's ear.

"I hope I remember where everything is," she said to him. "They're pressing me for a tour. I don't want them to see we live in separate rooms."

"I can go with you if you like."

"No. Stay out here and entertain the men."

She walked back into the house. "Ladies, are y'all ready for the tour?" she asked. "Deposit a dollar in the jar when we're finished."

"Ha-ha," April chided.

Nikki looped her arm through her mom's and led them back toward the front door. "To my left is the living room." Since she wasn't too sure herself what was in the rooms, she ad-libbed as she showed them the living room, den, and office downstairs. It was now time to show them the upstairs.

"Mom, do you need some help?" Nikki asked.

"No, I think I'll be able to make it up these stairs," her mother replied.

They were all amazed at the spaciousness of the house. After showing off the décor of other portions of the house, Nikki tried to steer away from the bedrooms.

Adrienne placed her hand on the master bedroom door-knob. "I want to see the master bedroom."

Ethel said, "Maybe she wants a little privacy."

"It's all right, Mom." Nikki walked forward. Adrienne moved out of the way. She sighed before opening the door.

Everybody was amazed at the high-post bed.

Nikki had to admit, this was the one room Byron had decorated perfectly.

"This is where I like to sit and read," Nikki said as she sat on the beautiful chaise in the corner by the window.

"I don't blame you. This is a nice view of the backyard too," Pam commented.

"On this side you can see the front yard," Ethel noted.

"I love your bathroom," Janice stated.

April added, "It's a little too manly for me, though."

Adrienne sneered. "Everybody is not into pinks and baby blues like you."

Ethel shot Adrienne a look. "Ladies, I think we've invaded Nikki and Byron's privacy enough."

They exited the room and Nikki closed the door behind them. Adrienne lagged behind and whispered while spreading her two fingers, "April is this close from me telling her off."

"You need to quit," Nikki told her.

"She thinks she's the only one who knows how to decorate."

Ethel said, "Shh. If I can hear you, she can too."

"I don't care," Adrienne stated.

"Please save it for another time," Nikki pleaded.

Adrienne moved past everyone and walked outside.

The men set up the tables and chairs. The kids sat at one table and the men and women at the other tables. Byron, Frederick, Nikki, and her parents sat at the same table.

Byron stood up. He looked down toward his right side at Nikki and smiled. "Nikki and I would like to thank everyone for coming today," he said. "With my job schedule, I know this is only your second time meeting me, but I feel like I'm part of the family already."

Frederick, who was sitting on his left, accidentally spilled his drink. Byron cut his eyes at him.

"Mr. Montana, will you bless the food?" Byron asked as he sat down and squeezed Nikki's hand.

Napoleon said, "Hold the person's hand sitting next to you and bow your heads please." He paused before praying. "Father, we would like to thank you for this beautiful day. Thank you for bringing my family together one more time. I know You are an all-knowing God. Please bless this union between my daughter and son-in law. . . ."

Byron looked at Nikki after she squeezed his hand a little too tight. He saw tears flowing down her face. He was tempted to reach over and wipe her face, but he refrained.

Napoleon continued to pray. "Watch over my grandkids as they deal with issues of this world. Bless this food we're about to eat. Amen."

Everyone said, "Amen."

"Let's grub," Napoleon said with a smile on his face.

Everyone piled food on their plates. Light conversations were made in between bites.

"I could kiss whoever cooked these beans," Byron said after eating a mouthful.

Adrienne blushed. "I'm glad you like them. Nikki begged me to make them for you."

"I'm glad she did. The barbecue would have been incomplete without them," Byron complimented.

Nikki was glad her family and Byron were getting along great. "I'll be right back. I need to get the dessert out of the kitchen," she said.

Byron stood and said, "I'll help you."

Frederick said, "It takes both of y'all—"

Before he could finish, Napoleon interrupted. "Let them be, Son. Newlyweds are strange creatures."

Nikki and Byron smiled as they walked into the kitchen. She sighed. "Whew. This has been a day."

"You're doing fine," he told her.

"I know, but Frederick almost—"

"He's pulling your strings. He likes to joke, and if he knows he's got you sweating, he'll continue to get in jabs."

They both turned when they heard a knock at the door. "Who could that be? Everybody I invited is here," Nikki stated.

"I don't know. Wait right here and I'll go see." Byron walked away.

Nikki opened the refrigerator and took out the banana pudding and lemon meringue pie. She was placing them on the table when Byron walked in with a woman she had never met.

"Nikki, this is Joyce." Byron hand-gestured. "Joyce, Nikki."

Nikki reached her hand out. Joyce pulled her in for a hug and said, "Girl, we're like family. Give me a hug."

"Nice meeting you," Nikki said.

"I would have been over here earlier, but my boys had a game."

"We're about to eat dessert, but there's still food outside, so help yourself," Nikki stated.

Nikki picked up the banana pudding and picked up the lemon meringue pie when Joyce said, "Let me help you with that."

Joyce grabbed the pie. Byron picked up the pound cake and sweet potato pie.

Everybody was eagerly awaiting the dessert. As they placed items on the table, Byron said, "Everybody, this is my cousin Joyce."

Some replied, "Hi," as they all dug in and helped themselves to the dessert of their choice.

The rest of the afternoon went by without any incidents, to Byron's relief. He didn't know what to expect after Joyce arrived.

"Nikki, we made it through the day," he said as he closed the door behind their last guest.

"I'm exhausted," Nikki responded.

"Me too. I'll get those dishes in the morning."

"I hate to leave dirty dishes, but I'm emotionally drained right now."

"You want to talk about it?"

"Let me go get out of these clothes and I'll meet you back downstairs."

"Meet me in my bedroom," Byron suggested.

"I don't know if that's a good idea."

"I promise. I won't bite."

"Okay."

"That is, unless you want me to," he teased.

33

Byron was dressed in shorts and a T-shirt. He was lying across the bed flipping stations when Nikki walked in. She lay down beside him and hugged him.

"Thanks," she told him.

"For what?" he asked.

"For going beyond the call of duty."

"When I agreed to be your husband, I took my duties seriously," he joked.

"You're so silly."

"And you're so beautiful." His eyes sparkled as he spoke.

She paused before saying anything. "The tour of the house was a trip. I had to make up stuff. And you know the ring leader, Adrienne, asked plenty of questions."

"Did you show them big daddy's room?" He laughed.

"Yes, we came in here. Thankfully, I didn't have to show them the other guest room, because my stuff was all over the bed."

"Why not?"

"Adrienne was about to tear into April and by then everybody was ready to go back downstairs."

"April seems cool to me."

"She is, but she said something to set Adrienne off."

"Well, the menfolk didn't have any drama. Your dad had us laughing with some of the stories he was telling. I'm beginning to love your family."

"Don't go getting too comfortable. In a few more months you'll be going about your merry way."

He turned over onto his back, placed his arms under his neck, and looked at her. "Don't even think about getting rid of me," he said.

"I'm not. I don't want you to feel obligated."

He pulled her down to his chest and began rubbing his hands through her hair. "Nikki, how many times do we have to go over this? Regardless of our little predicament, we're going to be together. Who knows? One day you may really become the real Mrs. Matthews."

"Who knows?" Nikki said before falling asleep in his arms.

Byron carefully moved her and placed her under the covers. She reached out to him throughout the night. He wanted her so much, and with her this close, it was making it harder for him to restrain himself. When he woke up, her legs were wrapped around him. He attempted to move without waking her, but as soon as he moved, she woke up.

She rubbed her eyes and yawned. "I'm sorry. I didn't mean to keep you up all night," she said.

"I'll accept your apology after I take a cold shower," he told her.

He jumped out of bed without giving her a chance to respond and headed straight for the shower.

This water feels good, he thought as he rinsed the soap off his body. *But it's not helping my situation. Nikki, we need to hurry up and do something about this. I hope things work out with this paternity test. Either way it goes, I'm going to be a man about it and accept my responsibilities.* When he stepped out of the shower, he called out for Nikki, but she didn't respond. *Good, she's left the room.*

He wrapped the towel around his waist and was startled to see her sitting on his bed with her legs crossed when he entered the room.

"I thought you had left," he told her.

"No. Then I would have missed seeing you walk out half naked."

He looked down and pretended to be covering himself. "I'm shocked."

"I'm aroused," she teased.

"Nikki, leave now or I won't be held accountable for what I do next."

"You promise?" she asked as she stood up.

"Don't have me call your mama," he said as she turned to walk out the door.

"Don't have me call yours," she retorted.

Nikki looked at the time and contemplated whether or not she would go to church. She hadn't attended in a while. She was lying to her coworkers and family, but she wouldn't dare go into the church sanctuary with the cross she had been carrying around. People would ask her about her husband and she would be forced to lie. She refused to be struck down on the church premises.

She poured herself a cup of coffee and began reading the Sunday paper. Byron walked into the kitchen dressed in a tailor-made gray pin-striped suit.

"What are your plans for today?" Byron asked while pouring a cup of coffee.

"Nothing," Nikki replied.

"What's wrong with you?"

"Why does something have to be wrong with me because I choose not to go to church?" she said with an attitude.

"Hold up, I didn't mention anything about church. I just asked one simple question and you're going off."

Nikki knew she owed him an apology, but instead of apologizing she said, "Have a good time at church."

"Why don't you go to church with me today? Besides, it'll give you a chance to meet my folks."

She thought about it and agreed. "Give me about thirty minutes."

Byron was proud to walk into the Tabernacle Baptist Church with Nikki on his arm. She was dressed in a light purple double-breasted designer suit. The sleeves were feathered and she wore matching heels. Her purse was the same color. Byron's dad was a deacon and Byron noticed him sitting near the front of the church. His mother was sitting in the front pew.

It was crowded, so the usher directed them to seats near the back where they enjoyed the sermon. After the sermon, his cousin sang a beautiful rendition of "Amazing Grace." He looked to his right and saw tears flowing down Nikki's face. He handed her the handkerchief in his pocket and whispered in her ear, "Are you okay?"

"I'm fine," she said between tears.

After service, they waited out front for his parents to come out. He greeted some of his relatives and other church members and introduced them to Nikki as they waited.

Some of the single women weren't too friendly.

Nikki enjoyed the service, but if one more woman turned her nose up at her, she would not be held accountable for her actions.

These heifers are crazy, she thought. *They shouldn't be coming to church looking for a man anyway. If he wanted y'all, he would be with y'all. Now get to stepping.*

She put on a fake smile and continued to shake her head at what seemed like appropriate moments as Byron talked.

I hope his folks hurry up and come out, she thought, *because my feet are killing me. I don't know why women like to torture themselves. All because we want to look cute and I know I must be looking real good for the women to act jealous and not even know me.*

Byron called her name a few times. "Nikki, this is my mom, Belle Matthews."

"Oh, I'm sorry. I don't know where my mind was," Nikki said as she reached her hand out for a handshake.

"Give me a hug," Mrs. Matthews insisted.

Byron's mom hugged her.

"This is my dad, Frank," Byron said as he gestured toward a six-foot-three inch bronze-complexioned man with piercing gray eyes similar to Byron's.

"I've heard so much about you," Frank said as he shook Nikki's hand.

"I hope it was all good," Nikki stated as they walked down the sidewalk.

"Any woman who can put a smile on my baby's face is all right with me," Byron's mom said.

"I'm not a baby," Byron said.

"You're my baby," his mother insisted.

Byron blushed.

Byron's parents invited them over for dinner and they accepted. Nikki got a chance to speak with his mother in private as Byron and his father retreated to the den. Nikki attempted to help with dinner, but Byron's mother motioned for her to have a seat.

"Nikki, Byron tells me you're originally from Dallas. Where are your parents from?"

"They're from this little town in Louisiana called Mansfield. It's about twenty miles south of Shreveport." Nikki wiped the perspiration from her forehead when Belle turned away.

"Never heard of it, but I've been to Shreveport to the casinos."

"I've been to Vegas a few times but don't frequent the casinos in Shreveport," Nikki informed her.

"I shouldn't be going, but the sounds of those machines can be addictive."

Nikki nodded her head in agreement. "You sure you don't need any help with anything?"

"Sit down. I would hate for you to get your pretty suit dirty."

"That's what cleaners are for." Nikki stood up, took off her jacket, and placed it on the chair. "Now what do you need me to do?"

Belle had a pleased look on her face, and handed her a knife. "You can cut the potatoes for me."

"Will do."

Belle told Nikki stories of the mischief Byron and Frederick often got into growing up. It was hard for her to imagine Byron being a chubby little kid. Her maternal instincts kicked in and she yearned to have a child, Byron's child.

Byron walked in. "How are my two favorite girls?" he asked. He kissed his mom on the cheek and attempted to open up a pot. His mom smacked him on the back of his hand. "Ouch."

"I told you I don't like anybody over my stove while I'm cooking," his mother scolded.

Looking like a dejected little boy, Byron said, "Yes, ma'am." He paused before saying, "Dad and I are going to the store. Do we need to bring something back?"

"Not that I can think of," Belle responded.

"Ladies, we'll be back," Byron said before winking at Nikki.

She smiled at him and went to the sink and cleaned the potatoes before placing them in a pot. She tried to figure out which knob to turn for the front burner.

"I got it, dear," Belle said. "Once these potatoes get done, I'll make the salad and we'll be ready to eat."

Although dinner went well, Byron sensed his mom wanted to ask him something. Nikki's ring sparkled brighter under the dining room light than he remembered. They were getting ready to leave when his mom pulled him to the side.

"Son, is there something you want to tell me?"

"No, Mom."

"You're not messing with a married woman, are you?"

"Of course not. You raised me better than that."

"I hope not. Nikki's nice and all, but I don't condone extramarital affairs," Belle sternly said.

"She's far from married."

She hugged Byron and he bent down and kissed her on the cheek. "Call me later," she said.

"I will. I better go before Dad talks Nikki's head off."

Byron rescued Nikki and they waved at his parents as they pulled out of the driveway.

"That was nice," Nikki commented.

"Yes, it was. Did my mom say anything to you?" he asked.

"We talked. Why, what's up?" she asked.

"She made a comment about you being married."

Nikki held up her right hand. "I guess I should have taken the wedding ring off. Sorry."

"Everything's cool. She knows we're not committing adultery." He laughed.

She wiped her forehead. "Whew. Good. I would hate for her to think I was messing around with her son."

"Her son wishes you were, though." He looked over at Nikki and smiled.

"Wishful thinking. And please keep your eyes on the road."

"Yes, ma'am."

When Nikki turned in for bed, she reflected on the weekend events. She wanted to believe her life was going well, but internally, she struggled with the idea she was living a lie.

How I wish Byron and I met under better circumstances and not in the middle of a lie, she thought. *I wish he were my husband. I see how he interacts with his family, my family. I know he cares about me or he wouldn't have agreed to live this lie. I don't know how much longer we can live like this. He deserves better.*

Tears streamed down her face as she pulled the covers over her head.

34

"I heard you were at church yesterday with Nikki," Joyce said to Byron the following morning while they sat in the company conference room.

"Did your sources also tell you that we had dinner with my parents?" Byron asked.

Joyce sat down in a chair next to him in the conference room. "No. How did Aunt Belle like her?"

"If you must know, they got along great."

"Good. I like her too. I think she needs to stop playing games, though."

Byron was about to comment, but some of his other coworkers began to pile into the conference room.

After the two-hour meeting, Byron avoided Joyce by rushing to his office and closing the door.

He checked his messages and returned a few phone calls.

"Hi, Nikki, sorry I missed your call," he said through the phone receiver as he left Nikki a voice message. "I've been tied up in meetings all morning. I'll be working in the field this evening, so if you need me, call me on the cell."

After leaving a message for Nikki, he unplugged his laptop, placed it in the carrying case, made sure he had his cell phone, and left the office.

He was barely in the car, when Joyce rang his phone.

"Yes, Joyce," he said, sounding exasperated.

"Now this could be business, while you're answering your phone with an attitude."

"I know you."

"Ha-ha."

Byron tried to sound annoyed, but couldn't. "I'm sorry. You can't help being a busybody."

"I'm offended." Joyce chuckled.

"Bye, Joyce."

"Bye."

Byron drove through the drive-through at Mickey D's and ordered a supersized number 3. He ate in the car as he drove to a potential client's site.

His cell phone rang as he pulled up into the parking lot. Byron recognized the number as Tara's. After the call went to voice mail, he turned the ringer off.

He took the last sip of his drink before popping in a breath mint. He blew his breath into his hands, and after being reassured his breath smelled fresh, he turned the engine off, grabbed his briefcase, and walked to the office building with confidence.

Nikki suppressed a yawn as she and eight coworkers sat in the conference room listening to her manager go over the past quarter's budget in their weekly Monday meeting. She threw a piece of paper at Kenneth to wake him up. She laughed when he almost jumped out of his chair.

"That concludes today's meeting. I'll be sending out an e-mail with this information," her manager stated.

Everyone was filing out of the room. Nikki lagged behind. When she walked out of the room, Tara was walking by.

"I was wondering where you were. I've been sending you

e-mails and I decided to walk over and see you in person," Tara said to Nikki.

Nikki continued to walk toward her desk. "We just got out of a forecast meeting. I haven't had time to check my e-mail today," she said.

Tara lagged beside her. "There's something I really need to talk to you about."

"Can it wait? Because I have a conference call I'm late for," Nikki stated as she placed her notebook on her desk and sat down.

Tara looked annoyed. "Sure. Let's do lunch tomorrow."

Nikki pulled out the keyboard and typed in the screen saver's password. She logged on to her e-mail and opened up her calendar.

Tara stood, tapped her foot, and waited for Nikki's reply.

"Tomorrow's not good. How about Wednesday?"

"It'll have to do."

Nikki pretended to be oblivious of Tara's mood. "Anything else? I need to log on to this call." She picked up the receiver and dialed 9.

"No. I'll talk to you later."

"That's what I thought," Nikki said as Tara walked away out of earshot.

She placed the receiver down. She picked up a piece of paper out of her in-box and began skimming through it. She dialed the number on the paper after placing the headphones on.

The phone beeped to indicate to the others someone was entering the call. Kenneth walked by and attempted to get her attention. She placed the phone on mute.

"What's up?" she asked.

"Tara is on the warpath. Word has it, she's about to fire Smitty. You know he's been here for twenty years!"

"Dang it. Hold on, Kenneth." She signaled him with her hand. "Yes. We'll be sending out reports on the ninth of each month going forward," she added to the call.

Kenneth mouthed the words "Call me" before walking away.

She nodded her head to indicate that she would.

After getting off the call, she scrolled through her e-mail. She deleted the messages from Tara. From what she could tell, they were not business related, so she didn't feel obligated to respond. In fact, they looked like chain e-mails.

Kenneth sent her an e-mail asking her to call him.

She dialed his extension. "Kenneth, tell me what's going on," she replied after he answered.

"Smitty was told he could either resign or he'll be asked to leave," Kenneth informed her.

"But he's close to retirement." She opened and closed e-mails as she spoke.

"Yeah, I think you're right. He said he's spoken with his attorney and they'll have to fire him before he ever quits. Apparently your girl was brought in to do some house-cleaning."

"Interesting."

"He's not the only one getting the ax. Somebody from our department is too, but nobody knows who yet."

Nikki stopped checking her e-mail and gave Kenneth her undivided attention. "Are you sure? You know how rumors get started."

"Yes, and apparently Tara made a recommendation to our manager from her own observations."

"I bet she has," Nikki said halfheartedly.

"You're not worried, are you?" Kenneth asked.

"Of course not," she lied.

She looked over her shoulder to confirm that no one was coming up to her desk. She logged on to Monster.com and performed a job search.

Kenneth whispered, "I'm about to update my resume just in case. I don't trust any of these people up in this place."

"Neither do I," Nikki said before hanging up the phone.

* * *

Byron greeted Nikki with a kiss as he unlocked the door and let her in. "How was your day?"

"You don't want to know." She paused before walking upstairs.

"I ordered pizza, so it should be here any minute."

"Okay," she yelled from the top of the stairs.

A few minutes later, the doorbell rang and it was the pizza delivery guy. Byron took the pizza and tipped him.

He grabbed two plates and some napkins and placed them on the coffee table in the den.

"Byron," Nikki yelled from the dining room.

"I'm in here," he said.

He noticed the formfitting red shorts she was wearing. They accented all of her curves. The T-shirt was a little snug and he could see the imprint of her breasts.

Byron immediately felt uncomfortable. "Nikki, please dress more appropriately," he begged.

"There's nothing wrong with what I have on." She sat down near him.

"From my point of view there is."

"Get over it."

"What's with the attitude?"

"I don't have an attitude. You're the one who made a comment on what I was wearing."

"Look, Nikki. I didn't mean to offend you. Take what I said as a compliment."

"It didn't come out like that."

"The problem is my libido is strained and when you walk in wearing something like that." He glared at her top and said, "It puts me in a very uncomfortable position."

She took a slice of pizza out of the box and placed it on her plate. She picked up a piece of pepperoni and ate it. "Oh, I see. Sorry."

"No apology needed."

Byron opened up a package of Parmesan cheese and sprinkled it on top of his three slices of pizza. "I hope you like pepperoni and Italian sausage."

"I do." She took another bite.

After they ate in silence, Byron asked, "What happened at work to have you come home in such an uproar?"

"It's a four-letter word."

He had a puzzled look on his face. "You got me." He held his hand up.

"T-A-R-A."

"Dang, what did she do now?"

"I found out today she was actually hired to come in and do an assessment on the employees and make recommendations on who to keep and who to fire."

"And?"

"And that means my boyfriend's ex-girlfriend is in control of whether I have a job or not."

"She wouldn't do anything like that."

Nikki seemed agitated. "So you're taking up for her now. I thought you despised her."

"Granted, she's not one of my favorite people in the world, but I can't see her jeopardizing her job by firing you."

"I wouldn't put anything past her. To think I did her a favor by babysitting her little bastard," Nikki said with a feeling as if she had been used.

"Whoa. Calm down, Nikki."

"I'll calm down when I'm good and ready. I'm going to bed now." She stood up.

"It's only eight o'clock."

"And it's midnight in some parts of the world." She angrily left the room.

Byron didn't know what to do, so he sat and watched her storm out of the room. A few seconds later, he heard the bedroom door slam.

I guess I'll call it a night myself, he thought, shrugging his shoulders.

He took the empty pizza box and threw it in the kitchen trash. He placed the dirty dishes into the dishwasher, poured some lemon-fresh dishwasher liquid into the spout, and turned it on. He then grabbed a beer out of the refrigerator, turned off the downstairs lights, and headed to his bedroom.

Nikki knew she owed Byron an apology for acting the way she did the night before. She woke up early after tossing and turning all night, got dressed, and went downstairs to cook a big breakfast. She made a note to stop at a grocery store because the food supply was getting low.

She mixed up several items, including cheese, and poured them into a bowl. She cracked a few eggs and made two omelets. She drank her fourth cup of coffee before putting on a fresh pot.

The coffee was brewing when she heard Byron walk into the kitchen. He barely got the words "Good morning" out when she went over and hugged him.

"Sorry about last night," she apologized.

He seemed unsure of what to say. "Okay."

"Sit. I hope you like omelets. I made you one with everything in it. Don't ask what, just enjoy it," she rambled on.

"Thanks." He sat down.

Nikki handed him a cup of coffee. "Here's your coffee just the way you like it."

He placed it on the mat in front of him. "Slow down."

"Do you want some juice before I sit down?"

"If I do, I'll get up and pour some myself. Sit and eat your breakfast."

"I can get it for you."

"Nikki, what's wrong with you?"

She sat and fidgeted with her food. "I must have drunk

too many cups of coffee. I get this way when I get too much caffeine."

"Remind me to get decaffeinated next time," he commented.

Nikki watched Byron eat. "You want some more? I'm not really hungry."

"You need to eat something," he said out of concern.

"I know, but my nerves are bad right now."

"Anything I can do to help?" Byron asked.

"Yes. Pray for me," she said with sincerity. "Pray for me."

Byron walked Nikki out to her car. "Meet me for lunch," he told her.

"I wish I could," Nikki said while fumbling for her keys.

"Make it happen."

"I'll try."

Before Nikki could open the car door, Byron's lips were over hers. Byron was the first to pull away. He opened her car door and said, "That should jump-start your day."

"In more ways than one." She reached up and wiped the lipstick from his lips before entering her car.

Byron closed the door and they waved good-bye as she pulled out of the driveway.

After making sure the house was secure, Byron left for the office. Traffic was nonstop as he headed to work. He put his headphones on and listened to his cell phone messages. Several were from Tara. He became irritated and decided to listen to the *Steve Harvey Show* to take his mind off his issues. He regrettably pulled into the parking lot before hearing what Pee Wee's pick of the day would be.

Nikki was swamped with work. Her computer kept acting up and her phone wouldn't stop ringing. To make matters worse, Tara made it her business to pass by her area what seemed like every ten minutes.

"Do you need some help?" Tara asked at the same time Nikki slammed down the phone.

"Everything's just lovely," Nikki said, sounding as if everything was just the opposite.

"You seem to be frustrated. If there's anything I can do, let me know."

"I sure will," Nikki said with a fake smile.

"I'll let you get back to work." Before walking away, she asked, "We're still on for lunch tomorrow, aren't we?"

Trying not to sound irritated, Nikki responded, "Yes. This time you choose the spot."

"I'll let you know." Tara winked and walked away.

"She's up to something. I know it," Nikki whispered to herself.

"I see you're talking to yourself again," Mya commented as she passed by Nikki's desk.

Nikki looked up and rolled her eyes at Mya. After making a few more phone calls, Nikki realized she hadn't called Byron to confirm lunch. Her cell phone rang and she scrambled to find it.

"Hello," she answered.

"You're the hardest person to reach," Byron blurted out.

"I'm sorry. I forgot to call you."

"That's all right. I picked up lunch. I'm downstairs."

Nikki stood up and began walking toward the elevator. "I'll meet you in the lobby."

When she got to the lobby, she noticed Byron leaning on the security guard station. He appeared to be in deep conversation. When he looked up and saw her, she heard him tell the guard bye and he met her with two Olive Garden bags in his hands.

They hugged. "Do you guys have a conference or visitors' room or somewhere we can go to and eat lunch?" Byron asked.

"Uh, I didn't know you were staying." Nikki looked around as if she was looking for someone.

"Now if you don't want one of these fresh garlic sticks," he said as he waved the bag under her nose so she could smell the aroma before continuing, "me and these bags can walk right back outside."

She reached for his arm. "I'll find us a room. We can go to the break room on the fourth floor. It shouldn't be too crowded."

Byron smiled at her and followed her to the elevator. He wanted to sweep her up in his arms the moment he saw her. Since they were in her office building, he refrained from doing so. He made a promise to stock up on her favorite perfume because the smell was intoxicating. Even with the aroma coming from the Italian food in the bag, her fragrance overpowered him.

He followed her into a noisy, crowded room.

"Maybe we should find another place. I normally go out to eat or take it back to my desk," she apologized.

"I'm following you," he said as she led him back out the door.

"We'll use one of the conference rooms," she suggested.

They took the elevator to her floor. Most people she knew were at lunch, so she didn't have to explain who Byron was. She found a vacant conference room and closed the door behind them.

"I hope it's not cold," he said as he took the items out of the bag and placed them on the conference room table.

"I can always warm it up in the microwave down the hall if it is," she commented.

"I think you might want to."

"Hand those to me. I'll be back in a few."

"I'm not going anywhere," he said, handing her a couple of containers.

She walked out and closed the door behind her.

Byron was deep in thought when the door opened. He assumed it was Nikki, so he stood to help with the door. He and Tara were both surprised to see one another.

She blurted out, "What are you doing here?"

"I'm having lunch with Nikki. Why?"

"It's a natural question to ask. Do you always have to have an attitude with me?" She twisted toward him.

He took a few steps back and sat down. "No. But I learned a long time ago that being nice to you comes with a price."

She laughed. "You need to let bygones be bygones."

"If you weren't up to your old tricks, I could," he snapped.

She walked closer and sat on the corner of the table. She went through the bags. "Hmm. I wish I had a man bringing me lunch."

"Don't you think you should leave?"

"You're at my job. I have more of a right to be here than you. I could call security and have you escorted out if I wanted to," she snapped.

"Like I really care."

"Oh, I know you wouldn't want your wifey to be embarrassed on the job." She took a bite from one of the bread sticks she had just pulled out of the bag and then threw it back into the bag. She swung her head so hard that her hair blew into her face.

Byron wanted to snatch the weave out of her hair. He stood up and put an arm on each side of her body, putting him in close proximity to her face. "If I ever hear of you doing anything, and I mean *anything*, to harm Nikki, you will answer to me."

Nikki walked in, apologizing about taking so long due to the fact that someone was making popcorn in the microwave. She stopped abruptly when she saw the closeness of Byron and Tara. "What the hell is going on here?" she questioned as she stood at the doorway.

Tara moved Byron's arm and walked around the table.

"Nothing," she said. "Byron and I were getting reacquainted. I'll leave you two lovebirds alone." She walked around Nikki and closed the door.

"You better tell me what's going on or you'll be wearing this food," Nikki said to Byron, meaning her every word.

Byron walked near her, but Nikki backed up. "I was making sure Tara and I were clear on a few things."

"It looked a little more intense than that."

"It got heated, but I think she realizes where I stand." He reached out for the food. She handed it to him.

"I hope that's all it was, because if I find out something else is going on . . ." She paused before continuing. "Let's just hope we don't have to cross that bridge."

Byron released his breath. "Have a seat. Your lunch break is going to be over soon."

Nikki watched Byron and still felt as if he wasn't telling her everything. She vowed to keep her eyes open. She loved Byron, but she didn't know if she could fully trust him.

After lunch, she walked Byron to the elevator and kissed him good-bye.

"Was that your hubbie?" Kenneth asked as she bumped into him.

"Yes," she said, plastering on a smile.

"Darn. I missed him by a few seconds."

She crossed her arms and began walking back inside the corridor. "I'm sure you'll get another opportunity to meet him."

"You don't look so hot. What's wrong?"

"Nothing." She detoured into the ladies' room before Kenneth could continue to pry.

Before Byron could get off the elevator, his cell phone rang. He allowed it to go to voice mail the first couple of times. After the third time, he answered.

"Will you please leave me alone?" he shouted into the phone.

"I'm not going anywhere and just as soon as the test results come back, you're going to be tied to me for *life*!" Tara exclaimed. She continued to talk. Byron removed the phone from his ear and kept walking.

He waved at the security guard as he walked out of the lobby's swinging door. He tried to contain his composure. Once he reached his car, he sighed, put the phone back up to his ear, and heard Tara still talking.

"I don't mean to interrupt, but my battery is low and I have to go," Byron said as he pressed the End button. "I swear if he's my child, I will make sure I get custody. She's not fit to raise a dog," he said to himself as he sped out of the parking lot.

Nikki heard someone in one of the other stalls. She originally came into the bathroom to get away from Kenneth, but her bladder indicated she should relieve herself.

She heard the other stall door open and someone wash her hands. She was about to flush the toilet when she heard Tara's voice after she answered her ringing cell phone.

"He doesn't know I can make his world come tumbling down around him," Tara gloated into the phone after her salutation. "His stupid wife doesn't have a clue."

Nikki knew she was talking about her. As much as she wanted to confront Tara, she waited and listened to the one-sided phone conversation.

"Girl, I'm in a position of power." She paused and after letting out a horrific laugh, Tara said, "I told Christopher last night, his daddy would pay for not acknowledging him. After this week, Ms. Nikki and Byron will be history."

What does she mean by that? Nikki asked herself. *I know she's not talking about . . . No, she can't be.*

Nikki waited for Tara to leave the bathroom. She flushed the toilet, washed her hands, and slowly walked out. She bumped into Mya on the way out.

"Are you okay?" Mya asked. "You don't look too hot. Maybe you should take the rest of the day off."

"You're probably right," Nikki said absentmindedly as she made her way back to her desk.

Out of habit, she turned off her computer, packed her laptop, got her purse, and locked her desk. She stopped by her manager's office to inform him she wasn't feeling well and needed to go home. He approved her leaving and she headed out to her car.

She drove toward Byron's house but decided to go to her own house because she needed time to think. She got her mail and threw everything in the living room.

Her cell phone rang. She looked at the display and saw it was Charlotte.

"Girl, I called your office and the operator told me you had left for today. What's wrong?" Charlotte asked upon Nikki answering the phone.

"Everything," she said as she threw herself on her bed.

Charlotte could hear Nikki's voice begin to crack with just those three syllables. "Now come on. Things can't be that bad."

"Where do you want me to start?"

"Do you need me to come over?"

"Yes, and can you bring me a wine cooler?"

"That bad, huh?"

"That bad," Nikki said as she hung up.

What did I do to deserve this? she cried. *I thought Byron was one of the good guys. How could he have a child and not own up to it? What if I would have slept with him and got pregnant? He would have abandoned me too.* Nikki replayed in her head the words Tara had spoken. *If she wasn't talking about Byron, then who was she talking about? It has to be Byron.*

Her head was pounding. She got up and fumbled through her medicine cabinet. She found a bottle of aspirin and went to the kitchen to pour some water. She popped two aspirins in her mouth and gulped down the water. She lay on the couch in silence. She closed her eyes, hoping she was over-reacting. A few minutes later she was fast asleep from mental exhaustion.

It was five o'clock in the evening as Byron maneuvered his way through traffic. After the run-in with Tara and their intense conversation earlier that day, he knew he needed to tell Nikki everything as soon as possible. He would tell her tonight no matter what the outcome.

He tried calling Nikki at the office and on her cell phone but got voice mail.

Nikki, I hope you understand what I have to tell you, the words ran through his head. *I love you and if he's my child, I have to do what's right. She's a sensible woman, so she'll agree . . . Who am I fooling?*

It was after six o'clock by the time he pulled into the drive-way. He was surprised to see Nikki's car not there. *She must be stuck in traffic,* he thought as he pulled into the garage.

After another hour passed and he hadn't heard from her, he began to worry. He called and left her several more messages on her cell phone.

"Are you in there?" Charlotte yelled out as she knocked on Nikki's door after ringing the doorbell.

Nikki opened the door. Her hair looked tossed and she had to wipe the sleep from her eyes. "Girl, I fell asleep and didn't hear you out here."

Charlotte walked in carrying a bag. "It took you so long that I was about to use my spare key to come in and see what was going on up in here."

Nikki ignored her comment. "I see you come bearing gifts."

They walked into the living room. Charlotte sat on the love seat and Nikki sat on the couch. Charlotte handed her a Sprite. "I thought you could use this."

Nikki stared at it. "This isn't what I asked for."

"But this is what you got."

Disappointed, Nikki opened up the can and took a sip. She blurted out, "Byron is a father."

"What?" Charlotte said as she halted her can of Sprite at her lips.

"I overheard Tara on the phone talking about it."

"Tell me exactly what she said."

Nikki repeated verbatim the end of the phone conversation she had heard. Tears flowed down her face. "I really thought he was one of the good ones."

Charlotte went and sat by her and placed her arms around Nikki to comfort her. "This could still be a misunderstanding. Have you talked to Byron?"

"No. I couldn't face him. I came straight home."

"You need to call him." Charlotte glanced at the clock. "It's after seven and I'm sure he's worried about you."

"I don't know why I let myself fall for him. We had the perfect arrangement, but somewhere along the way I fell in love." She cried nonstop.

Charlotte rocked her. "He loves you too."

"If he loved me, why couldn't he be honest with me? Why didn't he tell me about his child?"

"Frederick, I don't mean to bother you, but do you have Charlotte's number?" Byron said through the phone receiver.

"You got something to write with?" he asked.

"I sure do." Byron wrote down the phone number to Charlotte's house phone as Frederick recited it. "Thanks, man."

"You need help with something?" Frederick asked.

"Not right now. If I need you, I'll call you back." He hung up with Frederick and dialed Charlotte's number.

Charlotte didn't answer, but on her voice mail greeting she left her cell phone number. Byron dialed her cell phone and she answered on the fourth ring. "This is Char."

"Charlotte, I'm so glad to get you. This is Byron," he said, both anxious and worried. "Have you talked to Nikki? She hasn't come home and I was concerned."

"She's right here," Charlotte said.

"Can I speak to her?" he asked. His heart was beating a mile a minute as he waited for her response.

Charlotte's voice sounded muffled. She came back on the phone. "She said she'll meet you at your place in about an hour."

"Is she okay?"

"She'll have to tell you that," Charlotte stated before disconnecting.

"I hope this doesn't mean what I think it means," Byron said as he rubbed his head.

35

"You really need to go talk to him," Charlotte urged her best friend.

"I have no choice now since you told him I would see him in an hour." Nikki wiped the tears from her red eyes.

Charlotte handed her the phone. "You could call him back and tell him you won't be there."

Nikki stood up and brushed the wrinkles out of her skirt. "I might as well get this over with."

They walked out of the house together. Charlotte gave her a tight sisterly hug. "Call me if you need anything. I'm sure it'll work out."

Not believing her, Nikki said under her breath, "Yeah, right."

The drive over to Byron's was long and Nikki almost turned around several times. But then she told herself, *I have to do this. I need to know why he felt the need to lie to me. Anybody else I could see, but Byron. It's like we've been living a lie the whole time.*

A lightbulb went off in her head. "We have been living a lie." She laughed uncontrollably as the tears flowed down her face.

She parked in Byron's driveway. It took her a few minutes to gather her composure before walking up the walkway. She reached out to ring the doorbell but then stopped, inserted her key, and walked in.

It was dark in the house. She jumped when she realized Byron was sitting on the stairway.

"Oh, hey. I thought you were asleep," she said.

He stood up and hugged her tight. Her arms remained at her sides. "I was so worried about you," he said and she could feel it in his gripping embrace.

"I bet you were." She walked past him and up the stairs.

She could hear him behind her, but she didn't slow her pace. She went into her bedroom and looked in the closet. She picked up one of her Louis Vuitton suitcases and threw it on the bed. She began opening up dresser drawers and throwing stuff into the suitcase.

Byron grabbed her arm. "Hold up. What's going on here?" he asked.

Nikki jerked her arm away. "I'd advise you to keep your hands off me," she ordered him.

He backed up a little. "I wasn't going to hurt you."

Nikki laughed. "I would have rather you hit me than hurt me the way you have."

Byron stepped forward to put his arms around her, but stopped when he saw the expression on her face.

"Nikki, I don't know what's going on, but there is no way I would intentionally hurt you," he told her.

She plopped on the bed. "But it's okay for you to unintentionally hurt me?"

"I'm in the dark, baby. Please tell me what's going on."

She stood up. With one hand on her hip and using her other hand as she spoke, she was within arm's length of him. "Does Christopher ring a bell?"

Byron looked away. "Nik—"

She interrupted. "How could you sit up there and pretend that he wasn't your son?"

"Things aren't what they seem."

"When were you going to tell me? When the kid was eighteen?"

"Calm down. We can talk about this."

"Please don't patronize me. I trusted you."

"Nikki, there's a chance he's not even my kid." Byron tried to convince her, although he wasn't too sure of it himself.

Nikki shook her head in disgust. "You're pathetic. You won't even own up to it."

"I was going to tell you everything tonight," he insisted.

"Sure, and I believe in the Easter Bunny." She turned and began putting more stuff into her suitcase.

Byron was blocking her path to the bathroom, but when she reached out to move him, he moved out of the way.

"If you'll calm down, we can get past this," he said.

Nikki turned around, looked him up and down, and walked into the bathroom. She grabbed her toiletries from off the sink, walked back into the bedroom, and threw the items on the bed.

She pulled out her Louis Vuitton backpack from underneath the bed and threw the items into it.

Byron wanted to tell her everything he had been holding back. "Nikki, I love you. I don't want you to leave," he pleaded.

"You should have thought about that when you lied to me."

"This is a big misunderstanding."

"It sure is. I should have known you couldn't be trusted." She grabbed her bags and walked out the door.

Byron felt like his back was against the wall and before he knew it, he shouted, "You're the one to talk!"

She dropped the bags on the floor in front of the door and turned around. "And what do you mean by that?"

He continued down the stairs, but stopped on the last stair. "You're the queen of deceit."

"What else, Byron, since we're being honest?" she asked with a frown on her face.

Her words cut him like a knife. He calmed down before saying, "Now that I have your attention, I'm not sure whether Christopher is even my child. We had a paternity test done on the first. The results will be back this week and—"

She held her hands up in the air. "I don't want to hear any more. You've been talking to Tara behind my back after I told you the hell she's causing me at work." She picked up her bags and opened the door. "I'm out of here. I'll come back for the rest of my stuff later."

He yelled out to her as she walked, "But I'm your husband. What about your family?"

He heard her say, "Correction, my invisible husband. You don't really exist, now, do you?"

He watched her throw her stuff into her car. She looked up and their eyes locked. Even through the darkness of the night, he could see her pain. He tried to walk farther, but was paralyzed. She cranked the engine, backed up, and sped away.

He stood there for a moment before walking back into the house and shutting the door. Once inside, he let out a yell that would have woken the dead. He balled his fists and slid down the door onto the floor.

36

Byron couldn't sleep. When he finally did fall asleep, his alarm clock went off, indicating it was five thirty in the morning. He turned over. He thought about calling in sick, but didn't want to sit at home and wallow in his pain.

As he was driving to work, his cell phone rang. He looked down and saw the number on the display and felt disappointed.

"Hello," he answered barely above a whisper.

"I'd get a better greeting at a morgue," Frederick stated from the other end.

"Nikki found out."

"I take it she wasn't too happy with the idea of you having a son."

"Man, it's the way she found out. I still don't know how she found out, but—"

Frederick cut him off. "You weren't the one who told her?"

"Exactly." He blew his horn and blurted out a few obscenities at the driver in front of him.

"That's my ear you're yelling in!" Frederick yelled back.

"I'm sorry. People in Dallas need to learn how to drive." Frustrated, Byron continued weaving in and out of traffic.

"What are you going to do?"

"I hadn't thought about it. I got too much going on. I can't deal with this right now."

"I hate to say it."

"But you told me so. I've already beat myself up about not telling her about it."

"That's not what I was going to say. You guys did rush into things, so maybe this will give you some time to really think about what you want from your relationship."

Byron, annoyed at Frederick's comment, abruptly ended the call. "Hey, traffic is getting a little too thick. I'll call you later."

He hit the End button on the phone. He turned up the volume on the radio, but not even the *Tom Joyner Morning Show* crew and their jokes cheered him up.

Nikki dragged into the office wearing a dull beige pair of slacks and an off-white blouse. Her shoes didn't match her outfit and she still wore her shades.

Mya attempted to stop her, but Nikki held her hand up. When she got to her desk, she turned on the computer and put on her headphones.

Kenneth came over to her desk. "Are you all right? You look like Medusa's twin sister," he said with a look of disgust on his face.

Without removing her shades, she snapped, "I'm not in the mood, so I would suggest you leave me alone."

He backed away. "I'm sorry. Mya stopped by my desk and I was only trying to check up on you."

She forced a smile. "Thanks for your concern, but I'm fine."

"You sure?"

"Yeah," she said, not believing it herself.

She couldn't see the computer screen, so she was forced to remove her shades. She glanced at herself in the mirror she had on her desk. Her eyes were puffy and red from crying all night. *I do look bad.*

Her attention was on the computer when her e-mail indicator sounded. She went through her normal morning ritual by responding to internal and external e-mails. She deleted Tara's e-mail without even opening it.

She checked her voice messages. There were several from Byron. *Whatever, sucker. You had your chance,* she thought. She deleted them without listening to them in their entirety. There was one message from Tara. She deleted it and was about to call her and cancel their lunch date but paused. *There are a few things I want to say to that heifer. She's messed with the wrong woman. I'll show her who's in control of things around here.*

She typed up a memo and put it in her Save file. She would send it to her manager as a last resort. A smile came over her face as she plotted revenge on her nemesis.

Joyce walked into Byron's office carrying a steno pad and a cup of coffee. She handed him the cup. "I thought you could use this," she said.

"Thanks."

"I'm listening." She closed the door and sat down.

"Remind me to never hire another relative."

"Ha-ha. What's wrong?"

"I swear you act more like my mama than my employee."

"Avoiding the question will only prolong things." Joyce crossed her legs and leaned back in her chair.

Byron knew if he didn't talk to someone he would burst, so he told Joyce what happened and how he was feeling. "I don't know what to do."

Joyce uncrossed her legs and leaned forward. "Yes, that's a tough one."

"She's not returning any of my calls."

"Hmmm. Let me think about this and I'll get back with you." She stood up, picked up the steno pad she had laid on the desk, and began walking out.

"Thanks," Byron said to her.

She turned around. "For what?"

"For not saying, 'I told you so.'"

Joyce smiled and continued to walk out the door.

Byron kept hearing his brother's voice in his head. *Oh, what a tangled web you weave when first you practice to deceive.*

Byron picked up the phone and dialed Nikki's number. Just when he thought she was answering, her voice mail came on. Disappointed, he hung up without leaving another message.

Nikki looked at her e-mail and confirmed the location of her lunch with Tara. She looked at the time. She purposely decided to leave late. Their luncheon was going to be short and sweet and chances were that she might not have a job when she finished with Tara. She put on her shades, grabbed her purse and keys, and walked toward Kenneth and Mya, who moved out of her way after seeing the expression on her face.

She heard Mya say, "She looks like she's on the warpath."

No one said anything to her on the elevator or in the lobby, as if they all knew she was a woman on a mission.

She found her car, and when exiting the parking garage, she flirted with the parking attendant because her monthly parking pass had expired. He gave her a new one for free and she sped to the restaurant.

Nikki was able to find a parking space near the door. A gentleman walking out the door held it open for her. She smiled at him.

The hostess asked, "How many in your party?"

"They're already here," she stated as she walked away to look for Tara.

Tara waved at her. She walked slowly toward the table. *I can do this. Don't let her see you sweat,* Nikki repeated in her head with each step.

"Hi," Nikki said as she removed her shades and placed her purse on the chair before sitting.

"Thought you weren't coming at first," Tara said.

Smiling, Nikki commented, "I wouldn't have missed this for the world."

Tara handed her a menu. "I didn't know what you wanted, so I ordered us both iced tea."

"Thank you. That was very considerate of you." Nikki smiled.

Tara looked at her strangely. "Are you okay?"

"Yes. Why shouldn't I be?" Nikki leaned in closer as if expecting Tara to say something about the baby.

"You seem different."

While opening the straw, she confirmed, "I am. Things couldn't be better."

A waitress came over and took their orders. "Thanks for meeting me for lunch today."

Nikki sipped her tea and didn't comment. Tara went on to say, "I wanted to talk to you about something personal, but I changed my mind."

"Why? I thought we were becoming friends."

Tara spat out her drink. She took her napkin and wiped her mouth. "Excuse me?"

"You heard me. You e-mail me during the day. I've even kept your little brat."

Tara threw her napkin on the table. "Hold up. You can say what you want to about me, but *do not* bring my child into this."

"You mean yours and Byron's child."

"Who told you that?"

"So you're not denying it. All of this time you knew he was the father and you pretended to be this helpless single mother."

"I never said I didn't know who the father was."

"But you never told me it was Byron."

Tara had a gratifying look on her face. "I didn't feel it was my place."

"As a woman, you should have come to me and told me," Nikki said, getting a little loud and drawing some attention in their direction.

"What good would that have done?"

"I don't know, but at least I would have known you were on the up and up. You're just like Byron said you were, trash."

"Nikki, I wouldn't go there if I were you. I haven't turned in my recommendations to your manager on who I think should be downsized," Tara stated with a smile on her face.

"If my name is on the list, I'll make sure you're the one out the door. Now how would you take care of your little precious child then?" Nikki stood up.

Tara pushed her chair away from the table. "Look, b—"

Before Tara could get it out, the restaurant manager came to the table. "Is everything all right over here?" he asked.

They both looked at him and then back at each other. Nikki was the first to speak. "Everything's just lovely." She walked away.

Tara was about to walk behind her, but the restaurant manager stuck his hand out. Nikki heard him say, "Ma'am, you need to pay for the tab first."

Nikki felt a little relief as she walked out of the restaurant and got into her car. She placed her head on the steering wheel and thought to herself, *I'm losing control. I don't know what to do. My whole world is crumbling.* She was brought out of her state of confusion by a knock on her window.

"What the hell?" she blurted out.

Tara was yelling, "You need to get out of the car because we need to get this straight right now."

Through the glass, Nikki yelled, "I suggest you move out of my way." She started up the car and made the engine roar. She began backing up. Tara was yelling some obscenities and following her. Nikki came within inches from hitting Tara. She could see the surprise in Tara's eyes. She then put the car in drive and drove off. Looking through her rearview mirror, she saw a security guard walking toward Tara.

37

Later that afternoon, Charlotte and Nikki sat in her living room talking. Charlotte laughed at Nikki's reenactment of the day's events.

"Girl, she could say you tried to run her over," Charlotte informed Nikki.

"I wish she would." Nikki curled her legs up under her.

"So she never came back to work?"

"Nope. I was waiting on her too. I'm not through with her yet."

"Slow your roll. Your issue is with Byron. You can't be mad at her, because it was not her place to tell you."

"Whose side are you on anyway?"

"Yours, of course. As much as I would love to see a woman like that get what's coming to her, you need to channel your energy on getting things straight with Byron."

"I'm the one who was lied to and here you are taking up for him."

"I'm your best friend and when have you known me to lie to you?"

"There was this one time, when I asked you about my black-sequined sling-back pumps."

Charlotte laughed. "Other than that?"

"I don't remember."

After getting Nikki to laugh, Charlotte continued, "Byron lied to you. But he also tried to protect you. He's not even sure if the child is his."

"Have you been talking to Byron?"

"I promised I wouldn't say, but trust me. Byron is as torn about this thing as you are. Call him. Talk to him."

Nikki leaned her head back and sighed. "I can't. I'm afraid I won't be able to get past this if Christopher ends up being his."

"Do you love him?"

"Yes."

"Then make a way."

"I can't."

"You can't or you won't?" Charlotte asked.

Nikki held her head down and closed her eyes.

Byron was working up a sweat in his home gym when his phone rang.

"Hello," he said, out of breath.

"Hi, Byron, this is Adrienne. May I speak with Nikki?" she asked.

Taking his towel and wiping the sweat from his face, he responded, "She's not here."

"Do you know when she'll be in?"

"You need to call her on her cell."

"Anything wrong?"

"I suggest you speak with Nikki. I don't mean to be rude, Adrienne, but I was in the middle of a workout."

"I understand. I'll talk to you later."

"Sure," he said before hanging up.

I'm not going to be the one to tell your family we're not

together, he thought in his head. *How long will your little charade work now?*

He frowned because he knew how important it was for Nikki to save face with her family. He left his workout room and went and took a shower. While in the shower, he thought of a way to get Nikki back. *If she would only talk to me, I know I can get her to see things my way.*

He dried off. After putting on a pair of boxers, he picked up the phone and dialed Frederick's number.

"Freddie, I need your help," he said after Frederick answered the phone.

"Your wish is my command," Frederick responded.

He talked over his strategy with Frederick and felt much better after speaking with him. He knew it would be hard to convince Nikki to forgive him, but with Frederick's help, and he hoped Charlotte's, his plan might work.

"Who was that?" Nikki asked Charlotte after she had just ended a phone call.

"That was Frederick," Charlotte answered truthfully.

"He sure had a lot to talk about. Could it have waited until you left?"

Charlotte smiled. "No, it was important."

"I've done it again," Nikki stated before going on. "I've been so wrapped up in my own drama that I didn't even ask you how things were going with you two."

"We're only friends."

"That's what your mouth says."

"I don't think Frederick is ready for all of this," Charlotte joked as she framed her body with her hands.

"I see."

Nikki's cell phone rang. "Girl, let me see who this is." She looked at the display. "It's Adrienne. I'll call her back from the house phone."

Charlotte stood to leave. "Let me go. I need to make one stop before going home."

"Thanks, girl," Nikki said as she walked her to the door, hugged her, and locked it.

She dialed Adrienne's number. Adrienne picked up on the first ring, saying, "Girl, where have you been?"

"Hello to you too, big sis," Nikki replied with a chuckle.

"I called you, and Byron told me I needed to call you on your cell."

Nikki curled up on the couch, turned the TV on, and pressed the Mute button while flipping stations. "We're no longer together."

Sounding shocked, Adrienne asked, "What happened?"

"I don't want to talk about it."

"Do I need to go over and give him a piece of my mind?"

Nikki imagined Adrienne confronting Byron. "No. I can handle it."

"Running away from your problems is no way of handling anything."

"It's how I choose to deal with it."

"I told you rushing off to get married was a bad idea. Girl, marriage is serious. You can't up and leave the first time you have a fight. Whatever the problem is, you need to face it head-on."

"How can I?" Nikki asked.

"Take it from somebody who's been married over ten years." Nikki started crying as Adrienne continued to talk. "I remember when Edward and I had our first big fight. I packed my bags and was about to move back home, but Mama convinced me to stick it out. I'm glad I did. I know I might fuss and complain, but there's no other man out there like my Edward. I see how Byron looks at you. He has that same kind of love."

"I wish . . ." Nikki couldn't finish because of the tears.

"What, sweetie?"

Nikki almost confessed to her fake marriage, but couldn't. "I wish it was that easy."

"I'm here if you need to talk. Call Pam. She was concerned about you too."

"I will."

"Love you, girl."

"I love you too," Nikki said before they hung up. She dialed Pam's number and Louis answered the phone. "Is Pam still up?"

"She sure is," Louis said as he took the phone away from his ear. "Honey, Nikki's on the phone." He then placed the phone back to his ear and asked, "You all right over there? Your sisters have been on the phone all night talking about you."

"That's what I feared. Tell her to hurry up or I'll have to talk to her later."

"Here she is," Louis said.

"Girl, what's going on?" Pam said after taking the phone from Louis.

"It's bad, Pam. I found out something about Byron and I don't know if we'll be able to get past the lies."

"Hold on, Nik. Let me go downstairs so we can talk in private."

Nikki could imagine Louis listening to their conversation. She loved her brother-in-law, but he was as nosy as they came. He was almost as nosy as Kenneth. The thought made her chuckle.

"I'm back," Pam said.

"Girl, before I bog you down with my issues, did you ever confront Louis with your suspicions?"

Pam whispered, "No. I found out he's been so secretive because he's planning a Hawaiian vacation as a surprise for me for our anniversary that's coming up."

"Wow, that's great news. I'm glad he wasn't creeping."

"You and me both. I feel like a fool for having the thought cross my mind in the first place."

"Men will do it to you."

"Yes, they will. Now back to you. I'm all ears."

Nikki told Pam more details about what had happened. Some things she failed to mention. She left out the comments Byron made to her about being deceitful herself, though. "Now you have it," Nikki said.

"You need to talk to him and get his side of the story."

"I heard what he had to say."

"When Nikki gets upset, she says what she has to say and tunes out the rest."

"You know me, don't you?"

"All your life."

She hung up with Pam. She dialed Byron's number, but put the phone on the cradle before the first ring.

I'm not ready yet, she thought as she turned the TV off and went to bed.

38

When Byron walked into his office, he was startled to see the back of a woman's head in a chair across from his desk.

Tara turned around and Byron shouted, "What the hell?"

"Good morning to you too," she said.

He walked to his desk and picked up the phone. "You have one minute to get out or I'll be calling security."

She stood up. "I wouldn't do that if I were you or else everybody in this office will know your business."

"Tara, I couldn't care less at this point."

"If you don't want me to file charges against your wife, you won't do it."

He hung the phone up. "I'm giving you five minutes."

"Did she tell you about our confrontation?"

"Yes."

Tara smiled. "You're lying."

"Four minutes."

"I have to hand it to your wife, she's got some backbone. She had the nerve to threaten me."

"With due reason, I'm sure."

"I came over here so that we can work out a deal."

"You and your lame ideas."

She stood and waved her hand around. "See, if you agree to my terms, I'll make sure I don't press charges against your wife for trying to run over me."

Byron laughed. "Now I know you're out of your mind. Nikki wouldn't do something like that."

"I have witnesses. So I'll have my lawyer draw up some papers," she said as she turned around to head out of the door.

But before she could reach the door Byron said, "Tara."

"Yes." Her hair swung over her shoulders as she stopped and turned around.

"Go to hell."

Tara turned her nose up and walked rapidly out of the room, bumping into Joyce.

"What was she doing here?" Joyce asked with an attitude.

"You don't even want to know. Hold my calls. This is going to be a long day," Byron responded.

Nikki kept a low profile while at work. She reread the memo she had written the day before. She printed it off and was on her way to the copier when she saw Tara walking through the door. She glanced at her watch and thought, *It's after ten and here she comes strolling in like she owns the world.* She pretended that she didn't see Tara, but to no avail.

"We need to talk," Tara stated.

"I said what I had to say yesterday," Nikki said flatly as she kept walking. Tara came up behind her and put her hand on her shoulder. Nikki jerked back. "Don't you ever put your hands on me."

People began staring. Tara tried to talk low. "We're both professionals and we don't need everybody in our business."

"You don't want everybody to know you're a lying, trifling b—" Nikki said loudly.

Kenneth pulled Nikki to the side. "Girl, calm down. You're making a scene and this is so unlike you."

"Move, Kenneth, I'm just getting started up in here," Nikki said.

"No, Nikki, you don't want to do this," Kenneth assured her as he took her by the arm. They began walking away. Nikki could hear Tara say something in the background. She turned around and sneered at Tara. She and Kenneth continued to walk away. Tara ran up behind her. Before Kenneth or anyone else could intervene, Nikki did a karate move. She grabbed Tara's hand when she placed it on her shoulder and flipped her to the floor.

"I'd advise you to keep your hands to yourself the next time," Nikki said after brushing her hands together.

Tara was about to launch at Nikki, but Kenneth stood between them and said, "I wouldn't do that if I were you."

Onlookers gawked but didn't try to control the situation.

"Come on, Kenneth. I've had enough of this cow," Nikki said.

As they walked away, Tara yelled, "Go ahead and walk. You can run, but you can't hide the fact your husband is my baby's daddy."

Nikki refused to cry in front of Kenneth or anyone else. She pretended she didn't hear Tara. As soon as they got outside in the hallway near the elevator, Kenneth put his arms around Nikki and hugged her. She couldn't control the tears and they streamed down her face.

"Maybe you should take the rest of the day off," Kenneth suggested.

She hesitated. "I don't know."

"Our manager is out of the office today, so it shouldn't be a problem. I'll cover your accounts."

"Thanks, you're a godsend." She gave him a tight hug and released him.

"I'll go get your stuff and meet you downstairs," Kenneth said.

"I won't be able to show my face here again," she said in between sniffles.

"You can and you will. Now pull yourself together, girl," he said after punching the Down button on the elevator.

She dried her face and when the elevator opened up, she stepped on. Just as the elevator door was about to close she stuck her hand out and stopped it. "Kenneth?" she called out to him.

When he turned around he looked into the apologetic and grateful eyes of Nikki, and before she could start her spiel, let alone finish it, he said, "Don't even mention it." With a wink he gave her a reassuring smile as the elevator door closed.

Byron listened to his cell phone messages. He was relieved to hear that the doctor's office had called. He dialed Joyce's extension and when she picked up he said, "Joyce, the results are in."

Before he could hang up with her, she was in his office. "What did he say?" Joyce asked.

"I haven't called him back yet."

Joyce ran and closed the door. She walked back over to the desk and pressed the speaker button on the phone. "Dial the number, because I'm just as anxious as you are."

Byron pulled a card out of his wallet and dialed the numbers.

"This is Byron Matthews returning your call. Your message said our test results were in," he said to the nurse who had answered the phone.

The nurse put him on hold. Joyce paced in front of the desk. He looked at her and said, "You're making me nervous."

"Sorry," she said as she stopped and took a seat.

"Mr. Matthews, can you come into the office tomorrow?" the nurse asked. "We'll be able to give you the results then."

Disappointed, Byron asked, "Is there any way you can give me the results over the phone?"

"For something like this, the doctor likes to talk to the party, or parties, involved in person."

"What about this evening?"

"The doctor has surgery and has canceled all of his evening appointments."

Feeling dejected, Byron said, "Tomorrow's fine. Give me your earliest appointment."

He was placed on hold again. Joyce remained quiet.

"Mr. Matthews, we can see you at eleven o'clock tomorrow morning," the nurse said.

"I'll be there. Thanks." The phone disconnected and he looked at Joyce. "What do you think?"

"It's going to be a long night." Joyce sighed.

He placed his hands behind the back of his head and leaned back in his chair. "Tell me about it. Maybe once this is resolved, I'll be able to fix things with Nikki."

"Have you talked to her?"

"Nope. She's not returning my calls, so I decided to go to plan B."

Joyce stood up and asked, "What's plan B?"

"I don't know. I'm still trying to figure out plan A." A half smile crossed his face.

39

"Pam, I don't know what came over me. I used one of those self-defense moves and the next thing I knew, she was on the floor," Nikki said as she sat across from Pam at Pam's kitchen table.

"Sounds like she deserved it, and much more," Pam commented.

"I could have handled it better."

"Are you going in to work tomorrow?" Pam asked as she drank her soda.

"Tomorrow's Friday so I was thinking about taking a long weekend."

"You have to face the music one day, so I think you should go."

Nikki looked down at the table. "I can kiss my promotion good-bye."

"For now anyway."

"Thanks for the confidence."

"Hey, nobody told you to act like Foxy Brown." Pam laughed.

Nikki laughed for the first time in days. She put up her fists and moved them in the air. "I should have punched her in the face. That would have really made me feel better."

"No, that would have gotten your butt arrested."

"Probably. But it would have been worth it."

Adrienne walked into the kitchen. "Your husband told me you both were back here," she said.

"I was telling Pam about what happened at work today," Nikki said.

Nikki repeated bits and pieces of the day's events. Adrienne dropped her mouth and said, "Girl, you could lose your job over something like this."

"I'm not worried. I can get another job, but I refuse to let someone come in my face like she did," Nikki said.

"I'm shocked," Adrienne commented.

"I don't know why," Nikki said.

"Because the Nikki I know would have walked away," Adrienne explained.

Nikki looked at both of her sisters before she responded, "Well, the new Nikki is tired of living her life the way other people see fit. I'm tired of letting people get the best of me."

"What you should have done was call us and we could have jumped her as she got in the car," Adrienne said as she tried to lighten the conversation.

They all laughed.

"Thanks, but I got this," Nikki said as she grabbed her collar with each hand. Just then her cell phone rang, but she ignored it.

Pam asked, "Aren't you going to answer that?"

"Nope. It's probably Byron or Kenneth and I don't feel like talking to either one of them right now," she answered.

The phone stopped ringing, but it started up again. Adrienne stood up and said, "Where's your phone? This is ridiculous." Nikki pointed toward her purse. Adrienne unzipped it and picked it up. "Hello," she said into the receiver.

Nikki blurted out, "Give me my phone."

"No. You didn't want to answer it, so now I'm going to find out who's calling you."

"This is Frederick," she heard the voice on the other end of the line say.

"Does she know you?" Adrienne asked. She continued to say, "Oh, I remember you now. This is her sister. With everything going on, I had to make sure."

Nikki waved her hands and whispered, "No."

"She's right here," Adrienne said before handing Nikki the phone.

Nikki sneered. "Frederick, how are you?" She faked enthusiasm. "Uh-huh," she said as Pam and Adrienne looked on. "I'll call you back when I have a little more privacy." She looked at her sisters. "I promise." She pressed the End button on the phone and laid it on the table.

"So," Pam said as Adrienne looked on.

"He called to invite me to their mom's birthday dinner," Nikki stated.

"Really now?" Adrienne commented.

"Doesn't she know you two are having issues?" Pam asked.

"Apparently Byron hasn't said anything and I'm not going to either," Nikki said, folding her arms.

Adrienne leaned on the table and asked, "So are you going?"

"I don't know," Nikki said before she chugged down the last of her soda. She looked from one sister to another, hoping to see an answer on their faces. When she didn't see one, she closed her eyes and held her head back.

Pam reached out and placed her hand over Nikki's left hand. She offered words of comfort. "It'll work out, Nikki, it'll work out just fine."

* * *

Byron was working out when the doorbell rang. "Hold on, I'm coming," he yelled.

He didn't bother to look through the peephole. He opened the door and Frederick was standing there holding a bag. Frederick walked around him and scrunched up his nose.

"Ooh. Somebody needs to take a shower," he said.

Byron hit him with his towel. "I was working out. Make yourself at home and I'll be right down."

Byron left Frederick downstairs while he took a quick shower. Frederick was sitting in his living room eating chicken when he came back downstairs.

"Man, get that greasy box off my table," Byron ordered him.

With a mouthful, Frederick said, "You know you want some." He pointed at the box. "I bought enough for you too."

Byron sat down in the chair. "Yeah, I am kind of hungry."

Frederick passed him a box. "Eat up."

After eating and light conversation, Frederick informed Byron, "Nikki will be there."

Relieved, Byron said, "Perfect. Hearing what the test results are will help me with my next approach."

Wiping his mouth with a napkin, Frederick commented, "I still don't know why you're so hell-bent on getting back with Nikki."

"It's called love. Something you wouldn't know anything about."

"Now that's a low blow. I've been in love before."

"Name one time."

"When I was in the fifth grade I fell in love with Ms. Applebee."

"Silly, she was your teacher."

"You have to admit, she was fine." Frederick couldn't control his laughter.

Frederick's cell phone rang. While he talked on the phone, Byron finished eating. He then took his box and Frederick's and threw them in the kitchen trash.

I'll get Nikki a puppy, Byron thought to himself. *She's always wanted a dog. Maybe she'll forgive me then.*

Frederick had his X-box turned on when he reentered the living room. "Let me beat you at a game of football," he said to Byron.

"The day you beat me is the day I walk around in a skirt."

"What color pumps do you want to wear with them?" Frederick laughed as he handed him the remote.

After beating Frederick at a game of football, Byron felt a little relief.

"Thanks, man, for coming over. It took my mind off some of this mess," Byron said.

Frederick gave him a brotherly hug at the front door. "You know I got your back."

"I hope your idea about inviting Nikki to Mama's party works."

"It will. Trust me. I should have been Cupid in my other life," Frederick joked as he headed out the door.

40

Byron checked his messages the next morning before leaving for work. He was in the process of deleting one of Tara's messages when he heard Nikki's name mentioned. He replayed Tara's messages several times. He then went to his bedroom and found the piece of paper that had Charlotte's number written on it and dialed it.

After interrogating Charlotte about Nikki and Tara for two minutes, Byron asked, "Did you know anything about this?"

"Yes. She called me last night. I was surprised she told me, because it was so out of character for her."

"It's all my fault. If I would have told her everything, all of this could have been avoided."

"Don't blame yourself. Tara's the one to blame."

"If you talk to Nikki, tell her I asked about her. Pleassse," Byron begged.

"I will. She invited me to tag along to your mom's birthday party."

"I guess I should be glad she didn't turn Frederick down."

"She'll come around."

"I'll believe it when I see it."

"Pray about it. God will work it out."

"You're right. I'll let you go. Thanks for everything."

"I want to see my girl happy, and being with you made her happy," Charlotte added.

"Thanks." Byron hung up the phone. He called Joyce and left a message on her voice mail. "I'm too anxious about the tests to concentrate on anything. I'll be working from home today. Call me at home or on the cell if anything comes up."

He took off his jacket and lay on his back on the bed. He closed his eyes, but didn't go to sleep. His thoughts were on Nikki and Christopher. *Christopher, if you're mine, I want you to come live with me. I hope Nikki will love us both.*

He dozed off.

Nikki vowed to hold her head up high when she walked into the office. Some of her coworkers stared and didn't say anything when they saw her.

Nikki wanted to say "boo" and see what their response would be. She chuckled at the idea.

When she got to her desk, a yellow sticky note was stuck to her computer monitor. She picked it up and read it. *I need you to come to my office as soon as you get in. I heard about the incident yesterday, but I need to hear your side of the story.* It was from her manager.

"I might as well get this over with," Nikki said out loud.

She placed her purse in her bottom drawer and locked it. She headed to her manager's office. He was on the phone when she entered the doorway. She knocked on the door.

"Come in," he said to her.

She sat down and waited for him to get off the phone. When he looked up, he had a disturbed look on his face. He got up and closed the door.

"Ms. Montana, I need you to explain what happened yesterday," he said, cutting straight to the point.

Nikki explained yesterday's events. As she told him what happened, she felt embarrassed about her actions. She could barely look him in the face. "I know my actions were not appropriate and I accept any reprimand you hand out."

"I'm glad to hear you regret your actions. I have to say I was a little disturbed to hear about my best employee acting like that." Nikki looked down at the floor. Her manager added, "However, I understand Tara has some personal issues with you, and from what you've told me, an altercation or something would have erupted sooner or later. I just hate that it happened here."

"Me too."

"In light of what you've told me, we'll have to place you on temporary suspension. It will be without pay, but at least you'll still have a job."

"Thanks, sir. I understand."

"You can work the rest of the day, but take next week off."

Nikki stood up. "I might be out of place, but can you tell me what's going to happen to Tara?"

"Unfortunately, I'm not at liberty to say right now."

"Okay," she said. She dragged her feet as she walked to the door and opened it. She looked back at her manager and he looked at her and shook his head. She continued to her desk feeling like she lost her best friend.

Kenneth waved at her, paused, but seemed to have changed his mind about stopping. He continued to his destination as she walked back to her desk.

Not even Kenneth can face me right now, she thought.

Byron woke up feeling a little more relaxed. He had to gather his senses. He looked at the clock and it read ten thirty. He jumped up, hurried and used the bathroom, and washed his hands and face. He rushed to get to the doctor's office. He was surprised at how little traffic appeared to be on the roads, because Friday traffic was normally backed up no matter what time of day. Even with the light traffic, he barely made it to the doctor's office before his appointment. The receptionist checked him in and then the nurse came to the door and called out his name.

This is the moment I've been waiting for. Lord, whatever Your will is, let it be. I'm willing to live up to my responsibilities, Byron thought as he followed the nurse into a vacant room. He sat in a chair and waited for the doctor.

"Hi, young man. How are you?" Dr. Phillips asked when he entered the room.

Byron shook his hand. "I've been better."

"I see the nurse tried contacting—" He looked in the file. "Tara, but she couldn't make it today."

"She doesn't have to be here for you to give me the results, does she?" Byron asked.

"I wanted to go over this with the both of you. After going over the results, it's probably best you're here alone."

Byron held his breath. "I'm ready."

"You understand the test results are 99.9 percent accurate."

"Yes." Byron looked directly into Dr. Phillips's eyes.

"You are—" The doctor's pager went off. He looked down at the pager and had a sudden sense of urgency. "Hold on, Byron. I'll be right back."

Byron was hoping he left the file so that he could see for himself, but to no avail. Byron got up and paced the floor. Ten minutes later, Dr. Phillips walked back into the room.

"Sorry about that. A colleague needed my professional opinion."

Trying to sound nonchalant, Byron said, "No problem."

"As I was saying before we got interrupted . . ." he paused. "You are not Christopher's father."

Byron let out a deep breath. A part of him felt relieved. "Did I hear you correctly?" He wanted to double check.

"Yes. You are not the father."

Byron stood up and shook his hand. "You don't know how happy you've made me."

"I wasn't sure if this was good or bad news for you, so I wanted to see you in person."

"I know it's none of your business, but his mother and I are no longer together and this would only have complicated matters."

"I understand. If you need anything else or have any other questions, feel free to call me."

"Thanks, Dr. Phillips." Byron smiled as he walked out the door.

41

Nikki made sure she kept herself busy. It was easy, with customers ringing her phone off the hook. When the automated system crashed, she was forced to manually enter statistics.

She noticed Kenneth as he passed by her desk a few times, but he would only smile and wouldn't stop. This last time, she decided to follow him to wherever he was going.

"Hey, Kenneth, wait up," she said as she increased her steps to catch up with him.

As if he knew what was on her mind, he blurted out, "I didn't know if you felt like talking."

She looped her arm through his and they walked into an empty break room. "Thanks for what you did yesterday."

"I didn't do anything," he said, pretending to act oblivious.

She kissed him on the cheek. "If it wasn't for you, I would have lost more than my dignity."

"I know I can be a little pushy sometimes, but we are friends."

"You're the only one in here who tried to help. If nothing else, I know I can depend on you."

"I'm glad you feel that way." Kenneth opened his mouth to say something, but stopped as Mya and two other women walked in.

Mya joked to her companions, "Y'all better stay out of Nikki's way, or else she'll drop-kick you."

Mya laughed, but her other companions didn't. They pointed toward Kenneth and Nikki, who were now in clear view. The other women left the room.

"I'm sorry. I didn't know you were in here," Mya apologized.

"Apparently not," Kenneth said.

"Oh, I got this," Nikki intervened. "Mya, I'm glad to see you find all of this funny. But in the future, make sure the person you're talking about isn't around to hear it."

"Seriously, Nikki, I didn't mean anything by it. I never did like Ms. Thing. I was glad to see somebody put her in her place."

"Whatever." Nikki rolled her eyes and walked out of the break room.

Kenneth caught up to her. "Don't let Mya get to you," he said.

"I won't. I have bigger fish to fry, as my grandmother used to say."

They walked the rest of the way in silence. Before going to her desk, she turned and told Kenneth, "I'll be out of the office all next week on unpaid leave."

"They shouldn't have suspended you—"

Nikki held her hand up and interrupted him. "I would have suspended me too. I'm lucky they didn't fire me."

"If you need anything, call me."

"I will. I have a few more things to do and then I'll be heading out."

She sat down at her desk, but couldn't concentrate. She

looked at the time. Even though it was early afternoon, she felt as though she had put in a full day's work. She activated her out-of-office message on her e-mail account and voice mail.

After making sure everything was secure, she left the office. She decided to stop by Valley View Mall. *Shopping always takes my mind off my problems.*

Byron was paying for a pair of tennis shoes when he swore he saw Nikki pass by.

"I don't mean to rush you, but there's someone out there I need to catch up with," he told the teenaged cashier.

The cashier handed him his change. Byron inadvertently snatched the bag and walked quickly out of the store. He looked in the direction he had seen Nikki, but couldn't see her. He peered into some of the stores as he walked by. *I know I'm not seeing things. It had to be her,* he thought.

As he looked into another store, he accidentally bumped into Nikki. She looked as surprised as he did.

"I'm sorry," he said as he helped her pick up the bags she had dropped.

"I have it," she said as she motioned for him to stop.

"No, let me," he insisted as he picked the bags up and handed them to her.

Byron wanted to take her into his arms and hug and kiss her and tell her all of the things he didn't think to say when they were together.

"Thanks," she said in a soft voice.

"If you're not doing anything tonight, let me treat you to dinner."

She stuttered, "I'm meeting Charlotte. Thanks for helping me with the bags, but I have to go." She walked away.

He ran behind her. "You're still coming to the birthday party, aren't you?"

"I'll be there," she responded without turning around.

"See you then," he said, unsure if she heard him as she increased her pace.

After the mall encounter, Nikki didn't feel like shopping anymore. It took everything she had not to reach out and hug Byron. She missed him so much, but she didn't know if she should trust him after the Tara fiasco.

What if the child is his? she thought. *I don't think I could stand it. Little Christopher's adorable, but there's no way I can be nice to anything that belongs to Tara.*

She beat herself up about it all the way home. Charlotte was sitting on her steps when she pulled up.

"What is she doing here?" Nikki asked out loud.

She turned off the engine and exited the car. She grabbed her bags and Charlotte met her halfway. She handed a few to her.

"I had just got here right before you pulled up," Charlotte said. "I was about to leave, though."

"That's why you should call before dropping by unannounced," Nikki said as she unlocked the front door.

"I was in the neighborhood."

"Yeah, right," Nikki snapped as they went into the house.

"Where do you want these?" Charlotte asked.

"They go in my room."

They walked into her bedroom. Charlotte laid the bags on the bed and sat on the edge. "So what did you buy me?" she asked.

"The same thing I bought you the last time I went shopping," Nikki joked.

She removed clothes from the bag as Charlotte sat and watched. She held up a short black dress.

"That's cute. Let me see it," Charlotte said before standing up.

Nikki held the dress in front of her as she admired herself in the mirror. "I bought it for Mrs. Matthews's party."

"So you really are going?"

"Yes."

She held up another dress that Nikki had laid across the bed. It was a hot-pink short floral dress. "Can I borrow this?"

Nikki smiled. "I'll think about it."

After informing his mother, brother, and Joyce about the test results, Byron tried to find a way to relax. He flipped from station to station, but nothing was able to hold his attention for long. Frustrated because he couldn't get his mind off Nikki, he went upstairs and worked out. His body was sore, but he refused to stop. If his phone hadn't rung, he would have worked out until he fell out.

"Hello," he answered, sounding out of breath.

"Don't hang up," Tara said barely above a whisper.

Byron laughed as if insane. He sat on the bench wiping sweat off his forehead. He remained quiet.

"Hear me out," Tara begged.

"There's nothing else we have to say. You've lied and tried to manipulate your way into my life for the last time. How could you use an innocent child? You're not fit to be a mother."

He heard Tara crying. He felt no sympathy.

"I'm sorry. I didn't know what else to do," she cried.

"Your tears won't work. You knew exactly what you were doing. I don't know when you told Nikki about the situation, but because of you, she's gone. I'm sure that should make you stop crying."

"I didn't mean to—"

He wouldn't let her continue. "Like you didn't mean to jump her at her job."

"You got it all wrong. She's the one who threw me on the floor. Do you know I lost my job because of your wife?" she yelled.

"That's your problem, not mine."

"Byron, please talk to her. She could talk to them and maybe they'll give me back my job."

Byron laughed. "You seriously need some help. I pray Christopher grows up to be sane with an insane mother." He hung up the phone without waiting to hear Tara's response. *Lord, thank you for not letting me be tied to that woman for life.*

He took a shower, and for the first time in days, he was able to sleep peacefully.

42

It had been a few weeks since Byron ran into Nikki at the mall. After countless sleepless nights, Byron woke up refreshed and ready to begin the next stage of his life. He had a lot of errands to run before his mom's birthday dinner. He was excited and was surprised Nikki had agreed to come. It gave him hope about the state of their relationship.

For the first time since she'd left, he entered the guest room Nikki had occupied. Her fragrance still lingered in the room. The sun was beaming through the blinds. The sparkle of the ring he gave Nikki caught his attention. It was sitting on the nightstand. *I don't remember her taking it off,* he thought.

He felt a sense of sadness deep within his soul. He picked up the ring and placed it in his pocket. He walked out of the room, not sure if he should hold on to the hope that he and Nikki would reconcile. *I must snap out of this. Things are going to work out. Be positive. Isn't that what I always tell others? I need to take my own advice.*

Byron walked to his room and opened his dresser drawer

and pulled out an envelope. In the envelope was a receipt for the ring. He tucked the receipt into the same pocket as the ring.

Nikki, I love you and no matter what it takes, I want you back.

After turning on the alarm, he left the house to run some very important errands.

Nikki ignored her alarm clock. She hit SNOOZE several times. It annoyed her when it went off for the fourth time.

"All right, I'm getting up," she fussed at the clock. She threw the pillow off the bed before turning the alarm off. She wiped the sleep from her eyes and dragged herself out of bed. She stumbled to the bathroom and turned on the shower.

"Maybe this will wake me up," she said as she stretched. She heard her phone ring, but didn't have the energy to run and answer it. "Whoever it is, I'll call them back."

She stepped into the shower and let the hot water run over her body. With her eyes closed, she remembered how Byron felt in her arms. How special he made her feel. She had never felt this type of bond with any other man.

When she was twenty, she thought she was in love, but when she told the guy she was a virgin, he began acting funny. He always made excuses about why he was busy. It hurt her because she was at a point where she was willing to sleep with him and suffer the consequences. Fortunately, he saved her from what would have been a big mistake. From that day forward, she vowed to remain true to herself and save herself for the man who would be her husband.

Although she had dated a lot of men over the years since then, not one came close to capturing her heart. In a short time, Byron was able to break down all of the barriers and melt her heart with his kind words and demeanor. Up until the fiasco with Tara, she was willing to forsake her virginity and give in to Byron's needs. For once, she was willing to put someone else's needs over hers.

Even with the confusion of the past few weeks, she knew in her heart, it would be difficult to get Byron out of her system. When Frederick asked her to attend their mother's birthday dinner, she started to decline. For some strange reason, though, she didn't.

She had been in the shower so long, the water was becoming lukewarm. *Ugh. I guess it's time I start my day,* she thought. She turned the water off and dried off. She went through her closet and chose a red jogging suit. She found her matching tennis shoes and threw on an old baseball cap. It was time for a new hairstyle, and although she hated going to the beauty shop on a Saturday, she had to look her best.

After calling her beautician and confirming she could be squeezed in, she left the house.

"Happy birthday, Mom," Byron said after singing to her on the phone.

"Thank you, dear," she replied.

"I promise not to be late." He pulled up into the parking lot of Valley View Mall.

"I'll hold you to it. You're bringing that pretty girlfriend of yours, aren't you?" she asked.

Byron paused before responding. "She's coming, but she's driving her own car."

"Is everything okay? I sense some hesitation."

"Everything's fine. We had a disagreement, but we'll work it out." He tried to sound confident.

"I hope so. She's a special young lady."

"Yes, she is. Not to change the subject, but I'm glad the baby issue worked out."

"I am too, sweetie. I feel sorry for the poor child, though."

"If I knew who the real father was, I would contact him and let him know he should seek custody," Byron said, turning off the ignition.

"Baby, that's not your responsibility. Just make sure you don't make me a grandmother before you're married. Okay?"

"Yes, Ma," Byron said as he rolled up the windows. "I'll see you later."

"Bye, Son."

Byron got out of the car and went to several stores looking for the perfect gift. He finally found what he was looking for. He had the clerk wrap it. He walked out of the mall with a smile on his face.

Now it's on to the bakery. I have to get the right dessert for this thing to work.

Nikki admired her new hairstyle in the mirror. She would have to get used to the length. Her family and friends would all be surprised. She went from a short hairstyle to a shoulder-length curly hairdo.

I hope Byron likes it. I'll only wear it like this to see if I want to grow my hair out.

Her beautician told her it would be easy maintenance and if all else failed, she could always pull it back into a ponytail until she could get it professionally done.

Looking in her closet, she pulled out the short black dress she had purchased specifically for today's event. She sprayed her favorite Calvin Klein fragrance on before putting on her stockings and dress. She removed the long dangling earrings and replaced them with a pair of pearl earrings her mother had given her for her sixteenth birthday. When she got ready to put the matching pearl necklace around her neck, her hand stopped. She felt the diamond necklace and reminisced on the day Byron had given it to her. She took a Kleenex and wiped the tears that streamed down her face. She placed the pearl necklace back in its case. She reapplied her makeup and faked a smile while looking in the mirror.

The doorbell rang. Nikki looked at herself one last time. Before leaving her bedroom, she picked up her shoes and her miniloop handbag she'd recently purchased from DGP Enterprises.

"I'm coming!" she yelled as she heard a loud knock on the door.

When she opened the door, Charlotte stood there looking annoyed. "Girl, what took you so long?" she fussed.

"I was getting dressed."

Charlotte looked at her and stood with her mouth open. She took her hand and ran it through Nikki's hair. "You bought some hair."

Nikki swirled around. "You like it?"

"Yes, but I thought you didn't like weaves."

"I want to grow my hair out, but wanted to see how I would look first." She leaned down and slipped on her black-sequined sling-back, three-inch-heeled sandals.

"I'm jealous." Charlotte pouted as she brushed her hand through her own hair.

"Girl, please. You know your hair *always* looks good."

"I know." Charlotte giggled. "I wanted to bring the attention back to myself."

"You need to quit." Nikki moved things around as she looked for her keys.

"I can drive," Charlotte said.

"Cool, but I still need to find my keys."

"You mean those?" Charlotte pointed to a set of keys on the coffee table.

"Thanks. I thought I looked there."

"If it had been a snake, it would have bitten you."

"Ha-ha."

"I almost forgot the gift I bought his mom."

Nikki grabbed a beautiful floral gift bag. After locking up, she and Charlotte left her house and headed to Byron's parents' house.

43

Nikki was nervous as Charlotte parked. "Turn around," she ordered her.

"I will not," Charlotte protested.

"I don't think I can do this. I'm tired of pretending."

Charlotte turned and looked at her before turning off the engine. "Girl, you got issues. You've been pretending with everybody for months, so what's one more day?"

Charlotte opened the car door. Nikki was pissed. "If you weren't my best friend, I swear I would drop-kick you."

"Like you did Tara?" Charlotte laughed as she reached in the backseat and grabbed the gift.

Nikki felt as if she had no choice. She picked up the gift bag and got out of the car and followed Charlotte up the walkway.

"Are you going to stand there or ring the doorbell?" Charlotte asked.

Nikki turned her nose up at her. "Move out of the way." She rang the doorbell, plastered a smile on her face, and waited for someone to answer.

She could hear a man's voice from the other end. When

Byron opened the door, she felt like running into his arms. Neither moved until Charlotte cleared her throat and said, "Excuse me, but it's hot out here." She then nudged Nikki inside. "Hi, Byron."

"Hi," he responded.

"I will leave you two alone. Byron, please direct me to where I need to take this," Charlotte said as she held up a gift.

He pointed toward a room to the right of him. Charlotte headed out of the room, leaving Byron and Nikki standing alone. Neither spoke.

"Let's go in here so we can have some privacy," Byron stated. She followed him into a spare bedroom and stood as he closed the door. "Have a seat."

"I'll stand," she insisted.

"Thank you for coming."

"Your mom's sweet. I hope she likes the gift." She held up the gift bag.

"Whatever it is, I know she'll appreciate it."

Byron's dimples made Nikki want to melt. They stood and stared into one another's eyes for a brief moment.

Nikki commented, "This is awkward."

"Only because you want it to be."

"Byron, you're the one who lied. Why couldn't you be up-front with me?" Nikki asked.

"Because I knew you would run."

"You left me no choice." She had one hand on her hip and the other holding the gift bag.

"You had a choice. You could have trusted me and talked to me about it before leaving me high and dry."

"I'm sorry, but hearing the man you're with is the father of a one-year-old with a woman you can't stand is enough to push anybody over the edge."

"Are you through?"

"No. I'm just getting started. I almost lost my job because of you not telling me *everything* about Tara. If I had known about Christopher, I could have dealt with the situation better."

"For the record, Christopher is not my child."

She clapped her hands three times. "Whoop-de-do."

"We're not getting anywhere, going back and forth on whether or not I could have or should have told you."

She folded her arms. "Whose fault is it?"

He walked closer to her. She stepped back, finding her back up against the wall. With a kind, gentle look on his face, Byron stared into her eyes and said, "I hope you can accept my apology. I love you and I did not set out to deceive you. I found out about the baby after I met you." He paused. Nikki remained quiet, so he continued. "I had planned on telling you everything the same night you left. I didn't want to risk losing you, but you left me anyway."

Nikki couldn't control her emotions. Tears began flowing down her cheeks. What could she say? She was a big emotional crybaby.

Byron reached down and wiped her tears away as he had done before. Before she knew it, he was kissing her. She kissed him back. A knock on the door interrupted them.

"Anybody in there?" Byron's father asked as he attempted to open the door.

Byron shouted, "Yes, Dad. We're coming out."

He looked at Nikki as she walked over to the mirror and wiped her face. He unlocked the door. Frank smiled at them as they walked out.

"I'm glad you made it, Nikki," Frank commented.

Nikki, embarrassed, replied, "We had to talk and needed some privacy."

Frank held his hand up. "No need to explain. I try to stay out of my sons' business."

"Is everybody here?" Byron asked his father.

"Yes. I was coming in here to get the gift I bought for your mom."

"We'll meet you in the dining room." Byron held one hand on Nikki's back.

Nikki attempted to gain control of the situation. Ever since she set foot across the threshold, Byron had her under his spell again.

Byron knew if his father hadn't interrupted, he would still be tasting the sweet nectar of Nikki's lips. Although she didn't verbalize it, he knew she had forgiven him. At least he hoped so.

When he had opened the door for her and Charlotte and seen her standing there, he could not help but notice how beautiful she looked. The dress she wore accented her shapely legs. She had changed her hairstyle and it was becoming to her. He admitted to himself, she would look beautiful to him no matter how her hair looked.

A few of his aunts, uncles, and cousins, along with Frederick and Charlotte, were in the den when he and Nikki walked in. When they entered, Belle walked up to Nikki and gave her a hug. "I'm so glad to see you, dear. Thanks for coming."

"Now you know I wouldn't miss seeing you today of all days." Nikki winked. She handed her the gift bag. "This is for you."

"You shouldn't have. But since you did, give it here," Belle joked.

They laughed. Byron was happy to see Nikki and his mom smiling.

"Follow me, I want you to meet some of the family," Belle said, taking Nikki's hand and walking away with her.

Byron watched as his mom made the introductions. It appeared his family was going to like Nikki too. Frederick snuck up on him. "Boo."

"Man, what's your problem?" he asked his brother.

"Are you two back together? You looked quite chummy when you walked in the room."

"Not quite. I'm hoping by the end of the day, we will be."

Frederick patted him on the back. "Like a wise man once said, 'Keep hope alive.'"

Byron walked to where Nikki stood and placed his hand around her waist. "I hope you're not telling her any bad stories about me," he addressed his uncle Raymond.

"If I was a few years younger, I would take this young lady away from you, son," his uncle joked.

Nikki looked into Byron's eyes and said, "As handsome as you are, your competition is tight."

A huge smile swept across his face. "Move over, Uncle. A new kid's on the block."

They continued to laugh and talk for a few minutes. Frank walked into the room and announced, "Ladies and Gents, let's eat."

Everyone walked to the dining room. The long, conference-room-like table was beautifully decorated and was set to seat twenty.

"Hey, cousin. Since my family's not here, I'll sit next to you," Joyce said after giving him and Nikki a hug.

"Where's the family?" Byron asked.

"Everybody in my house is sick and I didn't want to bring them around your folks," Joyce said as she sat down.

Byron leaned down and whispered in Nikki's ear, "I want you to sit next to me."

She didn't object. He held out her chair and waited for her to sit down, before sitting beside her.

"Where will the kids eat?" Nikki asked.

"We set up a few tables in the kitchen."

Frank addressed Byron. "Son, I know you're the baby of the family, but today I would like for you to say the grace."

Byron looked and saw the smile on his mom's face. Frank looked around the room before saying, "Bow your heads please."

Everyone held hands as Byron prayed, "Thank you, Lord, for second chances." He gently squeezed Nikki's hands and continued. "And for allowing us to be here to celebrate another year for my mom. We know we're all blessed to be able to give thanks to You and to take part in this special day. Bless this food we're about to eat. Amen."

"Amens" were heard around the table.

As everyone piled food on their plates, Byron watched Nikki from the corner of his eye. He could sense she was uncomfortable. "What's wrong?" he asked her.

"I'm fine," she said.

He didn't believe her, but continued to talk and joke with other family members.

44

Byron noticed Frank trying to get his attention. "Excuse me," Byron said as he stood and walked to where his dad was sitting.

"I want you to get everybody to come in the den so Belle can start opening her gifts," Frank said as he pulled back his chair to stand up.

"We're moving this party back to the den. It's time to open up gifts," Byron shouted. "Mom, you come with me."

He linked his arm with hers. He smiled and winked at Nikki and they left with everyone following behind.

When they walked into the room, Frank was standing in the middle by a black leather recliner with a big red bow on top. "Dear, I know you've been talking about that old recliner for months. I hope you're not too disappointed," he said to Belle, who walked over and hugged and kissed him on the cheek.

"This is perfect!" she said. "After cooking and cleaning all day, I need something I can put my feet up on." She sat down in it. The chair reared back and caught her off guard. "Oops," she said as everyone laughed.

Byron watched and waited for everyone to give her their gifts. Nikki stood next to Charlotte. He could see them saying something after each gift was opened. Joyce handed Belle another bag. Belle read the card. "This is from Nikki."

Byron caught Nikki looking at him. She glanced away once he looked her way.

"Nikki, come give me a hug," Belle said as she held up a beautiful scarf and pendant to go along with it. Nikki walked over, hugged her, and kissed Belle on the cheek. "Y'all, I swear this is one of the best birthdays in my life." She beamed as she looked around the room.

Joyce handed her a small Tiffany's box. Everybody was quiet as they waited for her to open it. She read the card first. "Hmmm. This one's from my boys," Belle said. "What's this?" She held up a key chain with a key. She looked at Byron and then at Frederick. "You didn't?" She stood up from the chair and they watched her walk to the living room window.

"Follow us," Byron said as he and Frederick walked with her outside and everyone else followed.

"Somebody catch me because I'm going to faint," Belle said as she walked up to a silver Cadillac. She hugged both of her sons. In between tears, she said, "You boys shouldn't have."

"Mom, you deserve this and so much more," Byron said.

"Open it up and get inside. Feel how it sits," Frederick added.

She opened the door and sat inside. "Boys, you have outdone yourselves," she said as she leaned back in the seat. "Frank, did you know anything about this?"

"I plead the Fifth." Frank laughed and people laughed around him.

She got out and locked the door. "I don't know how much more excitement my heart can take." Belle glowed.

Byron walked by his mother's side as they went back into the house.

She stood at the door and hugged everyone as they walked back in.

"His mom is so happy," Nikki commented to Charlotte.

"I would be too if my sons got me a Cadillac," Charlotte said.

"Shhh," Nikki hissed, afraid someone would overhear her and Charlotte's conversation.

Nikki didn't notice Frederick coming up between them. He placed one arm around her and the other around Charlotte. "What are you ladies doing later tonight?" he asked them.

Nikki could have sworn she saw Charlotte blush.

Charlotte responded, "Nothing. Why, you got something planned for us?"

"Speak for yourself. I have something to do," Nikki exclaimed. She removed Frederick's arm and began walking away.

"I'm sure you do," Frederick said as if he was in on a secret.

"I'm going to the bathroom," Nikki snapped. *I don't see what Charlotte sees in him. He is nerve-racking,* she thought to herself as she walked away and went to the bathroom. Before she could exit the bathroom, someone knocked on the door. She yelled, "I'll be out in a minute."

She flushed the toilet and washed her hands. She reapplied her lipstick before unlocking the door. Joyce was standing to the side of the door when she walked out.

"Girl, I guess we all had to use it at the same time. Both bathrooms were being used."

"It must have been all the tea I drank," Nikki said.

Joyce moved around uncontrollably. "Good seeing you again, but duty calls." She raced into the bathroom, shutting the door behind her.

Nikki walked back into the den.

"There you are," Byron said as he wrapped his arm around her shoulders.

"I didn't know I was missed," she flirted.

"More than you'll ever know," he flirted back.

He grabbed her hand. "Hang out with me tonight. Please."

"I don't know if it's a good idea."

"It's obvious you're not mad at me anymore."

"I'm curious to hear how you came to that conclusion." She folded her arms and placed her index finger on her chin.

"Number one, you showed up even when you didn't have to. Number two, you didn't slap me when I attempted to kiss you in the room earlier. Number three—"

Nikki smiled and unfolded her arms. "You love lists, don't you?"

"I only do it to annoy you." Byron chuckled.

"I figured that much." She blushed. "I will hang out with you tonight on one condition."

"Your wish is my command."

"We meet in a neutral place."

"Name the place and time and I'll be there."

She thought for a moment before saying, "Meet me at the Broadway Café around eight thirty. I'm in the mood for some jazz tonight."

"It's a date."

One of Byron's cousins tried to get his attention. "I think they're calling for you." She pointed.

"I'll see you later," Byron said as he hugged her and kissed her on the cheek.

Nikki looked for Charlotte and found her in a corner talking to Frederick. She felt the intensity between them. She stood and watched them for a minute and then cleared her throat. "Char, are you ready to go?"

"Sure," Charlotte said as she broke away from Frederick.

"I'll see you ladies later," Frederick said.

"Bye, Freddie," Nikki teased.

"It's Fred-er-rick," he responded.

"Wait a sec, Charlotte, I need to say bye to Belle and Frank before I leave," Nikki said.

"I'll meet you at the car," Charlotte said as Frederick followed her out the door.

Nikki watched the interaction between Belle and Byron. Byron looked up and motioned for her to come over.

"Mrs. Matthews, happy birthday again," Nikki said. "I'm heading out and wanted to come say good-bye."

Belle hugged her tightly. "I'm grateful you're in my son's life. He needs someone like you by his side," she said with sincerity. She wrapped her arms through Nikki's before addressing Byron. "Leave us alone for a minute."

"I'll let you ladies talk," he said before departing.

As they walked arm in arm, Belle commented, "Byron hasn't told me everything, but I sense you guys are having some problems."

"I won't lie to you. Things have happened that made me question our relationship," Nikki replied.

"I know all about the baby situation."

"You do?" Nikki was surprised.

"Yes, and I told him he should have told you about it the moment he found out. But he didn't, and I hope you'll be able to forgive him."

"I don't know."

"If you don't remember anything else I tell you, remember this. My son loves you with all of his heart and I can tell you love him."

Tears formed in Nikki's eyes. "It's complicated."

"Search in your heart and the answer you seek will be there." Belle hugged her.

"Thanks, Mrs. Matthews. I hope to see you again."

"You will." She winked.

Nikki rubbed her nose. "I better go or Charlotte will be sending the cavalry after me."

"See you later, Nikki."

Nikki walked away and headed to the door. She heard Byron's voice behind her.

"Oh, you were going to leave and not say bye?" he said.

"I thought we said our good-byes earlier." She continued toward the door.

He cut her off at the door. "This is how you properly say good-bye."

Byron leaned down and kissed her passionately. For a moment, she forgot where they were. She was brought back to reality when a few people cheered.

"I better go," she said as she brushed past him and out the door.

Charlotte was in the car and Frederick was standing at her window talking to her. Nikki climbed inside. "Char, let's get out of here . . . *now,*" she said.

"Frederick, I'll call you later," Charlotte said as she started the car.

He waved at them as they drove off.

45

"You ran out of there like a bat out of hell," Charlotte commented as she drove Nikki home.

"I have some things I need to take care of before I go out tonight," Nikki replied.

As they pulled into her driveway, Charlotte said, "You didn't say anything to me about going out."

"That's because I *didn't* invite you." Nikki removed her seat belt.

"Do tell."

Opening her door, Nikki said, "Call me tomorrow. I might have something to tell you then."

Charlotte rolled down the passenger window and shouted, "It's Byron, isn't it?"

Nikki waved her hand in the air and yelled, "I'll tell you tomorrow. Bye."

She heard Charlotte yell before pulling out of the driveway, "You're not right."

Nikki laughed to herself. "It'll teach you to stay out of my business." She unlocked the door and immediately removed her shoes. She rubbed the bottom of her feet. "These are some cute shoes, but I don't know when I'll wear them again."

She walked to her bedroom with the shoes in her hand. She threw them on the floor by the bed. Before sitting down, she saw her message light blinking on her home phone. She picked up the receiver and scrolled through the caller ID.

She dialed Pam's number. She answered on the third ring. "Girl, where have you been?" Pam asked.

"I went to Byron's mom's birthday dinner," Nikki answered.

"I didn't know you guys had made up. That's good news."

"Slow down, we haven't exactly made up."

Nikki told her what had happened at the birthday party. "Tell Adrienne because I don't have the energy to repeat myself."

"I will." Before hanging up, Pam asked, "Will Byron be coming with you to Sunday dinner?"

"He'll be out of town."

"Maybe if he didn't have to travel so much your relationship would be more solid," Pam commented.

Nikki knew that was her cue that it was time to go. "Pam, I hate to rush you, but my husband and I have plans tonight."

"Do your thing, girl. I'll see you tomorrow. Too bad he couldn't stay until after dinner."

"No, he can't. Good night." After hanging up with Pam, she got undressed. *I need another shower.*

Byron helped clean up at his parents' before heading home. Once he got home, he took a quick shower and changed clothes. He then headed back out to meet Nikki.

When he arrived at the Broadway Café, he didn't see Nikki's car in the parking lot. He decided to meet her inside, just in case she had parked somewhere else.

The music inside was smooth and soothing. He declined being seated until he was sure Nikki was not there. After looking around, he asked the hostess for a seat for two. He left his name at the door.

Several women at the next table made it a point to flirt with him. He smiled and continued to listen to the music.

"The lady at the table in the back told me to send this over," a waitress said as she placed a glass of Courvoisier on the table in front of him.

"Who did you say sent this?" he asked.

The waitress pointed toward the back, but no one was there. "She was there a few minutes ago."

Before she could say anything else, Nikki walked up and asked, "Is this seat taken?"

Byron stood up and held Nikki's chair as she sat down.

"Thanks," he said to the waitress.

"I'll be back to take your orders," the waitress said before walking off.

"You look exquisite," Byron commented.

"Thanks. I see you have a fan club," Nikki said as she glanced at the table full of women next to them.

"I only have eyes for one woman."

"If another woman had bought you the drink, would you have accepted it?"

"No. I would have sent it back."

"That's what your mouth says."

Byron held his hand to his heart. "My heart says I would."

Nikki got quiet. Byron took a sip from his drink. He watched Nikki as she moved to the beat of the music.

"Would you like to dance?" he asked.

"Not right now."

"Let me know when."

"I sure will." She smiled as the waitress came back to take their order.

* * *

When she walked into the club and saw Byron sitting by himself, she knew for a fact that there was no way she could go on without him. Being around him and his family the entire day showed her he was the man she needed in her life. She watched as the women at the table next to him flirted. He was polite, but not once did she see him flirt back. The idea to send the drink came up at the last minute. Now as she sat across from him, she wanted to feel his arms around her and his lips on hers.

"Nikki, are you okay?" he asked.

She shook her head and came back to reality. "Yes. Would you like to dance?"

"Sure. I thought you would never ask." He winked at her.

Byron pulled out her chair. Nikki noticed a couple of the women turning their noses up when they passed by their table.

"Eat your hearts out, ladies," Nikki said as Byron wrapped his arms around her waist.

"I've wanted to sweep you off your feet since the day I met you."

"Is that why you spilled that drink on my brand-new shoes?" She pulled back from him a little and looked in his face and smiled.

"I had to do something. How else would I have gotten your number?"

She leaned in closer to him. "You're right. I never would have given you my number."

He blew in her ear. "Never?"

Nikki found it hard to keep her balance. "I would have if you asked."

He stopped blowing in her ear. "Glad to see I haven't lost it."

"You haven't lost me either," she said softly, not sure if he heard her over the music.

They danced for the next two songs. Byron held her hand

as they walked back to the table. After they got seated, the waitress brought out their food.

"This looks good," Nikki said about her stuffed shrimp.

"I hope it tastes good."

They ate in silence while enjoying the café's ambiance.

Nikki glanced at her watch. "Byron, I've had a nice time, but it's getting late and I've had a long day," she told him.

"This has been a long day." He stood, walked around to her chair, and pulled it out for her.

She waited for Byron to pay for the meal and drinks. After placing some money on the table for the tip, Byron reached for her hand and they walked outdoors.

"I'm parked right over there." She pointed.

"I'll walk you to your car."

Nikki didn't want the night to end. For a few hours, she was able to forget her problems at work and all other issues. She found her keys and turned off her alarm. "I guess this is good night," she said as she opened the door.

"Nikki, wait," Byron said as he reached for her arm. She turned around. "Come back over to my place so we can really talk. I know it's late, but I feel there are some other things we need to clear up."

Nikki took her hand and placed it around his neck and pulled his lips onto hers.

"Everything is cool now. I have dinner at my folks' place tomorrow, so I'll call you afterward."

He exhaled. "I'll be waiting on the call."

She got into the car and waved at him as she backed up and pulled away.

46

"Are you sure you're doing the right thing?" Frederick said through the phone receiver to Byron, who had just pulled out of the driveway.

"How many times are you going to ask me the same question? I was prepared to do it yesterday, but I didn't feel like the time was right," Byron stated.

"Better you than me," Frederick said.

"I called you for encouragement."

Frederick imitated Kermit the Frog as he spoke. "I'm sorry. I couldn't help myself. Me and commitments don't get along."

Byron had to laugh. "You must have cheated your way through school, because I know your retarded behind didn't earn a 3.5 GPA on your own."

"I plead the Fifth, and on that note, I'm about to let you go," Frederick said.

"Wish me luck."

"You don't need it. She loves you. And I love you too, man."

"Is Freddie getting mushy on me?"

"Bye, *Byron*," Frederick said before hanging up.

I know I wasn't invited to dinner, but this can't wait, Byron thought as he put the pedal to the metal. He turned on the wrong street at first, but ten minutes later, he parked right behind Nikki's car. He hoped her folks wouldn't mind an extra mouth to feed. He checked his pants pockets and walked up the walkway.

After he reached the door, he had second thoughts. He had turned to walk away when he heard Napoleon say, "Son, where are you going? I know you didn't come all this way to turn around."

"Sir, I wasn't sure if I was welcome," Byron said.

Nikki's father reached out to shake Byron's hand. "I saw a shadow come up the driveway and when I didn't hear a knock I came to see who it was. I see I almost missed you. No need to turn away. You're always welcome here, son."

"You still don't know, do you?" Byron asked.

Napoleon had a puzzled look on his face. "Know what?"

Byron stopped. "Maybe we should talk out here." He pointed to the chairs on the porch. "You should probably sit down."

"It must be serious." Napoleon sat down and didn't blink an eye.

Byron was nervous and made sure he was standing a few feet back. If Napoleon's reaction to him and his daughter's deceit was what he thought it would be, he didn't want to be in arm's length of his wrath.

"I don't know where to begin."

"The beginning always works for me," Napoleon said sternly.

Byron looked up in the air and then back into Napoleon's emotionless face. His palms were sweaty. How could he tell this man that Nikki and he were not really married and had been living a lie for the past four months? He took a couple of deep breaths and began telling him how he and Nikki had met. Once he got started, it became easier and easier to tell

Napoleon everything. He left out certain things such as Nikki being a virgin and the situation with Tara claiming to be the mother of his child. After confessing to Napoleon how he felt about his daughter and his intentions, Byron waited for a response. Napoleon remained quiet. Byron couldn't figure out whether it was a good or bad sign, because his face still held no emotion.

"What's taking Dad so long? I'm hungry," Adrienne exclaimed.

"I'll go see," Gerald said.

Nikki was oblivious of what was happening around her. Her heart was heavy from all of the lies. She had missed church again because she didn't want to lie in the sanctuary. Her mom looked at her disapprovingly when she walked into the room.

"Nikki, if you can go out, you can get up in the morning and give the Lord a few hours of your time," her mother scolded.

"I watched one of the TV ministries," Nikki said in her own defense.

Ethel shook her head. "Now, child, there's nothing wrong with doing that. But the Lord likes for us to fellowship with one another. You've said yourself that going to church gives you the fuel you need to deal with your hectic week."

Nikki looked down on the floor. "It does, but there's so much stuff going on. I don't feel right."

Before she could finish, her dad said, "Look who I found at the front door."

Nikki looked up and saw Byron standing between her dad and Gerald.

Byron hugged Ethel. "Hi, Mrs. Montana," he said.

"Hi yourself. Nikki told us you had to work," Ethel said.

Nikki couldn't bring herself to look at anyone. "I'm glad you're here," she said softly.

"I bet you are," Napoleon commented.

Ethel ignored Napoleon's comment. "Nicolette, what are you waiting on? Go get an extra plate and silverware out of the china cabinet," she instructed her.

Nikki wanted to ask Byron why he was there, but didn't. She obeyed her mom and followed them into the dining room. Her family was happy to see Byron.

Napoleon stated, "Byron, you sit up here next to me. Nikki, I want you sitting right next to him."

"Yes, sir," Nikki said bashfully. *Something's not right.*

Nikki squirmed in her seat. Adrienne was watching her when she looked up and gave her a curious stare. Nikki wanted to stick her tongue out at Adrienne, but she knew that was an immature act. So she straightened up.

Napoleon stood at the head of the table and said, "I'm glad to see everyone is here once again safe and sound. Before we start dinner, I want to give Byron a chance to say something."

Nikki whispered in Byron's ear, "What's going on here? You're not supposed to be here."

"Baby girl, let Byron speak please," Napoleon said firmly.

Everyone looked at Napoleon as if wondering why he spoke so harshly.

Byron stood up. She heard him clear his throat a few times. She felt like fleeing the room, but she didn't have the nerve or the strength to stand up.

"Thanks, Mr. Montana," Byron started. "I'm here today to clear up the mystery. I will no longer be invisible in this family. I'm here today because there is no other woman in the world I would rather spend my life with."

Nikki watched Adrienne pull her chair closer to the table and put her elbow on the table and her hand under her chin so she wouldn't miss a word that came out of Byron's mouth.

Nikki turned and looked at him and said, "Byron, don't."

"Nikki, I know I promised you I wouldn't say anything to your family," Byron said regretfully, "but I want to do this right. I tried doing it your way and it didn't work. I probably should have talked to you about it, but I'm the man and I must stand on what I know is right."

Nikki held her breath. She looked at her father and noticed a smile. She looked up at Byron. "What are you saying?"

As if they were the only ones in the room, Byron looked into her eyes. He reached into his pocket and took out a black velvet box. He pulled the chair out farther, got down on one knee, and reached for Nikki's hands.

"I've asked your father's permission, so, Nicolette Montana, will you take me, Byron Matthews, as your husband, to have and to love you all the days of my life?"

"I thought y'all were already married," Pam said curiously.

"It's too late to be proposing now," Adrienne shouted.

"Y'all be quiet!" Napoleon shouted as he slammed his fist on the table.

"What's going on here?" Ethel asked.

"Trust me," Nikki heard her father say.

"Nikki, did you hear me?" Byron asked, holding his breath.

Tears fell from her eyes. She looked around the table at her family. She saw her father nod his head. She smiled and looked at Byron and in a light whisper said, "Yes."

"What was that, baby girl?" Napoleon asked.

"Yes," she repeated. "Byron, I will marry you." Byron placed the two-carat diamond-cut ring on her finger.

"Now will somebody tell me what's going on?" Ethel asked.

Byron got off his knee and sat down beside Nikki. Not once did he release her hand.

Nikki got the courage she needed from the strength she felt in his hands.

Napoleon said, "I'll let Nikki tell you. The floor is yours, baby."

Byron added, "He knows."

"Everything?" Nikki questioned. Byron nodded. "This isn't going to be easy."

"Spill it out," Adrienne said as she sat back and crossed her arms.

Nikki sighed and began telling her family about her and Byron's relationship. No one said anything as she spoke. Byron put his arms around her shoulders for support.

"I know you're wondering why we, I mean *I* did it. I'm not making any excuses, but I hope you all can see it from my point of view," Nikki concluded.

"It's hard to figure out why someone would lie to their family for months and then get other people involved," Pam stated as she looked between Nikki and Byron.

"Every time we get together," Nikki began to reason, "the first thing out of everybody's mouth is 'when are you getting married?' 'Why isn't Nikki married yet?' Or 'something must be wrong with her if she hadn't snagged her a husband by now.'" She looked at her mom and noticed tears in her eyes. "I actually did think something was wrong with me until I met this guy." She looked at Byron. "I had already lied about being married, but he was my knight in shining armor. He was willing to do whatever it took to make me happy."

Ethel spoke for the first time. "He shouldn't have lied for you."

"I know, Mom, but he did. It might not be right, but he was only trying to make Nikki happy," Nikki said in defense of Byron. "For the first time a man put me first. Even when he thought it was a crazy idea."

"You got that right!" Adrienne shouted.

"Hold on, Adrienne," Nikki said. "Don't go judging me. You're the one who kept telling me I needed to hurry up and get married so I could have kids. For six months straight, every conversation we had revolved around me being single. You tried to fix me up with every guy you knew."

Adrienne looked away. "I was only trying to help," she explained.

Nikki looked around the room. "I know and I love you for it, but couldn't y'all see the anguish you put me through? Yes, being over thirty and not married came with a price. I've had the opportunity to travel and do plenty of things being single, but you guys made me feel like my world wasn't complete unless I was married."

Her hands began to shake and tears streamed down her face.

Ethel stood up and walked over to her. "Dear, I'm sorry for any part I may have had."

"It's not your fault, Mom. I shouldn't have lied. I bowed down to the pressure."

"Give us a minute, y'all," Ethel said. Nikki stood up and followed her mom. Adrienne and Pam walked behind them.

47

The tears wouldn't stop flowing from Nikki's eyes. Her mom handed her a handkerchief. "Nikki, you have to stop crying," she told her.

"I know. I feel like a big baby," Nikki replied.

"That's because you are," Adrienne joked, but stopped when everybody shot their eyes at her. "Sorry. I know this is the wrong time to be joking."

Nikki noticed that Pam was the only one who hadn't said anything. "Pam, I'm sorry."

"You should be." Pam frowned.

"You've all done some crazy things, but I must admit, Nikki, you got them all beat." Ethel halfheartedly smiled.

"I promise to cook the next four Sundays if y'all forgive me," Nikki said.

"Girl, there's nothing to forgive. I wanted to see how low you would go," Pam said, hugging her.

Ethel went and poured her some water. "You need to pull yourself together and go back out there to that wonderful man of yours. Don't worry about anything else."

Nikki took the water and drank a little of it before heading back into the dining room with her mother and two sisters on her heels. When they reentered the room, Nikki noticed everyone in side conversations, but then the room got dead silent when she walked back in.

Napoleon stood up and hugged Nikki before kissing her on the cheek. "Everybody, hold hands so we can pray and eat this cold food," he ordered. A few chuckles were heard around the room. "Father God, please forgive us this day for the sins we have knowingly and unknowingly committed. You know our hearts, Lord. Thank you for my family and soon-to-be son-in-law. You know his heart was in the right place when You sent him to protect my daughter from herself. Bless this food we're about to eat and keep us close to you as we travel on this journey we call life. Amen."

Nikki kissed her father on the cheek before sitting down next to Byron.

After they warmed up some of the food, the rest of dinner was uneventful. Byron marveled at the strength Nikki's father showed during the entire ordeal. He reminded him of his own father; and he vowed that day if he ever had a son, he would teach him the same wholesome values.

"A penny for your thoughts," Nikki whispered in Byron's ear.

"Give me a quarter and I might tell you," he replied.

She opened her mouth to say, "I remember when—" before Byron bent down and kissed her.

Napoleon walked over and pulled them away. "Save that for the honeymoon," he said.

"Daddy," Nikki said bashfully.

Byron enjoyed the time he spent with Nikki's family. He knew the love he had for both Nikki and her family was genuine. Even knowing what they did, they welcomed him again into the family.

Nikki bent down and wrapped her arms around Byron's shoulders. "Are you ready to go?" she asked him.

"Only if you are," he responded.

"Mom and Dad, we're going to leave now. I'll call you later." She picked up her purse.

"Now that we know you're not actually husband and wife, you guys need to be living in separate quarters," Ethel said as she walked them to the door.

"We already are," Nikki said as she hugged Ethel and Napoleon.

"Don't be a stranger now, son," Napoleon stated. "You're welcome over here anytime, whether Nikki is with you or not."

"I won't be. I promise," Byron said. Then he and Nikki walked to their cars.

"Your place or mine?" Nikki asked.

"Yours. I'll follow you," Byron said with a smile.

While driving home, Nikki called Charlotte. "I couldn't wait to tell you. Byron and I are engaged."

Charlotte laughed. "Girl, you need some serious help."

"I'm serious," Nikki said before telling her how Byron had proposed.

"I know Adrienne had something smart to say."

"She did at first, but afterward everybody was cool. I probably won't be able to live it down, though."

"I'll remind you *every day* if you like."

"That's okay." Nikki laughed.

"I'm going to be a bridesmaid," Charlotte sang.

Nikki drove down her street. "I want you to be my maid of honor."

Charlotte got quiet. "Are you sure? What about one of your sisters?"

"You're my very best friend and besides, you know they would argue if I chose one over the other."

"In that case, girl, I'm honored."

Nikki smiled. "I'm at home now, so I'll talk to you later."

"Later, girl."

"Bye."

Nikki parked and threw the phone in her purse. Before she could get out of the car, Byron was opening her door for her. "Thanks."

"You're quite welcome," he said as they walked to the front door.

"I still can't believe everything is out in the open." She sighed as she unlocked the door and let them in. "I feel like a ton of bricks have been lifted off my shoulders," Nikki exclaimed as she threw her purse on the chair.

Byron swung her around. "I'm glad you agreed to be the real Mrs. Matthews."

"How could I resist with lips like these?" Nikki stated as they kissed passionately.

Byron was the first to pull away. "Uh, Nik, if you don't stop, I don't think I can control—"

"You don't have to," Nikki moaned.

"Yes, we do." Byron took her hand and led her to the couch and continued to say, "We've waited this long, so there's no reason why we can't wait until we say our vows."

"But—"

He placed his finger on her lips. "No buts. You're a virgin now and you'll be one when I marry you."

She pouted. "But what if I'm not good enough?"

"Oh, there's no doubt in my mind that making love to you will be the most extraordinary thing for both of us. I'm not saying I'm an expert, but I'll teach you what I know. And what I don't know . . . well, there's always a video."

She playfully hit him with her hand. "You're something else."

"What's on TV?" he asked as he kicked back on the couch.

She picked up the remote and turned it on. "How about a Lifetime movie?"

He couldn't help but laugh. "I've lived a Lifetime movie," he said with a smirk on his face.

"There's nothing else on," Nikki said, flicking channels.

He reached for the remote, turned it back on Lifetime, and placed it on the coffee table. "Come here." He pulled her into his arms. Nikki placed her head on his chest. She smiled, because she felt at home.

They watched the movie and fell asleep in one another's arms.

48

It was well after midnight when the ringing of Byron's cell phone woke them both.

"Nikki, I'm sorry," Byron said. "It must be an emergency for someone to be calling me this late."

"What time is it?" she asked with a yawn.

"I don't know exactly, but it's still dark outside," Byron said before answering the phone. "This is Byron."

His facial expression changed. Nikki asked, "What's wrong?"

Byron reached for her. She snuggled up to him. "No. I don't have any of that information, but I'll find out what I can and get back with you. How's the ba—?" Byron went to ask before obviously getting cut off. He nodded his head and then hung up the phone.

Nikki seemed scared. "Who was it? What's wrong?"

"It's Tara."

"What?" Nikki pulled away. "Why is she calling you at this hour?"

"Calm down, baby. It wasn't Tara, it was about Tara. That was the hospital. She was killed in a car accident last night."

"Oh my God!" Nikki exclaimed while putting her hand over her mouth.

"It comes as a shock to me too."

"What about Christopher? Is he—" Nikki couldn't finish asking her questions.

"No. His car seat saved him."

"What is that sweet little boy going to do without his mother?" Nikki asked as Byron rocked her in his arms.

"I don't know, sweetie. I don't know."

Nikki sat up. "How did the hospital know to call you?"

"She still had me listed as Christopher's father. I guess she never got around to changing the contact information."

"We need to go get him. I know he's scared out of his mind. I would be, too, after a horrible accident."

"Nikki, Tara's mom can take care of Christopher."

"I don't know. Tara and I weren't the best of friends, but I feel she was serious about the type of woman she described her mom as."

"Her mom is a character," Byron confirmed with a look of doubt.

Nikki stood up and grabbed his hand. "Come on. We have to go check on him."

"Nikki, I don't know."

"It's weird, but even after all that transpired with me and her, I feel like it's the right thing for us to do."

Byron looked up at Nikki, who had the deepest look of concern in her eyes. "I love you, Nikki Montana."

"I love you too. Now grab your keys."

Nikki held Byron's hand the entire way to the hospital, and as they entered the emergency room. She watched Byron take control of the situation. The nurse pointed them toward a set of elevators. Tears flowed down Nikki's face when she saw some of the infants in the emergency room. One of the nurses was holding and playing with an infant that looked like Christopher from a distance.

The closer they got, Nikki said, "That's Christopher. He looks to be all right." Christopher reached for Nikki. She held him close to her chest. "I'm so glad you're all right." For a moment, Nikki forgot Byron was standing there. "Do you want to hold him?"

He paused and reached his arms out. Christopher smiled and almost jumped into his arms. "Hey, little fellow. I'm Byron," he said.

"Ma-ma," Christopher said.

Nikki noticed the tears forming in Byron's eyes. She patted him on the back.

The nurse brought out some release forms. "I need you to sign here," she said.

Byron looked at Nikki and back to the nurse. "There's some misunderstanding. We didn't come to—"

Nikki interrupted him. She looped her arm through his and asked the nurse, "Can you give us a minute?"

"Sure. I'll be right over there," the nurse said as she took Christopher and walked to the other side of the room.

Byron whispered, "Nikki, what are you doing?"

"Let's take Christopher tonight and we can decide later on what to do with him," Nikki suggested.

"Are you crazy? He needs to be with his real family."

"If we leave him here, there's no telling what will happen to him."

"Tara has sisters. She has a mother."

Nikki pouted. "But where were they when she really needed them? You dated her. You should know better than anyone else what kind of family she came from."

Byron listened and knew Nikki made some valid points, but he wasn't prepared to take on additional responsibilities. "We take him home with us tonight and then what? We have our own lives. We're getting married."

"I know. I'll probably beat myself up later. But my heart is telling me we need to take Christopher. I'll take care of him until we find a home for him."

"What if we don't?"

Nikki didn't have an answer to his question. "We'll cross that bridge when we come to it. For now, I think he needs to be around at least one familiar face. I feel it's the right thing to do under the circumstances."

Byron hesitated. He saw the compassion in Nikki's eyes. He couldn't bring himself to go against her wishes. "We'll do it. Let me get the nurse."

Nikki hugged him. "Thanks, baby. I know it's going to be hard, but we'll make it through this. I promise."

Nikki held Christopher as the nurse gave Byron some papers. Byron signed several forms. Before he was finished, an officer walked over and talked to him. He handed him a few items they were able to recover from the wreck, which included Tara's purse and some papers from her glove compartment.

He took the items. He looked at Nikki as she played with Christopher. He said a prayer before walking in her direction.

Lord, I need You right now. I don't know what I'm supposed to do. I need You to direct my steps. I pray I'm able to hear your answer when it comes. I'm temporarily in charge of that little boy's life. Whatever Your will is for him, please give me the insight and the strength to endure. Amen.

Byron wrapped his arm around Nikki and smiled at Christopher. "Let's go home," he said.

"Your home or my home?" Nikki asked.

"It doesn't matter. Home is where the heart is," he said as they walked hand in hand out the front door of the hospital with Christopher lying on his shoulder.

EPILOGUE

Nine months later

"Nikki, hurry up. He's not going to wait on you all day," Ethel said as she helped Nikki remove her veil.

"Wasn't this the perfect May wedding?" Nikki asked as she looked at herself in the mirror.

"You made a beautiful bride. Now I know you don't want to keep that handsome husband of yours waiting."

Charlotte walked into the room and added, "Girl, you better hurry and throw the bouquet. You know how we planned it, right? I'm going to shake to the left and then you throw it to the right, okay?" she teased.

"So you can marry Freddie?"

"I told you Frederick and I are only friends."

Adrienne walked in behind her. "If you two are just friends, then I'm single," she said.

"Ladies, it's time," Pam added as she walked in.

"I'm so happy right now I want to cry," Nikki said, looking at her mother, best friend, and sisters.

"I think we've all done enough crying for one day," Ethel said as she hugged her.

They walked out to the reception area of the hotel. When Nikki saw Byron she smiled, and he flashed her one of his sexy smiles, showing off both dimples.

"Ladies, get ready," Nikki said as she turned around and threw the bouquet. People laughed because the lady standing next to Charlotte pushed her out of the way to grab it and then had the nerve to have an attitude. Nikki and Charlotte exchanged looks.

Charlotte mouthed, "Can you believe that?"

Nikki shrugged her shoulders and tried not to laugh.

"Byron, don't even think about throwing that garter my way," Frederick yelled.

Nikki's eyes sparkled as she watched Byron remove the garter from her leg. "We might need to skip out early," she whispered.

"I'm hurrying as fast as I can," he teased.

Byron stood up and turned around. "Who's the lucky man?"

The garter landed directly in front of Frederick. "No way. I'm not picking it up," he refused.

Byron yelled, "Don't fight it. You're next."

Everyone laughed around them as Frederick bent to pick it up.

Byron turned his attention back toward Nikki. "Are you ready?" he asked her.

"I'm beyond ready," she said. Before Nikki could respond further, she felt a tug on her dress. She reached down and picked up Christopher. "There's my little man. You be good for Grandma now."

"O-tay," Christopher responded and then reached out for Byron. Byron took him from Nikki and held him up in the air. Christopher drooled on him and said, "Da-da."

Byron exclaimed, "He called me Daddy."

Nikki smiled. "My two babies."

Belle, Frank, Ethel, and Napoleon walked over and stood near them.

Belle reached for Christopher. "Come to Grandma," she said. "These two have some business to take care of." She winked at Nikki.

Nikki hugged her parents and her in-laws. Byron's soul felt at ease. He watched his new bride say good-bye to her family.

Napoleon tapped him on the shoulder. "Son, you did good. You're the perfect man for my daughter."

"I'll do my best to take care of her," Byron assured him.

"I'm proud of both of you. Agreeing to adopt Christopher is an honorable thing to do, especially under the circumstances."

"I wish I could take the credit, but it was all Nikki's idea."

"She's always been the creative one in the bunch," he joked.

Nikki walked over and looped her arm through his. "What's so funny?"

"A joke between men, baby girl," Napoleon said. He kissed her on the cheek and continued to say, "You guys better get going if you don't want to miss your flight."

Nikki looked at her dad and said, "Bye, Dad."

"Bye, precious." He waved back.

The family followed them to the waiting limousine. The bride and groom waved from the windows as the limousine pulled away.

Byron poured two glasses of champagne and they toasted.

"Mr. Matthews, I love you," Nikki said as her eyes sparkled.

"I love you too, Mrs. Matthews," Byron said as they clicked the two champagne glasses.

My Invisible Husband

Reading Group Guide

1. Nicolette Montana was thirty-four and felt pressured to get married. Do you think a lot of women and men feel that way? Why?

2. Nikki went to the extreme by faking a Las Vegas wedding. Do you understand why Nikki decided to deceive her friends and family?

3. After Nikki told Byron her dilemma, he could have responded differently, but instead decided to go along with her charades. Why do you think Byron agreed to go along with Nikki's scheme?

4. Adrienne seemed to annoy Nikki on several occasions. Why was Adrienne so suspicious from the very beginning?

5. Do you believe her coworker Kenneth was really looking out for Nikki?

6. Although they were coworkers, do you think Tara had the right to ask Nikki to babysit for her? Would you have babysat Tara's son if you were Nikki?

7. Should Byron have told Nikki about the Christopher situation as soon as he found out?

8. Why do you think Byron came clean with Napoleon about his and Nikki's situation?

9. After tragedy struck, Byron and Nikki did something unthinkable. Would you have adopted the baby?

10. Nikki took her situation to the extreme. Do you think something like this can happen in real life?

http://www.sheilagoss.com